THE DURATION OF A KISS

Peter Wells won the 1991 Reed Fiction Award for his first book *Dangerous Desires*, which went on to win the 1992 New Zealand Book Award for fiction. He is also a writer/director of films, including the internationally acclaimed *Desperate Remedies* (1993). Another film, *A Death in the Family*, won the prize for Best Drama in the 1986 American Film Festival.

*Also by Peter Wells
and available from Minerva*

Dangerous Desires

Peter Wells

The Duration of a Kiss

Minerva

A Minerva Paperback
THE DURATION OF A KISS

First published in New Zealand 1994
by Reed Publishing (NZ) Ltd
The Minerva edition published 1995
by Mandarin Paperbacks
an imprint of Reed Books Ltd
Michelin House, 81 Fulham Road, London SW3 6RB
and Auckland, Melbourne, Singapore and Toronto

Copyright © 1994 by Peter Wells
The author has asserted his moral rights

a CIP catalogue record for this title
is available from the British Library
ISBN 0 7493 8615 0

The author gratefully acknowledges the assistance of the Literature
Programme of the Queen Elizabeth II Arts Council of New Zealand and
the University of Auckland.
An earlier version of the story 'The Duration of a Kiss' was published in
the anthology *Erotic Writings*, edited by Sue McCauley and Richard
McLachan (1992).
'The Happy Cadaver' first appeared as 'The Good Tourist and the
Laughing Cadaver' in the anthology of the same name, edited by
Michael Gifkins (1993).

Printed and bound in Great Britain by
BPC Paperbacks Ltd
a member of
The British Printing Company Ltd

This book is sold subject to the condition
that it shall not, by way of trade or otherwise,
be lent, resold, hired out, or otherwise circulated
without the publisher's prior consent in any form
of binding or cover other than that in which
it is published and without a similar condition
including this condition being imposed
on the subsequent purchaser.

Contents

Author's Note

This collection was written during the time I co-directed the film *Desperate Remedies*. I make no great claims to being at the cutting edge of an international dialogue; it is simply the ongoing output of a working writer, the collection of the voyager moving through the terrain as he imaginatively finds it. What I offer here is a break in the hills, and a small view.

The Law of Relativity

What on earth did he think he was doing? It was as close as you could get to murdering someone. He loved Ethan, he recognised this in the shock he felt at his own actions the following morning. Yet at the time, at night, it had seemed right, flowing. It was like something both of them had separately been thinking of, in silence. And when the moment had come he, Eric, had simply grabbed Ethan by the harness of his outspread legs, pulled him down to the end of the bed with a pleasurable degree of vigour, then prepared to penetrate him. Penetrate him! How can language be so insufficient to express what both men felt at that moment?

Eric had looked down into the face of his young lover, this man who had brought new purpose into his life. Ethan was lying back against the sheets, his head crooked just slightly sideways as if to catch a better view of Eric — someone who had felt himself to have fallen from grace at one time, a man who had lost the savour of existence. Yet now this young man lay, face flushed, eyes looking up into Eric's with so much warm trust that Eric had undergone — he told himself later — a momentary fit of madness: a kind of willed amnesia, the lunacy that they both existed in a safe world.

Yes, yes, later the following morning, when his hands shook, Eric told himself he had been only thinking of momentary penetration. He had wanted only — he now told himself — to feel for one second the deep pleasure of his flesh inside Ethan's warm, sinuous, waiting body. He would have withdrawn quickly and at this time the clumsy negotiation of latex and penis would begin. Yet would he have withdrawn? Would he have been able to? It might have been one of those times when suddenly, like a sudden sob, you came unexpectedly, the pleasure too sharply rapturous. Besides, there was also the question of pre-cum (spelling itself signifying the dangers of the new world they all existed in).

It was impossible, what he had been on the very brink of doing — committing. It was as near as you could get to committing murder. Unsafe sex with your young lover, a boy-man who adored you so much that he trusted you at that moment. Not of supreme acceptance, because this was to make too much of a simply sexual act. Yet how significant the act had become, since the disease! How complicated, how gradated with hesitations and equivocations, sudden tunings of the fork of the mind, the conscience, where before there was only, and always, the gush of sex, the haunt and hunt of appetite. *What on earth had he been been thinking of?*

No, Eric thought as he took a long, pensive shower — as if he sought, in the cleansing water, to clarify his thought. He sought, in fact, at that private moment under sheets of water, to admonish himself, to teach himself almost a lesson. With Ethan, his new lover, it was as if he was tentatively having to discover or locate a new self. And this new self had its own form of memory. Or was it amnesia? *How had he been able to forget?* This was what was truly remarkable: he had been able to forget.

It was as if the last ten years had not happened. As if Perrin were not dead.

Isolated inside the bell of water, in the cell of silence, Eric tried to analyse his feelings. *What had he been doing?* He felt ashamed of himself, startled by his own actions. He saw himself as a man who knew himself. Surely the odyssey of Perrin's death had taught him nothing, if not that? The importance of knowing your own behaviour, of having no pretences. Of living naked with your own self. But now, at this moment in his life, he stood again revealed — flawed. He had acted spontaneously. Spontaneity, which had once been the flower of the old sexuality! Yet his actions were ones he would have hated in someone else: he was trying to murder his young love.

Thank god, he thought, allowing the water to dash and bash his face. Thank god that in a way he had become so carried away, he had pushed too quickly into Ethan so that Ethan's face, one moment a shining lake of trust, a shimmering sea of confidence and union, had suddenly altered: beneath the surface rose up a mask of pain. Ethan returned to being a small boy who had stubbed his toe. He didn't cry out. But it was at this point that consciousness fully returned to Eric, when he felt an instant regret for causing pain to this young man he, yes, loved; he had to admit it. But also one moment later, as they lay together cradling and kissing each other, Ethan's hand irresistibly feeling down for Eric's cock, it was at this moment Eric fully understood what he had been about to do: he had been about to fuck his boyfriend not even using a condom.

What on earth had he been thinking of? Eric looked in the metal faucet and inspected his own face slowly. It was an act of denial, of cruelty too. As if he wished to drag Ethan into his own shaded world, a world of loss, of uncertainty. But it was more than this: it was an act of madness, a *folie d'amour*, the sort of madness which love was meant to be, an intoxication. Or was it simply sex? It was often at those moments hard to tell, yet so important.

Was the impossible happening? Was he forgetting his old love?

It was true, Eric felt a mixture of emotions about the death of Perrin, his closest friend. He felt sadness, naturally, that Perrin was no longer there. It still seemed shocking, especially now two years later, when time had given him enough space to recollect that yes, Perrin had finally and forever gone. Fear too, that he, Eric, might actually be able to forget him: forget not only the mad and happy times they had had together, their peculiar fit and closeness, the symmetry of their mutual queerness, but a deeper fear that he might forget those final months, the haunted time, stark in its pain, extraordinary in the depth to which he had been riven.

Could he forget it? The process of living — the necessity to continue living — meant you simply had to obliterate the worst. He *needed* to forget the spilt blood, the hoicked phlegm, just as he needed to obliterate the sight of Perrin's face, a face throttled red with anger, pain. He wanted to forget all this. Yet he was frightened, too , of forgetting. Frightened of letting Perrin finally go.

In meeting Ethan, it was as if Ethan's fleshly form, the delights of his body, his outspread thighs, his soft cries when he came, the almost abstract drop of his hand on to Eric's back after orgasm, the lazy drizzle of his fingers stroking Eric's spine — it was as if all these intense sensations, the actual physical shape of his small and randy lover, stood between Eric and Perrin: as if the curtain of the living divided him off from the horrors and the extraordinary emotions of his too painful recent past.

Ah but, Eric thought, soaping between his legs, there was the elasticity of desire, the illusion. He was only too happy to bury himself in the textures of Ethan's flesh: his thrush-like freckled limbs, the sturdy nature of his musculature. Ethan was like a small discus thrower, compact, purposeful, concentrated. Besides, and this was peculiarly satisfying, there was no end in sight. There was not even the sense of danger, of impending shocks. Neither had managed to anger the other, both were extraordinarily courteous towards each other's emotions. Whether this could last the battery and intent of a lengthy relationship Eric did not know. But he did know he felt an extraordinary degree of tenderness towards his young lover, rescuer of his hope.

It was extraordinary, he thought then, allowing the water to hammer out his thought, how Ethan never asked for details of Perrin's illness and death but listened thoughtfully to whatever Eric might have to say. He accepted the anguish unspeakingly. He soothed it away, like thoughtful hands smoothing a page. Ah yes, now this was what was so extraordinarily satisfying to Eric's soul: that a sense of mystery, of pleasurable anticipation, could exist, like the shortening distance in each other's footsteps as they hurried to meet each other. The gap between their hands as they met and fingers clasped one another, the space between their lips as they leant together to kiss, tongue touching tongue, probing, meeting, satisfying, greeting. It was this space between pleasurable anticipation and whatever lay ahead.

Whatever lay ahead.

What was he doing? Falling for this young man with a shy laugh and strong, persistent gaze. Who turned up at his house regularly, even eagerly, with an unembarrassed laugh. *What was he doing?* Up until now, Eric felt he had been sleepwalking, dreaming: now, this morning, he felt he had woken up. Wasn't it jaded and manipulative to believe he had a second chance?

Could it, would it, ever settle down? Would there be a time when he wouldn't be driven to grab Ethan in a corridor, going up stairs — anywhere where a vague notion of privacy existed? As if they could never ever get enough time together. Yes, he knew it would settle down.

Just as he had seen, one night as Ethan had undressed in front of him, the impending shape of an older man. But this perception, this sensation almost, was one of overpowering tenderness. Perhaps, he thought, quickly calculating the years between them, perhaps they might grow old together.

Grow old! What on earth was he thinking of? Once feared, it had become an impossible luxury, an unattainable dream. To grow — together! When Perrin's sickness engulfed his life, Eric had bit by bit assumed that there was a simple logic to all their lives. Suddenly one day you got sick. Then you died. You died. Tomorrow, or the next day, or the day after, but soon: you were dead.

This was Ethan's inestimable gift to Eric, a sense of there being not merely a future but a hugely enjoyable one, one which could, if it could not actually eradicate the past, at least place it in some kind of relativity. Yes, that is what he must grasp hold of — that slim chance, of hope: the relativity of all objects.

Eric finally turned the hot water off.

He pulled aside the curtains in his bedroom and hurriedly dressed. *What had he been doing?* He was seeking to forget, he was attempting to obliterate the past. In loving Ethan, he was forgetting Perrin. But it could not be like that. No, he thought, pulling up the covers of his bed, smelling, in that one moment, a sharp scent of his lover, almost acrid, a perfume of his absence. It could not be like that. That was not the relativity he sought.

He returned gratefully to his world of work — grateful, because it had nothing to do with the dereliction of his thought. Midway through an assignment (working on a script for a new food show — 'olive oils, virgin, or promiscuous?') the phone went. It was Gwen, an old friend from university. She was coming to stay. He had forgotten. Amnesia again, he told himself.

He thought of Gwen: he had known her now for close on twenty years. They had met at university, at that time of swift change when one took for granted an idea of freedom, the malleability of change (underscored, perhaps, by the accelerant of drugs). Time had proved both Eric and Gwen had a hardening set of characteristics; it was impossible, with time, to overlook patterns of behaviour. Eric was fastidious about times for meals, courtesies like letting people know arrival times. Gwen was more random, still 'spontaneous' as perhaps suited an 'artist' (she was a singer/composer). Besides, now there was a new element. She was pregnant.

When Eric inspected his own thoughts he tried to work out whether his lack of empathy expressed the bitterness of those who would never breed. But more than this, perhaps, he feared Gwen succumbing to the piety of motherhood. He feared the faintly sickening sanctity of 'family' resettling itself, simply in a new form. He was not a fifties reject for nothing.

Could the rock star manqué be like this? She had succumbed; she had got pregnant. It didn't matter that her boyfriend was chosen, like a stallion, then kept at bay. The demands of parenting soon smoothed that out. But anyway, faced with her voice on the phone, its old and dulcet magic, he felt seduced again, back towards her. Besides, he had his own news. Ethan.

During the day, subconsciously, he waited for a call from Ethan. But just as the call didn't come, so the pleasure grew, deepened, like a form of climax pleasurably delayed. They would meet, they would talk. It was all certain.

At times of boredom, Eric found himself stalked by daydreams. Moving into focus, like a vast image in close-up, he simply saw flesh, freckle on freckle, like a bird's wing, thrush's fleck. This became his landscape. He saw Ethan's long sandy lashes which, in candlelight, trailed a sail across his cheekbone: eyes looking downwards, grazed open, like his lips. His lips soft pillows, pullulating, tongue wet, tart, darting. He heard Ethan sigh. This became the real world, his polar centre.

The most unexpected thing awaited Eric at the airport: Gwen, on time. Eric had taken a novel with him to read, so routine were the searches which greeted the rock star on arrival at New Zealand Customs. He was used to an almost empty airport where he and a puzzled cleaner would be greeted by a hoyden-ish figure, henna-haired, dragging behind her a mountain-weight of sound equipment. Spitting out behind her, at the closing Customs doors — 'Fuckwits! Bastards! Fascist pigs! Why does New Zealand always have to be like this!' Eric knew. He lived there.

She was already large. More surprisingly, she was wearing glasses. Eric knew she was so chronically short-sighted that if she lost her contact lenses she was sent, in a mimicry of blind-ness, searching by touch round all the flat surfaces. Glasses were usually exiled to her private moments. Now she wore a dense pair of spectacles, nonchalantly. This was a whole new image.

In his car (he slid the chair back so it could accommodate her) he looked at her intently. Her skin had a special sheen, glowing. But perhaps more than this was a change in equilibrium. Whereas before she appeared slightly frantic, even fractured, now she seemed oddly composed, as if she was standing on a high promontory, taking an overview of all that surrounded her. She appeared relaxed. He kept glancing at her. She filled him in on the minutiae of her life in LA: she had found a flat, a car. Gigs had come her way, a recording deal was almost lined up. Things were falling into place.

She smiled at him. 'And how are you, dear?' Normally he had to wade through several volumes of the misadventures in her life, the lapsed promises, the almost-signed contracts, the duds, the fools, the flakes for Gwen to look up, even notice he was right beside her. It was one of those things which contributed to the metal fatigue of their friendship. But now she was actually look-ing at him. Same old arrowed gaze, now enlarged by glasses.

'Well . . . ,' he hesitated, then looked at her and smiled. 'My job seems to be going really well. It's quite worrying, actually. And . . . ,' he took a deep breath. Was it dangerous saying this? Challenging the fates? 'I've met someone . . . really nice. Someone who is good for me. His name is Ethan.'

She asked a few specific questions. She was most like a gay

man in that regard: she wanted detail, facts. Sizes, almost. But emotions too. Eric went through his brief inventory.

'You'll meet him later on. He's turning up tonight.'

'Well, I'm really glad for you dear,' murmured Gwen, easing her back into the chair. She was looking out at the strange tussock paddocks near the airport, so signal of their country. It was dimpling down into a glamorous darkness, still and silent out there. But her voice was transparently sincere. Then the unexpected, which embossed the bonds of friendship — the longer-term perception, based on intimate knowledge. 'You've really earned it, Eric.'

Earned it? He didn't know about that. He computed this as he went on driving. He had kept his pace beside Perrin for as long as he could. But as the dementia hit and Perrin's voyage into the unknown accelerated, hadn't he dropped back? Hadn't he reached a barrier he could not pass beyond? Or was this death itself? An interlude before entering that darkened country, where god knows what voyages, patterns and paths occurred, or did not happen?

Perrin had occupied that landscape, made it his own. Eric had gone with him as far as he could but the fact was, the slightly criminal fact, one which still haunted him: he had held back. He was still alive. Perrin was dead.

Back at his flat he gave Gwen clean linen, towels.

'These are Perrin's,' he said, dropping them on Gwen's bed. He did so with the hint of irony. 'He always was a quality control queen. Everything had to be of the very best.'

Gwen picked one up. She was sitting on the edge of the bed, momentarily exhausted. Her hand did its own small choreography of contact. Pad of finger massaging. Thick as fur, soft as moss, enwrapping, comforting.

The towel was the deepest variant of, ironically, Virgin Mary blue. Gwen held it to the side of her cheek, cradled.

'You know when Lionel died,' Gwen was speaking of a musician friend in LA, a Maori, 'and we were clearing out his flat, it was so strange and sad all the things we found.'

She told him then about her friend dying: the laughter, when

14

there could have been crying; the crying, when there might only have been loss. This was a mixture Eric knew: a compound of exhaustion, exhilaration and a deep underlying sadness. Lionel had left her his saxophone. It was to this saxophone that Gwen traced all her changed luck. She had played it at her first major audition, the one that landed what looked like being a contract. She intended naming the baby after Lionel.

This softened something obdurate in Eric.

'Oh Eric,' for a second Gwen took on Audrey Hepburn's gamin charm, 'it was so funny in the end, emptying out all of Lionel's personal things. The last thing we threw out was his dildo . . . a giant one, a real whopper . . .'

They had laughed at this, companionably. It was all rather ridiculous in the end. Or rather, you had to savour the ridiculous. We were only humans, after all: a bit of a joke on the cosmic scale.

Eric was on the phone when Ethan arrived. Eric felt at that moment a kind of panic, of indecision: would Ethan wait? He had known young men who had never been able to wait one second as they chased after the powder-keg explosion of their intuitions. But no. Ethan was not like that. He had his bag with overnight things, a book on Arts-and-Crafts silver, a bottle of chilled champagne.

He put his things down. Then simply looking at Eric, as if he couldn't wait any longer, as if the moments apart must be lessened, as if any time apart was simply not worth living, he walked straight towards him in an undeviating line. Smiling slightly and butting into Eric with his hot lightly sweaty, fleshly discus-throwing body, he leant into him. Ethan fitted against him as purely as joints are made to fit, as machine parts cohere to function efficiently. Eric was still holding the phone and maintaining the semblance of a business conversation. Ethan's face came closer, closer to his as the soft cushioned plane of his lips moved up his neck and found Eric's lips. Eric's eyes momentarily lost their focus and he tried, quickly, quickly, to make his decision: always to be fair with Ethan, never to risk his life, to hold all things in relativity, try to maintain that balance. To remember, to forget, to relax and accept that memory did not disappear. And having made that decision, Eric let himself go loose, abandoning himself to the epiphany of desire, relaxing as he set off, falling whichever way he fell, whispering as he went: *Thank you for opening a door and entering my heart. Make yourself at home.* Then: *O god, don't trust me. Don't!*

But prove me wrong, I beg of you.

He had found a new form of relativity.

The Duration of a Kiss

1

Y's sister had, supposedly, committed suicide when I met him. He did not find out because the telegram lay unseen for five days. At the time I spent a day depressed for him, longing to see him so I could hug him and talk to him about it: telling him the beads of my suicides — suicides I have known. (A happy subject.) Gradually, however, as his excuse to me — that he always wanted to be alone to think about his sister — later turned out to be nights on which he went out to openings and parties and took part in genial, late-summer debauches, I began to doubt about the sister. Then I decided it could not possibly be true. It was simply another part of the melancholy landscape of his lies. Yet there is another way of looking at this: *all* his behaviour was dictated by his sister's suicide.

2

The nape of his neck I have a particular passion for. It is almost negroid, its gentle incline, the way the hair is prickly under the tongue, and runs away, like sand under a wave, into the firm cartilage at the top of his spine. That first morning I gathered the flesh of his neck into my mouth, I sucked on its warmth, I closed my teeth about it. His body was on top of mine — his back arched on my chest, his arse grazing my cock, and slowly, with a leisurely power, I began to bite him, harder and harder as he flailed away from me, caught at his neck, pinioned.

I knew I had his consent, so I decided to leave a mark on his

17

body which would exist there for days, hours when we would be apart, a bite which, by its very placing and obviousness, created a form of ownership by proxy; a mark which says to everyone: this is where I have been. So I bit him. And he, in his turn, he bit me.

3

I could not stop laughing. First of all this disconcerted him, he was suspicious. Am I laughing at him? I gather him down to me and kiss him silent, kiss him blind, kiss him dumb, then I say I am laughing because I am happy. He begins to laugh too. His laughter has some kind of wild glee in it, a percolation of manic joy in it which I can't quite explain. We laugh at all kinds of things, and during moments which, properly, should be charged with silent passion. Afterwards I think our laughter has a kind of staggered relief to it, like two men escaping danger, or death.

4

Soiled arum, coal-dust lashes, the hair on his body an intricate black lacework made by no human's fingers it is so feathery. His cock is thick, good to grasp hold of, firm, more dependable than anything else about him: his face white, moon-white. His eyes, he says to me, laughing when I say they are so beautiful, are 'cows' eyes'. 'Cow's eyes watching a train go by.' His laughter at this is cynical, yet delighted too. Another lover has told him the same thing. He tells me this as if he has, at long last, been caught out.

5

He has two moles on his back. I felt these in the dark, and in the light I ascertained they were two small raisins of black, charming imperfections in a boy-man whose body, in many other respects, creates its own standard of beauty.

Yet there is another thing. He bites his nails. This is the first sign to me of something which bodes ill. We are lying together his hand inside my hand, we are scissored together, lightly sleeping. Under the guise of sleep I investigate his body. I run my fingers over his fingertips. There are no nails. I think of a lover long ago, a hopeless love affair, a fixation, an addiction. This other lover was a charming psychopath, a liar. So I lie in the bed and try and ponder this conundrum: an achingly beautiful man who bites his nails. What can be the source of his anxiety? What can a beautiful man have to worry about?

We who are ordinary-looking, even perhaps ugly, cannot imagine this. To us, beauty is its own absolute, an imperium which creates its own laws, just as it defines its own territories, bends everything to the sway of its glamour: which is where he moves: that zone within which he breathes. I long, from this moment, to occupy that area within which he breathes. This becomes the essential oxygen for my life. I decide to overlook the fact that he bites his own fingernails. Willingly I abdicate the responsibility of listening to my own instincts. I give up, almost without noticing, what is essential to self-survival. Indeed, I lay it, without comment, at his feet.

He does not notice. Why should he? He is used to it. More than this, he is bored by the surfeit of it.

6

Call him Y. His name is of no importance. Nor his country. He was simply foreign, from a country which summons up the idea of glamour, from an ancient city synonymous with beauty, civilisation and taste. Suffice to say, he was, in this country, adorned with all the virtues of his native land. This made it more difficult, rather than less, to perceive the person beneath. Besides, he was such a capable manipulator of artifice and advantage, he knew too well how to use his foreignness as a way of creating his own safe passage.

So he cut a swathe through our small city, sleeping with many men, an occasional woman. Most of these found him, at least on the first occasion, irresistible.

7

You ask me precisely what he looks like? Well, dear reader — and this is the good part (as people snicker, handing you a well-scuffed paperback) — I have found people's ideas of what constitutes attractiveness to be so infinitely individual that I am safely leaving a description of his physicality to you. Simply think of the last person you were intolerably attracted towards. Imagine not being able to breathe deeply unless your eyes are upon his or her face: imagine doing things like waiting in a street so that you might accidentally meet. You supply your own details. The compulsion towards chaos and disaster is nearly always the same. The object of desire differs. But the important thing about him is the fact he is appallingly beautiful. Please reader, take pity: imagine the last person you felt an intolerable attraction towards. This is him.

8

The first time he came in my face, suddenly, splattering all across my forehead, the bridge of my nose, my hair. I closed my eyes quickly and gasped. He was pinning me down, thighs up by my neck, a brace of flesh. He bent over me, laughing at me scornfully.

'You are worried about the carpet?' he said.

Later he said, 'You want to fuck only in bed,' as if this confirmed my petit-bourgeois nature.

9

I would abandon my oldest friend willingly. I would betray any confidence. I would turn a marble ear to an old parent.

This is how I know I have changed: this is the alchemy of his desire.

10

The first night what I remember most and what I can recall this instant, as I write this here, as instantly as if he were now doing it, was the pressure of his lips on my toe. He was at the end of the bed, he was naked and crouching, athletically, down. He was sucking, gently at first, then with almost childishly impatient insistence, so his lips seemed to be crying out, even as they suctioned round my toe. I looked down to see his lowered nape, his cock hard and thick against the black hairs of his belly. It was my left foot, I am sure. (I hesitate to mention such an idiocy of sexual obsession.) What side of the brain does that relate to, now, I wonder? Is it that which made me more irrational? Was it that which made me, that night, decide to lose control? Decide to lease out the power of my control?

11

There was only one night.

12

The fourth time he came I saw his face in the early morning light and this was one time he looked older than his age — his lips clenched, his eyes puffy. He looked determined, a soldier in the eternally marching army of sex, a foot soldier, perhaps labouring.

He was least beautiful at this moment: most human, more ordinary.

I lay there watching him not one foot away from me, yet his face distant and removed, in his own immense solace of pleasure. This is when he was most naked. And I had seen him.

13

That unlucky number.

Obsession lies, perhaps, in inventing a meaning where none, in fact, may exist: in giving to a glance a whole subtext of meaning. In this, is there not a parallel to fiction? The fictional persona of Y which I am giving to you may in fact only be a construct of my imagination.

14

Have I told you that his mother is wealthy, has powerful lovers, that he has had a small but significant part (playing a drug dealer) in a movie by a film director I greatly admire? That he worked in the most fashionable bar in Sydney? Did I tell you this? Over a week, by apparently accidental questioning of his acquaintances who had no idea they were talking to a maniac, I found this out.

He is even a writer of stories.

15

This is how I see him. He has the face of a corrupt child, of a slut-angel, a kind of purity of dissolution refined to an exquisite point, expressed by his battered eyes, his bruised lips. That he is almost thirty is one of the fascinating things about him. The reality of his interior is so well hidden that to look at him, you would think you were seeing someone in their early twenties. He is an alcoholic. This is something he tells you himself, matter-of-factly. Yet there is no evidence of this in his face or body. After a night of debauch he simply seems most reassuringly himself: it is as if he has grown into his skin, stretched, yawned and felt sublimely comfortable. This makes him more irresistible.

So that night I conceived a terrible and mistaken passion: that here was a person for whom I had waited all my life. It was as if everything up till this point had been a preparation and now he had appeared and we were, meteor-like, together.

I did not understand that though Y needed love that night, and I provided it, he really existed in a world of surfeit. Too many men were attracted to him, too many men were driven to distraction by his glance, his 'self-destruct' eyes, as someone said of him. (The whole town — 'the whole town' meaning a small group of people who frequent a certain nightclub, bar, certain

22

parties — exchanged information about him, almost anxiously, as if he were a disease among us, and all of us must nervously, constantly take our temperatures.)

16

Now I began to hear further things of him: his name was spontaneously on everyone's lips. He was a writer of two successful plays, he was 'more intelligent than you and I', his understanding of human nature transcended our local levels of comprehension.

Between ourselves we laboured blissfully to create his aura: he was, not to put too fine a point on it, an angel.

Yet that night our transaction was, above all, earthly. We used each other well, I think. That was our agreement. What happened after that is perhaps my fault: yet did he not give me some leading clues? Did he not ask for my phone number, ring me repeatedly, ask me whether, at that time, I had a boyfriend?

And did he not, as if casually, yet with hidden portent, leave certain, expensive clothes at my house, taking in their place worthless items from my wardrobe? Was I a fool to believe that this marked a transition point, almost a cinematic dissolve by which, in the end, his entire wardrobe would be at my place: and he would be in my life?

Now I pick up his shirt, breathe in deeply. I smell him: a curiously clean, even vaguely perfumed smell. This is an irony for he is, as a pornographic story would say unctuously, a 'really dirty fucker'.

17

Have I told you he is liar? Have I told you that? That he is a charming cheat, fickle and incapable of ever telling the truth? Yes, but he is beautiful. His beauty is truly appalling. All over town men are falling in love with him and among ourselves we talk of him, wonderingly, as if we seek to convince each other that he is not what he perhaps really is.

Besides, when a man possesses such astonishing beauty, can he not be forgiven everything? I hear, in a crowded restaurant, he must come from a certain valley, near a certain city: for that valley, in the whole wide world, provides the most beautiful of men. A woman tells me this.

When I finally send his clothes back, I keep one shirt which I wear defiantly yet with a real sense of exhilaration. He asks me about it ironically. What has that shirt become, he asks, supremely bored with the transparency of my games. A hostage?

18

He wanted no boundary in the sex between us, he demanded it impatiently, even angrily. And I was pleased to be absolved from careful, clumsy love-making. I wanted his fury. I wanted it wild.

We began kissing on the dance floor, then, unaware of anyone around us, rammed up against a wall. This continued in the taxi home, this hunger of our mouths for each other, this need to consume each other's face. I looked up at one point and saw a middle-aged Polynesian driver, stoic in the night, driving us home. I imagine he was like a barge-poler, in some dark twilight, Auckland changed into a Venice of the imagination.

It was in the light grey of morning, when I looked at him I realised he had led me whirlingly along on a dance of forgetfulness, of escape — to an area of oblivion in which I happily lost myself, lost everything about me. It was at this moment I grasped what sex really was: it was losing the weight of humanness, divesting myself of the persona known as 'me' and in the maelstrom, in those moments of loss, locating a centre, a source, a central vitality. 'This is what I really like. So this is who I really am.'

Yet two men together cannot ever, any longer, lose control totally. Not without, that is to say, acknowledging that it is permissible to lose control. In this sense, there is no loss of control. Only a lending of loss, a teasing, an extentuation of the rights.

That night we agreed to lose control.

19

In the morning our clothes were like snakes' skins, sloughed aside; in contorted configurations, suggesting the escaped vacuum of being human.

20

Later, driven to see him again, to refresh my memory with the actuality of his face, I went to see him where he worked in a café — a fashionable café, the most fashionable café in the small city. He had not told me he worked there, though this is where I first saw him and conceived of my rash design. Yet meeting him now, after we had actualised this fantasy — this dream — was a disaster. He did not like me seeing him, perhaps, only as a waiter — one who could not stop to talk. I felt awkward and ugly — ugly with emotion. I wanted to say I only wished to match his face with my memory, to confirm its dimensions. Yet already it was hopeless, as if by removing his physical form he left me with only one thing: memory.

21

So the placid surface of my life collapsed effortlessly. I, who prided myself on the carefulness of my painting, its artful subtexts and painfully worked surfaces, I who had at long last arrived at a point of confidence in myself — a promontory from which I might launch off on a new departure: what more perfect point to meet a disaster.

For days I dropped everything, lied to old friends, capriciously broke long-standing appointments. Shamelessly I duped people with the fullness of my days which were, in fact, spent relentlessly — with the true monotony of obsession — in trying to see him; and in trying to see him, to return to that one point at which we had met.

Artfully now, he began to elude me. Carelessly he made appointments which he then broke, without so much as an apology. Yet he continued to make these appointments, as if their sole point was to disappoint me. So I became involved in his own game: and is it not flattering to have someone helplessly in love with you? It aids your sense of self-esteem. It is even useful, for you need never indulge the obsessed lover. Indeed, by not indulging him, you make sure the legend of your love grows greater. So, with his permission, one might almost say connivance, I began to operate in the zone of a neurosis.

22

All other men became unattractive because they were not him. And he looked at me as if I repelled him utterly, had killed all desire in him. Or better still, to hurt me he openly made love to men who later, embarrassed, explained to me they were only friends and that the theatre — to dissuade me or encourage me? — was entirely for my benefit.

When he admonished me, demanding that I stop staring at him, I asked him, surprised, where else I should look. Then I mimicked the emptiness of space around him, the vivid vacuum in which he was enclosed. He laughed at this and for one moment we occupied the space we had known that first night.

Even the imperfections of his English I worshipped.

23

I sat with his waiter friends, cursing myself that I was not a waiter and could join in the fragmented discourse of their lives: parties, drinking, sex in toilets, all the beads in the rosary of cheerful oblivion. I had recently had a success with my painting, I was to go to Venice to the Biennale. Yet to all these people, and hence to him, all my accomplishments — everything I had worked for and worked at — were meaningless.

At that moment I conceived the wish to trade everything to become a waiter, simply so I could join in their conversations, broodily bored, edgily witty as they were: so I could be Y.

The summer was passing and with winter coming there was a kind of furious activity, because nobody knew who might not be there, at winter's end. Nobody said this, of course. It did not need saying. But it was there, in the crueller gun-metal grey of the waves, in the singular blue, almost of a ladybird, in the sky. The colours of our town now took on a peculiar palette: volcanic rock black and, across the harbour, the uniform khaki-green of the volcano, striated with cloud. The sea turned chillier shades of green. You could see right up the harbour to the land outside the city — its emptiness was an intoxication. How many summers would it be before the tourists finally got here? Or was this, in fact, the last?

Inside the city, the parties took on a peculiar frivolity. It was that summer that sadomasochism became *de rigueur*, I think.

25

Gradually I began to meet other men, all over town, at parties, in late hours at the nightclub, and our conversations, always, as if to the central point of the compass, turned to Y. It was in this way that I found I was not alone: it was as if an entire erotic life of a city was focused on this one, slight man. Many were the men obsessed with him, for he had slept with all of us, once, twice, three or four times perhaps, then he had broken appointments with them just as he had, effortlessly, 'broken my heart'.

One man warned me of the danger I was in: that it was only a matter of time before Y would have to retreat from our town: that sooner or later someone would physically take to him, perhaps scar his beauty forever.

All this news came to me as a reprieve. I who had forgiven him everything made up my own excuses for him: crouched down at his feet in the shape of a hideous griffin, tormented by jealousy, effulgent with thwarted love — a hunchback of the Waitemata, one might say.

As if to help me Y began to show himself in a less than ideal light. He even cried out to me one night, when we talked, 'How can you love me when you don't even know me?' And it is true, I knew almost nothing of him apart from what he showed me that first night: yet that night together was so profound it held his essence, with the almost savage purity of alcohol, a distillation of his life.

Yet, now, in the brilliant limning of early autumn light I saw how he had a sore at the corner of his mouth. And his skin, so white, had bruises beneath it, as if he was wounded internally and they were a long time working their way to the surface. He was also painfully thin, I decided: dangerously thin. And he could never give a straight answer, or be spontaneous, except in his deceptions. But he was fecklessly charming, a real cavalier of the heart, deeply cynical beneath the surface but a lover practised in all forms of giving pleasure. I became an embarrassment, one of the many men, I suspect, to be thus discarded.

Yet this is the truth: he needed this obsession as a pauper needs a warm cloak. He needed all these spurned men to long for him, to surround him constantly with the heat of their suppressed love: this created him, almost. In fact I suspect if none of us were there, he might collapse internally into the rather pathetic boy-man he in fact was. For he wants love, of course — he who is so cynical about it, and uses it with shocking bravado. He wants to be loved desperately.

This man whose sister has killed herself in a moment of despair. He wants only and endlessly to be loved. And is this not the cry of us all?

27

Then it happened.

Over the length of a summer — the duration of a kiss — an entire town had been enamoured of him. Suddenly, like echoes across a lake hitting their widest circumference only to return, disruptively, towards the centre — perhaps an intimation of the tininess of our social province? — his sexual reputation reached its apogee and inside the concatenation of our mutual discovery (he had slept with you!), to our consternation his reputation — or was it his beauty? — collapsed.

The time of his discovery was over.

Now a silence fell in his presence and in everyone's eyes was an accusation. Surrounded by supercilious glances as steely as shields presented, edge to edge, so that he could no longer escape, he, the prince of my obsession, found himself trapped in the distant country of provincialism.

He discovered our world was no bigger than a dance floor, no wider than the carpet on the floor of the bar, more claustrophobic than a cubicle in which he now lay, awaiting any stranger. Was it true to say this visitor to our shores had finally arrived? And what more perfect time, perhaps, for him to make his own too-late discovery.

So it is at this moment, in the middle of a dance floor on which he dances not exactly alone, but accompanied by his swain, the bottle, that he comes to me and says — did I imagine it? The music was so loud, yet I know from the formation of his lips they were the words I had ached to hear for so long. He said to me, simply, abjectly, confirming his defeat: 'I love you.'

And what did the pitter-patter of my heart do?

28

I began the process of realising that though I lived in the small town and always imagined myself to be a refugee of a large and distant city — the city of the mind, of the incomparably free — in fact I had proved myself to be a provincial by my actions. I was as subject to the ordinances of the small town as anyone.

Y escaped our indifference soon after.

On the Day

Dreaming comes from much worrying, foolish talk from a multiplicity of words.

— *Ecclesiastes*

'How far away are you?'

Ephram, the director, knocked on the make-up door nervously. It was his habit each morning to look in on the actors being made up. They always had the earliest call, arriving on location at half past five in the morning. This was before anyone, or anything, moved in the flocculent dark.

Padlocks were prised apart and the studio door rolled back, sending a rumble of stage thunder echoing through space. A 75-watt bulb cast a wan light over a landscape of make-believe: buggies, canoes, moas made out of papier mâché. All looked as sad as left-behind luggage in the dim and dust-strobed light. Barely awake, hardly talking, the actors and make-up women, advance guard of the unreal, climbed the rickety staircase to the make-up room, put on the heaters, boiled some water then set, somewhat heroically, to work.

Nobody spoke much. It was, after all, the very beginning of what was almost certainly going to be a long and exhausting day. Fifteen hours later would see this same make-up wiped off, eyelashes carefully prised off, wigs dismantled and tissues flung carelessly, with a residue of sweat, heat and hopes, into the bin. Each day risked disaster, each morning offered the possibility of triumph. But it was the role of Ida and Merlene, the make-up women, every morning to inspect each actor minutely for signs of psychological wear-and-tear: extra-fine lines under the eyes from a sleepless night, puffy cheeks because of a period, tension lines beside the mouth. And in these moments, precious confidentialities were traded: a symbiotic traverse of the film's shadowy heart.

But today the door to the make-up room was almost emblematically shut. Like anyone else on the crew, Ephram had been reduced to petition by nervous knock.

Getting no response, he turned the door handle and entered the room with its unforgiving light. It was queer, he thought, how he felt himself to be increasingly an actor on his own set. His incessant bustle, the pursing of his lips thoughtfully, the faraway look in his eyes; all this was now a meretricious technique to cover his increasing sense of bewilderment. How could something which was going so right, suddenly turn so wrong? It was unexpected as weather, this quick reverse. But it was clear there was a crisis of confidence abroad the set. A nervous mood of apprehension, a lack of belief in him, was seeping in like acid, like a poison.

Once, in the early days of the shoot, they had exchanged cheerful greetings with one another, like happy members of a bus tour, secure in the knowledge that they were heading off to an exciting destination. But the rushes the night before had been inexcusably bad: the lights had come up and everyone was poleaxed to their seats. Eyes refused to meet, and silently, in single file, as if washing their hands of an incipient disaster, the crew had disappeared. Nobody lingered behind for a beer (40 cents in the jar, THANK YOU). Ephram had commented out loud: 'I like it. Good work everybody.' But not even this could hide from him the fact that the strain involved in obtaining the scene — a 'sex scene' — had not been worth it.

'What is this? *Amateur hour*?' Ephram had screamed to Waddington, his producer, after the rushes. Waddington had gone white with anger at being yelled at. 'Did I ask for ham on the bone?' Ephram was unstoppable. '*Did I*?'

It is a rule of film that everyone on the crew, from the runner to the director, has a chance to stage a nervous breakdown. This is one of the true attractions of film. Every form of behaviour, to a certain extent, is accepted within the ad hoc family which is a film

31

crew. But Ephram had lost control completely. And hence respect. He had shown himself to be merely human, like all the rest.

As he entered the make-up room, neither of his stars deigned to look up. Starling flicked over a page, while Gloria — head held stiff by Ida as she painted on a thin line of mascara — greeted him with a cold flick of her glorious green eyes. Ephram stood behind the two make-up women, both of whom presented their backs to him as they went on working. The silence was electric.

'How are we this morning, ladies?'

He talked into the mirror. Starling's face looked pinched in the glass: her hair was in rollers and perhaps it was this sense, of flesh being painfully pulled back and up, and into tight coils, which gave her features a vaguely disagreeable, sour look. She was, anyway, a startling mixture of a woman: without make-up she looked less than glamorous, positively dowdy in fact, yet with a painted-on scarlet mouth, false eyelashes and a flattering hairstyle, she came alive in front of the lens, blossoming with a rare chemistry which pulled the eyes towards her unswervingly, even when she was silent, or merely breathing.

It was this act of transformation on which Ephram daily relied: this talismanic act of magic by his ladies and their attendants in artifice. But now, tissues resting round her face like flakes of peeling skin, Ephram saw trouble. A very clear and discernible rupture was elevating itself towards the surface of Starling's left cheek.

A pimple.

This was an A-list crisis.

Ephram could not stop a bleat of despair escaping from his lips. He leant back against the wall.

Starling's eyes did not rise to meet his own in the mirror. But he imagined he saw a hint of moisture — tears of anger, mortification — spread in a film over her almost violet irises. She knew it was her big day on the set: it was her chance, ambitious as she was, to steal the film away from Gloria, a more established actress in the middle of a secure career arc. He knew this. She knew this. And it was perhaps this insoluble knowledge, this tryst, almost of Faustian ambition, which did not allow her to meet his gaze.

'How are you, Ephram?'

It was Gloria, who, the line having been completed with severity, now had a moment to relax. Her eyes swept past his in the mirror. They did not linger, he noticed.

'Oh, you — know . . . ' he suspended his words for comic effect. 'As well as can be expected. I *guess.*' His final sentence, however, unintentionally dipped down into soft depression.

He cleared his throat with a dry, hesitant cough.

'Yes, Ephram,' Gloria said, as if she were a teacher speaking to a backward child. 'You want to talk to us about the kiss.'

'Well —' Ephram twisted on his feet as if he had a terrible stomach-ache. He felt a hopeless wreck: he was a social misfit, anyway, he knew that. And here he was, trying to tell people how to represent human beings on a screen. It was a joke. A sick joke.

'If you don't mind . . . '

Silence.

The two make-up women went on with their work. It was as if previous warmth and intimacy were a memory, a mistake.

'Well, maybe if we just look through the lines. I mean. I know we'll walk through them on the set. But . . . '

He creased open his script, which had an air of unquiet desperation to it: dirty, dog-eared, pages squeezed in between, sketches, notes, call-sheets, memos.

Everyone is waiting, Ephram.

With a curiously vulnerable wobble in his voice, Ephram read the lines and directions aloud.

Scene 37. *Dawn. A beach. The tide is out. The women in grey silk. Eliza (Gloria) and Juno (Starling) walk under a cowling sky.*

ELIZA
But what if he . . .
JUNO
He cannot, I will not let him.
Or rather, I should say, his
heart will not allow him.

ELIZA

. . . his heart?

JUNO

You care whether he is hurt?

Eliza takes off her hat and looks down at it seriously, considering.

ELIZA

The point, surely, is that neither
of us . . . any of us . . . should maim the
other. Or do you want that?

Juno now looks at her own hat, seriously.

JUNO

The point is . . . if we need a point
which, indeed, I think we don't
. . . but our aim must be our freedom.
Either he stands aside . . .

ELIZA (*excitedly*)

But if he knew!

JUNO (*smiling*)

If he only knew . . .

The two women move closer and closer together.

ELIZA (*aside*)

He has no freedom!
We have taken it from him.
He is our prisoner.

JUNO (*disdainfully*)

You want him as your prisoner?

*The two women look into each other's eyes and move close together,
till there is no space between them.*

Ephram delicately laid his script shut.

Gloria shook her head a fraction of a millimetre. Ida, almost in
usurpation of Ephram's function, had gone back to working on
Gloria's mascara, her face intent, nervous as a jeweller splitting
a multi-carat diamond.

Starling simply lifted her eyes and stared at Ephram as if she
had forgotten everything that he had told her; he read into her
eyes the possibility that she might just respond however she
wished. She was an enigma, of constantly bubbling neurotic

possibilities from which she extracted some essence of a performance. Just as Gloria, on the street, or caught off guard, had an extraordinarily pensive vacancy in her features as if there were literally no intelligence behind her flesh: a light bulb awaiting luminosity. Both these women were to kiss, as lovers intoxicated with each other's flesh.

'Ida!' It was Gloria. 'Oh god! Red-hot needles. Hurry! *Please! God! Hurry!*'

Ida sped her hands over the nobbled encrustation of Gloria's head. She drew out hairpins, at random. 'This one? This? *This?*'

Starling's high brittle laughter vaulted out of her lips. Iridescent scales, snake-green, fell about the room, clattering.

A vague flush settled on Gloria's shoulders.

'I'm so glad . . .' she said with the coolness of mountain water, 'you find *something* about me amusing.'

The two actresses looked at each other for a mini-second of stalled fury.

'It's just . . . it's just . . .' Starling took on the affectation of speaking with a cleft palate, 'your expression, dahling. So funny. Sorry. No offence.' She grew almost mournfully serious in swift ellipsis.

In the mirror, Merlene arched her eyebrows in significant portent to Ephram, who withdrew.

He was surprised to be followed out by Merlene. She leant against the door soundlessly, face heroically stripped of make-up.

'*Oh god, why in heaven's name on today of all days!*' Ephram cried in a crucified voice.

'For heaven's sake don't let anyone comment on it,' Merlene whispered. 'We've already had tears this morning.' She paused, assessing the damage. 'Close-ups?'

'ECUs.' His hands shot apart, to a maximum width. 'Vistavision. You know. *We're going in!*' he crowed, like an intrepid explorer in a B-grade jungle movie.

Merlene's face was deep in thought.

'Shoot from one side?'

'No can do. *Impossible.*' Soon it would be the desperate hour. Another one of them. 'Cover it. Plaster it over. Make a fucking fresco out of her face.'

'I can only cover up so much,' Merlene said. 'You'll still see it.'

They looked into each other's eyes and they both shrugged simultaneously. Ephram found himself smiling wanly at Merl.

'How far away are you?'

She thought for a moment.

'It'll add another hour.'

'An hour,' Ephram said, with an odd dislocated look. He began to climb back down the stairs, feeling an old, old man.

'A fucking useless bastard'

Ephram walked in a wild zigzag away from the building. It was only when he cleared the portaloos that he felt safe. He slumped down on a damp bank and closed his eyes. He waited to think of something and when nothing came, he opened his eyes. He looked down at a corpse: a dead sparrow. Animal of flight. Felled. Dead eye, stale oyster. He touched it with his foot. A busy line of ants was carrying its flesh away. Bit by bit. A feast. There was something in their industry, their organisation, which fascinated him. The front ones in single file, frenetically working, a small army febrile with action — direction. *Direction*. That word. He watched them in silence for a moment.

A pimple! On today of all days — the kiss.

Scene 54. *The Kiss. 'Juno had never looked more beautiful.'*

The pale light shines down on her face fresh with hopes, dreams, ideals. All the time she darts glances at Gloria, a faint flush of excitement on her cheeks. Her hands keep changing their position on her hat. Her lips are parted . . .

Pimple.

Better not to think of it. Today is a fresh day. New start. He flipped open his script for inspiration. He gripped the page with white-knuckled intensity. He was terrified of losing his script: it had reached phobic point. In fact, he had had a classic anxiety dream about it the night before, symptom of his fallen state.

In the middle of the night, silent, inside a warehouse he found himself searching through racks of lost, forgotten costumes. Dust. Dirt. Despair. Finally, when he was on the point of giving up, he found his name stitched, yet misspelt, on the label of a black velvet jacket. When he tried it on, it was comically large. Five sizes too big. In its pocket he felt his script. In his palm it turned into a tiny pocket dictionary, of the type which is so small it is even difficult to open. When he prised it open, he saw a language he did not understand. Hieroglyphs had removed it totally from the Roman alphabet.

He dropped the dictionary-script into the sea, watched it zigzag away from him, catching in the light like the flailing underbelly of an octopus till it finally faded and settled into the murk of the bottom of the harbour. He felt an indescribable relief. It was over.

And then, of course, he woke up.

There were still another four weeks to go.

Everyone is waiting, Ephram.

Behind him the slurping splutter of a walkie-talkie, frosty with static.

'Where the *fuck* is he?'

It was the voice of Ashes, the third AD.

'Useless fucking bastard,' he heard. Or was he imagining it? Whose voice was that? His own?

He is our prisoner.

Do you want a prisoner?

Starling's mocking laughter.

He must go back.

The hour calls.

He carefully did a Hollywood curve around Ashes, so that he, or was it Ashes, might have the indecency of his indiscretion left intact.

Inside the dinosaur

Ephram walked on to the set. Purposefully, 'on a mission'. Past the extras, already glumly painted, seated on school benches and leafing through outdated women's magazines. Each one was covered, head to foot, in bright blue paint. They were to be the 'furies', but at that moment they were exhausted, having been made up for over three hours.

A sad plump fairy sat peeling an orange into a dustbin.

Deeper into the studio he walked, as if he were penetrating the intestines of some felled beast. He smelt wires burning. And something else, an ordure which was penetrating, a miasma rather than a scent. The set had never really lost the smell of horse piss. They had shot Gloria's arrival on a six-horse coach first up. Animals, corralled painfully, had released their bowels. Hoses of piss had feckled down the walls, run in tides across the floor; horses had dropped steaming dollops. Under the heat of the lights the smell had permeated, it seemed, the walls, doors; even the pores of their skin.

Ephram saw the bulging eye of a horse, glossy, clouded blue, rolled back in fear, trying to look behind it, its hooves stamping a primal tattoo on the stage-floor, wheeling, always trying to move backwards, to see behind it.

The slaughterhouse.

Fear of the slaughterhouse.

Ephram, hurry up please.

The horse's pink pleat had sagged open. A torrent, a Niagara of shit, had slushed out.

Decide, Ephram. The crew is waiting.

It was his two producers speaking. He was in their office, his back to them as he looked out the window. He was exhausted: it was the end of another eighteen-hour day.

The completion guarantor, Ephram, rang today.

He looked out the window at people hurrying home from work: catching buses, walking across crossings, buying dinner. Why wasn't he one of those?

He can take over the production, Ephram. He can sack you.

I'm only telling you this for your own benefit.

It just can't go on.

The voices echoed in his ears.

You just don't seem to understand.

Able Waddington was yelling now, leaning across his desk. Coronary territory, Ephram remembered thinking, *There-is-simply-no-more-money.*

'G'day mate.'

Up high on a rafter, like the most distant point of sanity,

Georg, a sparkie, dangled his legs over a strut, holding a cigarette. He was a sexy man, unreachable: they exchanged a greeting. Ebenezer Hulwood, director of photography, stalked by, one eye scrunched shut as his powers of the occult strained to pierce the gloom of his light-metre. Legs lowered into a crouch, he took on the unavoidable stance of Groucho Marx. Turning a sharp zigzag, Cyclops after Circe, he exited behind a fibreglass waka.

'Dim the number fives,' Eb yelled out.

The light changed to near apocalypse.

Over by the tea trolley a disgruntled group of technoes stood around, the beginnings of a mutiny. They watched Ephram pass in silence.

'Can I clear something with you?'

It was Carole, the continuity 'girl'. Mother of four, she had two pincer lines of a headache already on her brow. Eating an apple. Staying healthy. 'Stress-free'. Often she could be seen, lying flat on the concrete floor, listening to relaxation tapes.

Script held open, section underlined.

'Yes. In a minute,' he said curtly. 'I just want to walk through the set.'

Hammerings all around him. Erratic heartbeat. The carpenters had been working against the clock. Up since dawn. It was testament to his own insignificance that Ephram felt like an interloper on his own set. The set designer, Angus, was nowhere to be seen.

The witching hour

In his own mind he had always seen the set — a beach — as a limitless horizon which faded away into West Coast sand dunes. Two women stood, heads close together, their gossamer dresses fluttering in the breeze. Their glances to each other were momentary, fragmentary: lovers' glances.

The camera would move almost as if it were a sensor, responding to the heat, the ardour of each glance.

Behind the two women, a pearl-white sky. White gulls, white clouds, white surf, a continuous rumble. It would begin to rain. Pearls. Pearls of rain.

Distant thunder. Mahler, underscored with electric guitars. Drenched in a long, piercing Jimmy Hendrix screel of desire.

The two women would take shelter. A cave. Dark. Pale flesh. The rain increases. It falls on them. They get wet. And under the cover of proximity, intimacy, they would find their lips aching. It was then they would kiss.

The schedule said 1 pm: closed set. No visitors please.

He had talked it over endlessly with Gloria and Starling: in fact there seemed no other fugitive motive which could possibly be searched for, to delay this inevitable moment when a woman's lips would meet another woman's lips, and not in greeting or farewell, but in passion. But he had not countenanced one thing: the vagary of a body which could produce, on so little notice, something so deeply anarchic, so irremovable as — a pimple.

Over by a wing, Denton, the cameraman, seasoned trouper of so many campaigns, was easing his feet, lying back on the crane like it was a hammock, enjoying a cigarette. His assistant, Carmen, had just brought him his sixth coffee. In the early days when Ephram was still seen as a director with purpose and a vision, he had been awarded crew approval by a significant act: Carmen brewed in the privacy of her truck her own espressos. And since caffeine was the lingua franca of the perpetually awake, he had received recognition by being awarded, along with other selected members of the crew, not a polystyrene cup full of overboiled instant but a demitasse of mainline caffeine. He realised his stock had fallen when this benefit was silently withdrawn. Back to the gulag of styrofoam and instant for him.

Ignored now, Ephram moved past.

Strains of laughter — curtains of disbelief? — spread out around him, diaphanously enclosing him, sealing him off: isolating him. It was all his fault.

Angus, the set designer, appeared through an aureole of light. Covered in splashes of red and white paint, as if he had been shot, he paced round, head lowered. He barely looked at Ephram.

'Good morning,' Ephram said with what he hoped was model calm.

'JESUS CHRIST! Fuck!' Angus's reply was on the descant.

They looked at each other like two battle-hardened soldiers for whom there is little left to say. Few illusions remained. Between them stood the chasm, the enormous difference between the excitement of their ideas, at the beginning, and their realisation, happening right at this moment.

On the day.

'On the day' meant now, the present, that remorseless arena hemmed in by lights in which Ephram inevitably found himself surrounded by people all of whom wanted to know the answer to a limitless range of questions.

We're waiting, Ephram.

What is your vision, Ephram?

We only want to know.

'On the day' meant whatever gamble you could draw on at the moment: it was the compromise of the possible in the face of the impossible. 'On the day' meant one thing: no more dreams, no more visions. It meant *now*, that most horrible of all things to anyone who is a dreamer by nature. It meant *reality*.

Ephram sometimes thought he had been attracted to film simply because it offered unreality instead of reality. Hours which took you away from normal working people, demands which were absurd in their grandeur: your house, your daughter, your horse, your smile — can we hire them?

But now it was the witching hour: 'on the day' had finally, and repetitively, arrived like a dreadful knell which struck again and again, day after wearisome day, as if its sole purpose were to remove any lust he had for unreality, to pursue all the dreams out of his head. Was this the real reason he had 'got into film'? To bring himself back to reality by the most perverse means possible? Was this his insanity?

His head ached, his stomach was clenched in a knot, he felt as if he were constantly caught in a dry retch.

Reality. It was desperately trying to work out a compromise, any compromise, whereby you could get what you wanted in a way which was something like what you had hoped for, dreamt of, originally. And you had to hope, to pray, some small segment, sliver, firework of the original dream persisted.

41

'Where do they meet?' Ephram asked.

'Well you see — you did say you wanted them in silhouette.'

Angus pulled Ephram with him into a pool of burning light. At their feet a set decorator, Angie, an art school student, was crouched down, painting in broad washes an emblematic beach. Beside Ephram, throwing glitter around, was Evelyn, another conscript from the hopelessly idealistic empire of art. They had been working since five o'clock in the morning. Drugged with sleep deprivation and overwork, neither looked up nor spoke. If anything, they appeared to have arrived at that state of equilibrium which certain Indians attained: in the fury of noise, they worked on in a trance.

A fan the size of a jet propeller was being wheeled on to the set. Ephram shaded the light from his eyes with his hand. The light was burning, as if its aim were to fire unguent ideas into smoke.

'The way I see it . . . ' Angus walked out across the plywood beach, head down, Napoleonic.

Ephram saw, beyond the lights, Continuity waiting like a detective for him, the suspect. Beside her was Dimbleby, from Wardrobe. He wanted, Ephram remembered now, to know about the final costume the women would wear — hats and jewels? Dimbleby, having caught a fraction of Ephram's eye, raised up the hats and jewels, in either hand, urgently, an impromptu statue of Justice.

Ephram saw nothing: or rather he glimpsed the disappearing vision of an eternal vista of a beach, a quintessential blending of air, light, heat, water. It was to be like that most perfect moment in choral singing, a duet of women's voices, melding into seraphic air. Sapphic air. Or just plain intoxication with another person. Those moments when an affair seems boundless, timeless.

Precious moments.

On the day.

He saw instead: wet paint, wood, glitter, glass. Reality. The box of the possible.

And the kiss. Would Gloria and Starling forget their tacit enmity and kiss like two humans hungry for the flesh of the

42

other? Could they? Starling was the dark card: an Australian actress, celebrated in the tabloids for her star allure. Could she allow herself to be seen as Sapphic? Would she give good lip?

Ephram crushed his lids shut and through tears he saw the possibility of an abstract space. It might work. It *had to* work. For a second he pictured himself washing dishes in a restaurant in Melbourne. His face had no expression. He washed the suds off his face with the back of his hand. He was being shouted at. *You fucking useless bastard.* The vision darkened.

Iris down to: Angus describing the 'beach' scene to him, face serious as a boy with his first meccano set. The best thing, he was saying, for this feeling of infinity, is for Juno and Gloria to be lying down, and simulating walking. 'The camera goes up there.' He pointed to the dirty pitch roof, where Ephram could already see Happy working with pulleys and creating a landing stage, as it were.

'The wind will come from here.'

He pointed to the enormous fan six metres across. Inside was the propeller blade of an aircraft. Art department navvies would throw white silk petals into the wind, which would blow across the two women.

'It's not sync, is it?'

Angus suddenly drew to a halt.

A crazed laugh escaped Ephram's lips.

'Well. It was. Up till now. It's really key dialogue.'

'You can dub it later,' said Angus, amputee of dreams.

Ephram felt the regret of a dying vision: that a scene he had seen as intimate, relaxed, a duet of looks, now had to be accomplished by such tyrannosaurus methods. But the visualisation demanded it. With their budget . . .

He looked afresh at the set. It resembled nothing so much as a torture system, medieval in its sheer inventiveness. The spirit of Da Vinci's flight hovered over the production.

A tree wandered past. A man carrying a tree, a plaster tree, weeping crystal tears and nightingales of cut glass.

Sorry!

Ephram had stood on wet paint. Incriminating evidence. Footprint. Captain Scott. To Oates. Out into the snow.

'I'll show you where Gloria and Juno go.'

Ephram felt a kind of reciprocal warmth: so Juno and Gloria were real characters to Angus also. They existed in that nebula of inspiration, a cloud of becoming which each actor strained to define and articulate. They — he and Angus — provided the necessary artifice which allowed this articulation, but first of all, you had to have belief. You had to believe.

In two fictional characters. No. In the reality of their dilemma: which was, they could not declare their love affair. They must fight, dissemble and advance. Like Ephram.

Angus pulled him aside. They walked behind a muslin curtain towards a stand. Two art department assistants, Jules and Jim, were standing in for the actresses. Or rather lying. Ephram read the pain of the situation in their strained expressions. They were flat on their backs, their shoulder blades straining against gravity. A metal stand stopped them from falling. Above them, mandarin as an eye surgeon in the middle of a delicate operation, Eb overlooked their discomfort.

'Won't be much longer,' he murmured.

The two actresses, Ephram saw, would lie down, strapped to the surface. The camera would be above them. As the actresses pretended to undulate (or walk), the camera would pull away. Later they would add other effects. But it did mean, Ephram saw, going up on his own and looking at where they would be lying, that the actresses would be in positions of acute discomfort while essaying looks to each other of the greatest intimacy.

'Have Gloria and Starling seen this yet?'

'Not yet,' answered Angus who at the same time looked at him.

They started laughing.

For one second, and sounding completely like two men driven cruelly insane, they laughed. They laughed intently, bitterly, a passing fit. As suddenly, they stopped and looked at each other, criminals.

Eb suddenly appeared right beside them.

'Dim that fucking light, Happy.'

'How far away are you?' Ephram tried to make his voice sound assertive.

Ebenezer looked at him across a vast white plain, snowing.
'Forty. Fifty max. The paint's got to fucking dry, mate.'
'Sorry,' said Ephram, clearing the set.

Strictly pre-eruption

O sweet Jesus, Ephram saw in the far distance Bill Loman, hovering on the very edge of the set. *The writer*. He had specifically asked the First to make sure Loman was *never, ever* allowed anywhere near the set.

Ephram could see him standing there, an ingenuous smile of pleasure on his lips. Looking round. For him it was a kind of zoo visit — visit to the desperate. Ephram felt his stomach grow acid. The last thing he needed now was Loman finding out how his precious dialogue had been 'freshened up'. He quickly ducked behind a pillar, headed towards an impromptu plaster *whare*. Stumbling along, head lowered to watch for cables, he walked straight into —

'Ephram!'

He checked Bill's face out. Ephram couldn't work out whether the stress he was under was giving him an almost clairvoyant sight. But the writer's face looked like a shock image of pleasure. He clearly loved his visit down to the zoo.

'O Bill baby,' Ephram lied speedily. They air-kissed. 'So good to see you! I was hoping you'd get accidentally electrocuted. I mean —' he said and laughed.

Where did that come from?

'I want to see the kiss, Ephram,' Bill said, coming straight to the point. 'Check the dialogue out. That it flows. Sounds natural.'

Ephram looked at him standing there, backbone so straight, pullover of integrity unravelling.

'Oh?' Ephram smiled at him, a crocodile flick at the corners of his tense mouth. 'Unfortunately,' his eyes were elsewhere already, watching Continuity thread towards him, 'I would really love you to, Bill — if it were only my decision, I wouldn't hesitate . . . not for a moment! But it's a . . . closed set,' he put his arm on Bill's shoulder and walked him away. 'Respect for the

45

actresses' privacy. Makes it easier for them. Space for emotions.'
Now for the killer. 'Too many men.'

Bill appeared not to have heard. He had opened his script and
was standing there, calm as a priest, mid-Mass. A chippie wandered by, half naked, glowering with disbelief. He had been
working non-stop now for six hours. He had reached the point
of black hallucination. And it was still only 11am.

'What I want to clarify . . . '

Bill had the extraordinarily annoying habit of speaking very
slowly and enunciating extremely clearly, as if whoever he was
talking to was somehow an idiot, or at best, beset with hearing
problems.

Dimbleby approached. On his head, in complete seriousness,
was the tumescent wig-fest which Gloria was possibly going to
wear. Ephram checked out Dimbleby's unshaven face. Was it
that time in a shoot where a vein of madness opened up, and
everyone began to behave bizarrely? When men wore frocks or
lipstick, and women moustaches, or black eyes? Food might
appear cochineal-coloured, or strange elliptical messages would
be written on the call-sheet. All without comment, as if it were
an everyday occurrence.

Unreality. They had breached the unreality barrier. Too many
late nights, too many drugs to keep you going, too many early
mornings. Sleep deprivation. Dream removal. Reality rearrange-
ment. It took its toll. Besides, film always attracted a certain kind
of person, like night workers: those with a reason to avoid day-
light.

Now Dimbleby was wearing, completely unassumingly, an
elaborately coiffed wig. He was carrying long strings of pearls, a
diamond choker worthy of Queen Mary.

'I need a decision . . . ' Dimbleby was a large man, fussy as a
typewriter, meticulous. 'Gloria and Juno are down in costume,
waiting.'

Warning signal.

'How is Starling?' Ephram whispered to Dimbleby.

Dimbleby murmured: 'Her pimple looks just great.'

Bill looked at them both, from person to person.

'She's doing a great impersonation of Mount Vesuvius. Or is it

Mount Etna? Strictly pre-eruption.'

'The script says . . . ' Bill broke in.

'I don't give a fuck what the script says!'

The words were out before Ephram could stop them.

Bill looked at Ephram, pausing before he went on. Ephram saw his chance. He turned his back quickly.

'Wigs. Silver skirts. Hoops. Shoes. No gloves. Pearl jewellery.'

He spoke like a machine gun; they had breached the dangerous hour.

'I really can't afford the time, Bill, unfortunately,' he moved slyly away from Bill who was standing there, lectern-stiff, script (two versions old, Ephram alone knew) open on his upturned palms.

'But Juno has never worn pearls!' Dimbleby was scurrying after him, hip-hopping the cables.

The point, surely, is that neither of us ... any of us ... should maim the other.

'Maybe at lunchtime, Bill . . . ' (Ephram, hurrying).

Or do you want that? You care whether he is hurt?

'Gloria's pearls, anyway, were worn in Scene 34.' Dimbleby was right behind him, immovable, encyclopedic, efficient. 'The lake scene. *Remember*?'

'Yes,' Continuity had joined in the fox-hunt. Dob the director. 'I'm sure of that.' Her fingers efficiently flicked through her notes. Found the incriminating evidence. Bill closing in.

Continuity: 'The script specifies diamonds.'

Ephram felt winded.

'Shut that fucking hammering up!' he screamed out, attacked by the noise-storm.

'O sorry, boss.'

Up above was sanity: Georg. He now looked offended. Ephram returned what is described as a 'shit-eating smile'.

'Sor-ry.' He didn't mean it.

'. . . *her throat glittering with diamonds,'* Continuity read out. *'Juno strokes them, then kisses them, gathering the cold glass into her mouth.'*

'Pearls! Diamonds!' Ephram almost yelled. 'I don't give a fuck! All I want is some essence of shimmer, a suggestion of sea, of sun in a mist. You know. We have talked this through I don't know how many times.'

Involuntarily, as if at the sight of something ugly — ugly behaviour perhaps — Bill stood aside.

Ephram felt himself growing smaller and uglier by the second. Was that why he kept eating starchy food and drinking a relentless course of alcohol, as if he desired most of all for his physical self to manifest his sensed inner ugliness? He was a monster, a monstrous distillation of ego, power, unreality. If only he could be wildly drunk now. Dead drunk. Knockdown drunk. With a few members of the crew for company. Company. Comfort. Casualty.

Time to unwind. Even that had to be condensed, rushed by in a frieze of speed, alcohol. He must keep moving.

Ephram saw his chance. As if it were unpremeditated, he moved off quickly, talking to whoever tailed behind him.

'I know diamonds were specified but everything changes — changes all the time and we must retain the ability to be . . . to be . . . ' he felt the ghastliness of a skull's laugh transform his features, '*spontaneous!*'

'Spontaneous continuity!' Continuity murmured *sotto voce*, in the voice of an annunciate tragedienne. 'This I have to see!'

'*Ephram!*'

He had up a considerable speed now, knowing that Bill's dignity would not allow him to move at anything other than an amble.

'See you at lunchtime. Have to move,' Ephram threw out behind him as he fled away. 'Great to see you, Bill! Catch you later! See you round! Ciao, baby!'

Mater doloroso

The sight of the two women walking towards the set was always one calculated to make Ephram's heart beat. It was at this moment that the illusion of film seemed the strongest, the most fierce. There they were moving from dark to light, climbing obstacles, their dresses held up by women from the costume department, the make-up ladies, an ad hoc court: here was a

48

small image floating out of his childhood — beauty as its own terrain, its own terrible empire, full of the cruelty of glances and the imperatives of desire. If you weren't beautiful you were dead.

It was too late to change anything now. All you could do was ride with the moment.

As the impromptu court came closer, unreality flickered then set in. An abrupt shriek from Starling. 'It was the best diet I ever tried . . . ' he heard her gabble. She was speeding. On energy perhaps. Fear. Or . . .

Gloria greeted Ephram professionally. In her calm lay protection. She sat down quietly, opened a book. 'Tell me when you want me,' she murmured to Ephram. Ephram smiled at her. When he was not looking, Gloria subtly edged Starling's chair, with her foot, slightly behind hers.

Starling ignored Ephram, her eyes for a moment passing by him in mockery. She was talking in cleft palate, to Dora; in her hand was a paperback tome on Vivien Leigh, *mater doloroso* to the unbalanced and talented. Or was it untalented? Ephram was going to find out in a moment.

You have used up all your overtime, Ephram.

It was another 'conference' with his producer. At lunch-time. In the 'privacy' of the producer's BMW.

Why do I always feel, Ephram had thought, *that I've been summoned to the headmaster's office?*

'The crew want to have a meeting.'

'They don't mind working ten-minutes occasionally but it's getting to be a habit.'

'They'll walk off.'

'They've had enough.'

'There's only so much a person can take.'

Don't I know it? Ephram had mumbled in reply. *Don't I feel it? Aren't I human too?*

Ephram and Merlene exchanged a mute look. The pimple had become a minute stalactite, blending as near as possible into her skin-tone. It was still a catastrophe. It snagged its own shadow.

Suddenly he had a vivid hallucination.

A patch!

'Merl!' he whispered. 'I've just had a brainwave.'

She looked at him, suspicious.

'A beauty spot. Paint it black. No one will notice.' He whispered, in top-level conference. Merl's eyes widened. 'Make it into a crescent moon. A sailing ship. It doesn't matter. How long?'

She thought for so long it seemed to encapsulate all the time Ephram had dreamt of that film, that scene, this moment.

'Two minutes. Can do . . . er, Starling? Lovey? Would you like to come this way? Just behind this scrim, petal.'

Finally the actors were strapped in. Below them, crouched down, were two apprentice film-makers, learning their craft the hard way: twin Quasimodos in support of the gravity for the two lead actors. Everyone was in their position. The studio door, primeval as a castle's drawbridge, had been rolled shut.

'EVERYONE QUIET PLEASE!' the First roared through his megaphone. The duet from *Der Rosenkavalier* rose up, ethereal, silvery, sublime.

'Action!'

Hunched over the playback screen, Ephram watched. The camera edged closer, closer as the two women came together, hesitated a second, almost in concussion, then, tentatively began to kiss.

White pearls, petals began to fall.

It was a suspended second. He clutched his hands together, an impromptu prayer. Nobody move. Please god, do it now.

But at the last moment, a bump in the camera.

'Cut!' Ephram cried out.

'CUT!' the First echoed through the megaphone. Energy released, everyone relaxed.

'Back to Number Ones as soon as possible.'

The make-up women rushed in, undertook the serious surgery of cosmetics. The costume department fiddled with the folds in the fan of the dresses. The art department tweaked some of the silver bushes. Jules and Jim jumped out and stretched their legs.

'OK everyone,' the First's voice, via the megaphone, had a queer impersonality, at once powerful and direct. 'Everyone in their Number Ones. We'll go again, folks.'

The next two takes were almost there. On the third take, Ephram jumped up from behind the playback, energised. He went over to where the two actresses were lying, imprisoned, uncomfortable. He looked down at their painted faces, the small beads of sweat pearling on their foreheads. Eyes glazed.

'Not too much longer,' he murmured. 'We're almost there. *Almost!* I need just a teensiest bit more involvement. One more time, and I think we might have it. Thank you. Thank you.'

He gabbled this, his impromptu salaam, and went back to his protective fort. He abandoned them to the moment, to make of it what they could. It was up to them, and solely them, to create this moment of reality now. Everyone else, himself included, was unimportant. Hired help. Starling and Gloria were the point of illumination. Or not.

Before they went again, Ephram made a small prayer.

Please! Oh god — if only this works, I'll do anything. Give up film. Work in a shop, anything, please god —

'Action!'

Now he was living, now he was breathing, flowing, riding with the idea. Everyone around perfectly silent. No boom shadow.

'Let's go again,' Ephram said. 'We're almost there. *Almost.*'

Gloria cried out: 'I'm getting the cramp. Can I please just take a moment? Stand up?'

Merlene and Ida rushed towards her, unstrapping her and offering soothing cloths, relaxing her neck muscles, tut-tutting and kafoofling her along, delicately.

Ephram suffered an agony, an anxiety attack that time was disappearing. It was impossible, he was losing it, everyone was losing it. *Nobody move*, he wanted to yell. He wanted to scream. It was terrible the way film encouraged an almost czar-like sense of omnipotence. It was ridiculous. Absurd.

Oh god — please this time, please.

A curious silence fell, one which only occurs when people of the same sex kiss on a set — a sense of contravention, a swim against a tidal drift.

The two women kissed.

Now, *now* was the moment, and he felt a full sweep of adrenalin pass through him. *Now* was the essence. A curious silence had fallen. It was interesting. Of the two women, Starling was more eager. More searching to explore the moment. Keeping all the balances and speeds and equations happening. *Yes!* Starling had released herself from reality: she was making the jump. She was going for it: the kiss, which started off tentative, became real, lip met lip, met a struggle to find, dissolve . . .

He let the moment run.

Time ticked away . . . dissolved in silence.

He looked round the set, at the faces of the crew. Georg up in the rafters, lit from below. Ida, Merlene sitting on boxes, Eb, Happy, everyone concentrating on a quasi-religious moment of working towards creating a reality. From disorder, order; from meaninglessness, a form.

'Cut,' he almost breathed out the definitive word, the terminating secession. '*Cut!*' he whispered it to the First who now called it out: bruited it aloud: 'CUT!'

For one moment he, and all the actors, had held reality at bay — they had managed to create something which, outside of time, registered on film. There was still the anxiety of rushes: would it work out, on screen? But in terms of this moment now — yes, it was complete.

'Have we got the shot?' The First stood beside him, flicking through the long list of shots still to get. There was anxiety in his face, yet a kind of renewed confidence.

'Yes. We have got the shot.'

Already the set was being dismantled. The boards which made the beach floor were being wrenched up, nails shrieking, chippies abandoning themselves to the delight, the luxury which comes from destroying a used illusion. Lights were pinging off, the scorching heat dimmed.

The actors were in retreat, carrying their bustles over their arms. Ephram caught up with Gloria and Starling.

'Thank you,' he said fervently. '*Thank you!*'

Cravenly, he wanted to fall at their feet: kiss the hem of the hand-stitched garment.

'Our aim is to please,' said Gloria graciously. She already had the manners of a great stage queen; the humility. Starling was blitzed, silent.

'I might want,' he ventured, 'something — a little more; later. I will talk to you about it.'

Always there was the infinite possibility of more, of going further, of refining, adding, underscoring, *improving*. Insatiable. Did he catch a blankness of refusal from Starling? Her eyes, now dead, travelled to his face like an exhausted animal seeking an exit, and, finding only a blank wall, began to limp away, lathered in sweat, sick almost, possibly dying.

Starling.

She could not manage yes.

She was no longer a beauty. That moment when the lights were dimmed, whatever unique chemistry she had, was over. She was a collection of wig and paint and eyelash: a dullness.

She said nothing and turned and walked, less away than into a central void in which she dissolved, growing steadily less until there was nothing left, just a faint tang of powder and sweat in the air, an exhausted tang of nail varnish.

Clutching her Vivien Leigh biog. Her genius.

Hobgoblins relax

The studio had returned to the darkness from whence it primevally came.

All but the most essential of the crew had departed. A few exhausted technoes remained, enjoying a quiet beer. A kind of democracy had returned, the army was in recess.

Georg raised a tinny in salute: 'It was lookin' good, mate.'

So he was living again, for another day.

He passed Dimbleby, down on his hands and knees, washerwoman-like, brushing down the women's no-longer-so-white frocks. They exchanged a faint smile of communality, of shared labour.

'Vesuvio no erupt,' said Dimbleby in pidgin-English.

'No erupt,' murmured Ephram gratefully. He was exhausted too.

He brushed aside the washing line on which hung, like evacuated forms, echoes of their fleshly selves, the undergarments of Gloria and Starling: empty envelopes of soul.

The 75-watt bulb now reigned and ahead lay the half-opened maw of the studio door. From this was emitted the dull radiance of the coming night.

The coming night, almost as tinted as the coming dawn, interlocked into that strange unreal time zone in which they all came and went, moving to a central core of unreality, the studio. Hobgoblins of craft, fashioners of make-believe whose highest praise must be: 'It is so like life.' All this fakery to deliver a few moments of emotional clairvoyance.

It was a beautiful evening outside, exquisite beyond art; or expressing that epiphany which all art aimed towards. Ephram walked along, drained, no longer clasping his script so tensely. His step was lighter, and he was dreaming again, dreaming as he walked, in time to the rhythm of his feet. He did not see the concrete in front of him, or the studio around him: he was far away, speeding along through the air, feeling the serendipity of weightlessness.

He was smiling softly, almost tenderly, a companion to himself as he moved towards that arc beyond which lay the light, and the night, and the teeming, impractical, insoluble mystery of the world.

A Casual Kind of Incest

May you be the last of your line to perish
— Scots curse

'Slower! What are you trying to do? *Kill me?*' Elsa Elsworthy, née Wolfe, raised her heavily beringed hands before her as a mask.

Bonnington wondered if, in fact, he was.

He felt a familiar brush of irritation. He wondered if he was doing the right thing. As always with his mother, there was a tangled skein of emotions. He had wanted to give her a day out. He was feeling guilty because he hadn't been able to see her in well over a month. But the simple truth was he felt dread at being in her company, as if all time had evaporated and they were back again as they had been when he was an only child, before he knew any better; when he believed her to be the most knowledgeable person in the world, source of all his intelligence.

'I can never work out,' his mother began. Her tone had the air of a pronouncement, one in which was expressed all her assuredness of being a Wolfe; that is to say, someone who knew their place in the world. Not a great and noble place, it is true. If you had searched the annals of New Zealand history you would find no knights, no honourables, not even a mere city councillor. But the Wolfes, as was her wont to say to her Mah Jong partners, the Wolfes were the lifeblood of the nation, energetic people who through their own shrewdness had risen to a certain point so that now, in the closing years of the twentieth century, she, Elsa Bonnington Wolfe, great-granddaughter of the lowlands Wolfe who had landed at Nelson 'without so much as a groat in his pocket', as she picturesquely said ('lost in the Napoleonic wars' she added grandly, when Bonnington began trying to piece together the puzzle of his family) — now Elsa was in the happy position of being a rentier living in fear of one thing only: the demise of her capital preceding her own death.

Mother and son were off to Taupo to meet their mutual kinswoman. Ethel Groudge, née Wolfe, unhappily divorced, had added purpose to her life by becoming the Wolfe family archivist.

'I can't for the life of me work out,' Elsa took up again, in a tone which said she perfectly well could, 'why you, *a doctor!*' her voice never failed to make a genuflection before the word, 'why you, a doctor, should take it upon yourself to drive such a dreadful, a truly awful heap!' She glanced about it contents, gym shoes, old magazines of quite suspicious provenance, a musty towel.

'It's as if you're ashamed of *what* you are, *who* you are!'

She left this last statement lingering in the air. It was her idea of sensitive comment, of allowing an idea to float. She who was famous for her bluntness, her inability, some would say, to confabulate or lie. Or as others might have it, those unfortunate enough to fall under her glance (when for example a certain woman was found embezzling petty cash from the Ladies Tennis Club Fund), her opinions had all the delicacy of a branding iron on tender flesh.

Bonnington sighed a little. He felt proud of her that, at seventy-six, she was still so alert and dynamic. Yet he felt a deeper shame that he, aged forty, was still paying court to her, listening to her silly homilies when all he longed to do was shout out: *I am a grown man, a doctor who daily faces issues of life and death.* He thought of his own rooms (now it was he who was in control) and the men to whom he had to say they had come into contact with the virus. He thought of their reactions, watching their world suddenly immolate: from a stunned silence, to a rage of unseemly rapturousness, on towards an almost breath-taking casualness.

Yet here he was with an old woman, his own mother, the woman who had given him birth, his whole existence, and she was so casually spendthrift with life, careless with death. Where was the fairness in that? Who made this weird and unjust imbalance? He longed sometimes to shout this out to his mother. But, and he had to be careful here, he could not be too harsh to such an elderly woman, someone hesitating, herself, before the precipice of death. Yet at the same time this very sense of imminent end hastened him to make his terms, be honest — ask that they look at each other at these last moments, face to face.

Instead they sat staring ahead, the landscape streaming across the windscreen and flowing either side of them: landscape of his childhood, irredeemably changed now. Horse studs which had gone bankrupt, farms over-mortgaged; small signs almost hidden, like old feelings, deep within the erosion of a landscape.

He eased the window down. He needed fresh air.

'Don't Bonny, please,' his mother instantly said, shielding what remained of her hair. 'I've just had it set.'

Unwillingly Bonnington made a compromise gesture: closing the window so it didn't affect his mother's frail carapace, yet leaving it open just enough so he didn't feel he was suffocating. He had begun to sweat. He changed his position on the seat, hunching over the wheel. The violence of his feelings, familiar to him from any number of occasions when he had gone out with his mother, still surprised him. Almost imperceptibly, his foot pressed down on the accelerator.

'Your father and I —' she looked at Bonnington momentarily, as if daring him to notice her lapse in tone. But then they were safely alone, where any small sin could be forgiven. 'Your father and I stayed with Ethel's parents when your father returned from the War. Of course,' she sighed here, inspecting the pattern on her tweed skirt thoughtfully, 'I never realised growing up that our side of the family had so much *more* than hers. I never knew,' she almost whispered this, butting up pattern to pleat then pulling them swiftly apart, 'that Ethel's father was a problem drinker.'

Bonnington longed to say: you mean he was an alcoholic? You mean he made Ethel's life a living hell? He longed to be so deplorably specific, if only to wound and bruise his mother's soft and suffocating camouflages. But, on the other hand, he did not want to hurt her. He loved her.

He could smell her beside him now, her familiar flesh smell

compounded with that of the fresh scones she had baked for the journey, her parsimonious dabs of perfume behind ear and on wrist. He was aware of the water in her eyes, the blood running through her body. It was in this sense of her that lay his insensate beginning, and also knowledge of her end.

'Bonny, are you *listening* to me?' she now said querulously, turning in her seat with a certain stiffness to take a good look at him.

She observed his profile for a moment with mixed feelings of powerlessness and deeply familial pride. He had exactly the same brand of Ronald Colman looks her husband had had, the ones she had succumbed to and, of course, lived to regret. Looking at her son now, as she had done ever since that dreadful night over twenty-five years ago, when he had 'spoken to her' — made *his* truth clear — Elsa searched his face and body for signs that other people might be able to read only too clearly: that she had bred, as she said in the first instance, 'God forgive me: a queer!'

Time had softened this to a hesitant, unwilling, yet finally accepted nod, a descent as much as an acceptance of the changed world still in molten motion. 'What you and your friends like to call — I don't know why when it isn't at all — *gay*.' The last murmured, or savoured in her mouth, like an unaccustomed swear word, one of the famously Anglo-Saxon expletives exiled forever from her too genteel lips.

It was still a mystery to her how she, relentlessly normal, as she said to herself, down to the bottom of her stockinged feet, could have produced an only child who turned out to be, well, *abnormal* in this way. Yet, and here she had to say very quickly to her friends who shared knowing looks among themselves, she could hardly have had a more attentive child. Even her friends had to admit, grudgingly, Bonnington was that thing known as 'a good son'. Whether this would save him, or incinerate him, only time would tell. She let out a child-like sigh. Her fingers returned, trying to make sense of the tartan of her skirt.

Landscape whirred past at an increasing pace. Small towns where betting shops and the pub were the focuses of activity; empty windows by which knots of children huddled round the inspiration of a glue-bag. Then more remorseless green.

She gazed at it meditatively: that soft hysterical green of over-production, a memory almost of those days when New Zealand had been rich. Now she felt only the monotony of a single idea carried to a melancholy conclusion. She shifted her view, microscopically, till she saw, on a distant incline, a marae.

'*This*,' she pronounced cryptically, even amused as she indicated with a flick of her head the cyclorama beyond the glass, 'was where our ancestor Angus Guy Wolfe disappeared. He was eaten by the Maoris. You know,' she added, as if quoting. 'The Maori Wars.'

'The Land Wars,' he corrected her, his tone a trifle flat, as if worn down by repeated usage. Bonnington had heard this story a thousand times: from his early childhood, when it had thrilled him with its air of being a *Boys' Own* instalment of a radio drama, through to the present, of adult disillusion, when he could question and note carefully the small differences in her telling.

'What exactly happened, do you think?' he now casually laid the trap at her feet.

His mother was fossicking in her purse. She took out a barley sugar, unwrapped it, began to suck thoughtfully. This was followed — horrors! — by her getting another one out for him and unwrapping it, offering it to him replete on its own little cellophane napkin.

'Well —' she said, taking up her story. She relaxed. The claustrophobia of hills and river faded away. She had glimpsed the satisfaction of a far horizon. A small smile softened her features.

'He was a colonel in the army and — I don't quite know how — he became separated from his men.' Her tone indicated to Bonnington's expert ears the beginning of artifice. 'Then he was found by the Maoris who captured him and — *ate him*.' It was all quite simple in Elsa's world.

'Were his bones found?' Bonnington kept his eyes ahead, white lines leaping almost hypnotically towards him.

He felt his mother turn and glance at him, thoughtfully.

'No,' she murmured, her tongue gently suggesting to the barley sugar it had better begin to dissolve. (Better to dissolve than break apart.)

'Well, how did they know he was actually eaten?' It was Bonnington's turn to glance at his mother.

There was a moment of silence in which he heard, suddenly, her jaws break into the crystalline sugar. She had done this unconsciously, an indication perhaps of the pressure he was bringing to bear on her.

Very distantly, as if uninterested, he murmured: 'You said he was a colonel?'

Suspecting an ambush, Elsa moved uneasily in her seat and applied herself to the particularities of the land. They were passing the black-humped hill where Maori kings were buried. A spectacularly bleak and barren piece of landscape, she always thought. With that killer bend coming up for the unsuspecting Pakeha.

'I can't quite recall,' she murmured, as if she had lost interest in that line of thought. 'Ask Ethel. She's made it her life's aim to find out all that sort of tommyrot.'

'It's just that I know,' his tone of voice was ominously even. 'Maori only ate people of great mana. It wasn't so much cannibalism as a talismanic act: consuming the person's wairua.'

Unthinkingly, his foot had sunk down on the floor. He wanted speed, he wanted to move out of that safe middle distance, to arrive at his conclusions. But as if resisting now, or sensing to what cruel destination he might be taking her, his mother became almost childishly fretful. She even let out a small moan.

'Please don't speed Bonny. *Please.*' She almost whispered this.

'I don't mean to.' His foot pressed further down on the accelerator.

'Bonnington. *Did* you hear what I said?' She spoke in a voice which echoed out of his childhood: Mother as authority. It still had the power to make him sit up, then get angry at his own reaction.

'I've been driving, Elsa, since I was sixteen and I've never had an accident.'

They swept past a poignant home-made cross.

'There's always a first time.'

He shot a look at her.

'You just have to trust me, Mum.'

'*Mother!*' she amended furiously, as if he sought, this late in the day, to change the rules of the game. 'How many times . . . '

'Do I have to tell you!' he added, shadow to the body of her thought. He couldn't help it. He was laughing.

His mother, gripping her purse to her tightly, turned to look at him then looked back ahead. Road leapt towards her, a nauseating sprint.

'You may laugh.'

He balanced his fingers delicately round the steering wheel. The car began to curve round a corner. Yet as they finished what felt like the last careless curl of the bend, the car continued on, as if it had a mind of its own. Wheels lost contact with road surface. Outside, pine tree, clay bank, tarmac blended into a frieze.

The car rocked to a stop facing the opposing lane of traffic.

At that moment — it had the dramatic appearance of a demon in a Noh play, rising up through the floor — a stock truck began roaring down towards them, horn blaring. Bonnington did not know what to do. While he hesitated, or rather his indecision became his decision, the truck recklessly swerved out in a wide arc, taking to the wrong side of the road. A calf's face, frozen mid-cry, flashed by. Within a second a swill of excrement, steaming, lay on the road where they might have died.

Bonnington sat still in momentary shock. Then he grabbed the steering wheel, reversed the car back into its proper lane and they began, with surreal sedateness, to drive again. Neither he nor his mother said anything.

When she continued to remain silent — he had reached a point when he might even have welcomed an 'I told you so' — he glanced towards her. As if still stunned by what had almost happened, she was staring ahead. Aware of time, aware of circumstance, aware of the diminishing space between two irreversible points, he sought to re-establish some warmth. As the truck had hurtled past, she had moved briefly into some unknowable space, some area of infinite aloneness, one he could not specify but felt, perhaps, might be something like an apprehension of a final separation between him — the last of the Wolfes — and the woman who had given him his life.

'Now you know, Bonny, don't you,' Elsa murmured when they drew up outside cousin Ethel's house — a one-time bach now serving as permanent residence. 'Don't believe everything she tells you.' Bonnington watched his mother go through the ancient rite of her maquillage: a fresh mouth painted on, several fluffings of pastel-scented powder, adjustments to her coiffure. Presentable again, she turned to face him. 'She's got it in for us because her father never really amounted to much. Whereas of course, your grandfather . . .'

She left the last discreetly silent, an implied eulogy as she rewound her lipstick. Both of them assumed the bland faces of those who feel they may possibly be watched. They exited the car and proceeded up a narrow path of home-mixed concrete. If they were Maori, perhaps this was the moment when a silvern sprinkle of karanga might break out, summoning the spirits to help them: this would be followed by the pressing of temple to temple, as if to read in each other's eyes the shadow of the spirit of their ancestors.

Instead, together, a mother and her son, the last of the Wolfes, moved up the slender concrete path to the front door. The door chimes rang up and down the scales: shadow of Big Ben.

Ethel, when she opened the door, was a middle-aged woman his mother might have characterised as 'lacking in self-respect'. She had a face from which make-up was signally absent. Worse — and this was unforgivably bizarre, Bonnington could see his mother thinking as she shrewdly took in the socio-economic indices of her niece's apparel — she wore a slightly soiled tracksuit, as if this occasion, relatives visiting, was lacking in social significance.

But a sudden transformation, one of those characteristic acts of vivacity, or self-invention by which his mother never ceased to surprise him, seemed to have overtaken Elsa. She was suddenly a good old girl, the 'mad old bag' as she sometimes called herself, full of colonial spirit, ready to enjoy the moment on whatever terms, in whatever company she found herself. She leant forward, her face wreathed in smiles and claimed her niece's wrist.

'Good heavens, Ethel. I remember when you fitted on a trike!' Her hand was clasped tightly round Ethel's slightly rotund wrist. It was as if she, or memory, did not want to let go.

Ethel showed that slight queasiness all family members feel when they come face to face with the custodial nature of memory. Then she stood aside.

'Enter the surgery,' she said, a curious smile on her lips. 'Do.'

'I've only got teabags,' she called out through an open door after she had led them into the lounge, then abandoned them. Although it was a warm day, there was not a window open. Elsa moved quickly towards a sepia photograph of the family boot factory. 'I've laid the family tree out on the kitchen table,' Ethel called out. 'It's the result of a lifetime's skulduggery.'

She brought back a pot of tea and a plate of round wine biscuits which she placed carefully down on a glass-topped coffee table surgically stripped of all other ornament. More to Bonnington than his mother, she said, 'They call me the Detective down at the local library.' She laughed. 'Once I get hold of a fact, I never let it go.'

'We were talking on the way down,' Bonnington decided to open up the enigma of their family's past, 'about Angus.' His mother shot him a look of reproach. 'The Man the Maoris Ate.'

'Oh that old acorn,' Ethel cried gaily. 'You were brought up on that too!'

In Elsa's eyes she suddenly took on the emetic qualities of a nurse slipping on rubber gloves.

'It's a fascinating case of the way in which truths get distorted. Half a mo. I'll get the facts.' She went away and fossicked in a shoe box.

Bonnington exchanged with his mother a coolly charged look which hovered like a question mark — a taiaha over a word called *facts*.

His mother broke the silence by reaching across, as if impulsively, to take a biscuit.

'You don't bake, dear,' she said with genial irony to Ethel. 'You don't have the time, I expect.'

Ethel, however, was deaf to such subversive texts. A look of concentration had fallen across her face. 'Ah,' she said at last.

'Found you, you little monster! Don't think you can get away from me!'

She held in her hand a pale blue document of shiny governmental provenance. Its dense black script had the force of legality — of unexpected and uninspected clauses which, later in life, could wreak havoc.

'I got this from the Imperial War Office,' Ethel said airily, waving the document as if to dry its ink. 'This —' she paused for rhetorical effect, putting some dated spectacles on, which immediately enlarged her eyes to a slightly gorgon prominence, '— took me more than six months to locate.'

Elsa looked at her niece, her face betraying no emotion as her hand, almost with a ventriloquism of its own, relayed the biscuit to her mouth. She began, soundlessly as possible, munching. Bonnington listened to the little mouse-like mastications of his mother's teeth — still her own! — while she delicately reduced the fibre of the biscuit to pulp.

'Basically this report establishes that he wasn't captured at all. He went AWOL. The night before a battle.'

'It's their way of saying,' Ethel looked up, first at Bonnington, then, more lingeringly, at his mother, '— he deserted.'

There was the profound silence of a dying fall as Elsa's cup came to rest, in protest, bone chine to bone china, Royal Aynsley, Made in England.

'Well, I *certainly* never heard that,' Elsa Bonnington Wolfe said, as if loudly asserting her innocence.

'It was a good move, as it turned out,' Ethel said cheerfully. 'Heck of a lot of limeys got wiped out.' She let out a belly laugh.

Bonnington reached over, with an artful dissemblance of casualness, to snatch the document.

'He was a corporal, not a colonel!' he said a shade too brightly, waving the page at Ethel.

'His wife applied for charity relief,' Ethel continued. 'Thirteen kids. Husband scramarooed. In the next census she's listed as a laundress.'

Bonnington could not look at his mother. He was afraid she could read, wounded as she was by these *unspeakable* disclosures, a note of triumph in his eyes.

'In those days,' Ethel continued placidly, 'there was no dole of course. The women who moved round with regiments were often prostitutes. Even if they were called something else.' She shrugged philosophically.

Elsa Bonnington Wolfe stared at her niece intently, face a mask.

'But what about the lowlands?' she demanded. 'My father told me how his grandfather arrived in Nelson without so much . . .'

'. . . as a groat,' finished off Ethel. 'Oral history,' she said in a dismissive tone.

He felt rather than heard the sharp intake of his mother's breath.

'I can't get back far beyond the Wolfe who came out here. There was a lot of unemployment at the time. People went wherever they thought they could eat. They might have come from anywhere. I've a parish record of the birthdate of our ancestor who came out here. Before that, nothing. We may never know.'

There was a sudden and vertiginous silence, as if Bonnington and his mother were staring at a deep dark hole down which all the Wolfes were bit by bit disappearing; that black hole of the past, of want, of crime, of poverty — the dark borders of anarchy which surrounded them now, threatening . . . His mother appeared to be listening to some sound, apparently internal. Was it a pebble she had cast down the well, surreptiously, as if to test there was ever an end? She was caught up instead in a soundless blizzard: a vacuum of emptiness so powerful it might pull them all in. Shakily she pushed her cup away from her. A light veil of sweat covered her brow, beading her powder.

'Perhaps,' he said, fearing it might even be too much for her, 'we might take a turn round the garden?'

'I . . .' his mother struggled to her feet, a look of distress on her face. They both stared up at her.

An unmistakable sound of flatulence came from beneath Elsa's pleated tartan skirt.

'Ethel. The loo! Where?'

Sentinel against awful consequence, her niece pointed.

Her hand over the back of her skirt, genteel to the very end, mimicking sorrow, apology, yet with an acceptance of life's little ironies, Bonnington's mother retreated.

'It's those *bally* biscuits,' Elsa shot out by way of accusation. She had not finished the battle with her niece yet. 'Bought biscuits have *never* agreed with me.'

Outside, in the sharp air of the central plateau, Bonnington and his cousin walked and looked at her rows of staked-up dahlias. Bonnington suppressed his instant thought (and this, he mused, was where the rot of family snobbery never ended), that the dahlias were, every one of them, 'common', their colouring 'technicolour diarrhoea', 'vile'.

'How is the old girl really?' Ethel asked him in accomplice tones. 'Problems with the old plumbing?'

He felt now a protective sense for his mother: this woman who had fought for him to realise himself, to be as he was now, independent, well off; someone who even wanted to face the truth. The intricacy of her truths, her fictions, had helped him to understand life. He did not want to destroy. He wanted only, perhaps, to build a stronger boat. The world was aflood; her sort — his sort? — were sinking. It was a time of swim or drown.

'She's not so bad for her age,' he said carefully. And he left a small pause, as if describing not so much something which was of dubious ancestry as possessing a positive form of knowledge: a kind of carving, perhaps, which was dying out in the world, yet whose very rarity raised its value. She was, in her own small way, remarkable. He did not quite know why, but felt himself tremulously near to tears: of humility, or humiliation, he did not know.

'I'd better go and see if the poor old thing is OK,' his cousin said.

'Oh no,' Bonnington was alarmed. 'She'd much rather be left on her own. She'll make a comeback when she's good and ready.'

He dropped his mother back at her townhouse, in a poorer street, a 'better' suburb where she still lived alone, still proud, still independent. He put down by her feet the wicker basket in which the now empty thermos stood, sentinel beside the immemorially old biscuit tin which had held legions of home-made biscuits.

He turned to go. She hesitated for a moment.

Inside the house was dark and cool and she looked about her distractedly, as if she didn't quite know where she was.

'You alright, Mum?' he murmured.

She looked at him then, her son, Bonnington Wolfe, the last in the line.

'Bonnington,' she sighed. She passed a hand over her face.

'What, Mum?' He returned her gaze.

'It doesn't matter, does it?' she said doubtfully. '*We* know who we are, don't we, Bonny?'

He was uncertain what she was asking of him.

She smiled hesitantly.

'It's how we treat each other, isn't it?' she said then, as if she had thought of it on the journey back home. 'It's what we *do* to each other. That's what's finally important.'

For a moment there were traces of doubt on her face. He was clever, her son, he had a medical degree. But what did he know? What could he know? She smiled at him briefly, softly; then, the world held in suspension between two points, she leant forward slowly and gave him a farewell kiss.

His Eternal Boy

When I was a boy, the first man to seduce me was an antique dealer. They were synonymous with homosexuality in that simplistic, or was it savage, time. There were ballet dancers, hairdressers. Antique dealers were the slightly more macho end of the range. Mr Kernow, when I think of him now, had beautiful and uniformly greyed hair, a most expensive production. He wore a fine black-and-white houndstooth jacket, a yellow-buttoned waistcoat, and camel-coloured trousers. Brogue shoes.

I remember all this, in painfully enlarged close-up, because as a fourteen-year-old, approaching my fifteenth birthday, I took to going into his shop and looking blindly, it seemed at the time, at his wares. On Mondays and Wednesdays, he had Mrs Jolley, a distracted woman who knew a great deal about Georgian silver. I always made sure I went when she was still in the shop. It was as if I needed her presence, her guidance, almost, to persuade me to enter.

He was very careless about my seduction. The third week I went to the shop, he came out from the back room into which I had never, up till that time, been. There was a water-damaged piece of brocade, the colour of café au lait, attached to a kind of metal wing affair, which separated this back room from the shop. Behind this curtain, the lining had split and frayed; it was quite rotten. I came to know this lining well.

After a certain amount of agonised searching of objects in the shop, I glanced at him. He was looking directly at me. Grey eyes. He asked me in a bored kind of voice, 'Would you care to share a glass of sherry?'

We were standing about two metres away from each other, in the public area of the shop. I was almost as far away from him as I could manage. This struck me, however, as intensely erotic: we could encapsulate each other's bodies, totally, from head to foot.

The abrupt turn of the key in the lock, the sound of his leather soles growing louder as he made his way across the polished black and white linoleum tiles (mimicking marble), the slightly reddened, blunt-fingered hand, laced with long black hairs as he held the curtain aside for me: all of this caused revolutions of will-lessness to pass over in me in quick succession.

He came and stood about twenty centimetres away from me, but so directly in front of me I could feel the heat coming from his body. His smell caught me off guard: that of a very clean animal, mixed with a light silvery cologne. This seemed sophisticated beyond anything I had known up until that time. Unsmilingly, he reached his hand out and very delicately — this was his trick — he ran his fingertips up and down my penis.

I closed my eyes momentarily with the pleasure and let out an embarrassingly emphatic sigh. When I opened them it was to find his eyes staring into my face, offering then withdrawing a question. But with his continued sternness he now began to unbuckle my pants, and with an almost prosaic business-like yank he peeled them down my thighs. When I looked down, it was to see the novel view of the top of Mr Kernow's hair (parted and brushed back) and better still, to feel the attack of a hundred thousand moist butterflies entrancing me. His hands capably, after a few moments, lowered me back into an old armchair, covered in greasy blue brocade, whereupon he set capably, professionally, intently, to work.

His only words to me were abrupt orders to change my position. Efficiently he delivered me of an orgasm so intense it left me deeply shaken, yet grinning at the same time. He was standing, fully dressed, running his hands under a tap. He did not look at me. I think I was expecting some kind of endearment, even a kiss. But after a while I realised our transaction, such as it had been, was over. He was standing with his back to me, gargling and spitting. When he turned round, there was a faint hint of a flush on his cheeks, of moisture on his upper lip. But apart from that he had, almost immediately, returned to being the immaculate Mr Kernow I had always seen, in association with my mother's raids on the foreign territory of the past.

'Come back the same time next week,' were the only words he addressed to me as, embarrassed, I pulled my pants back up and wondered whether I had the right to wash myself. (I didn't, in my confusion.) I watched him as he peered out the brocade curtain then indicated to me, with a swift — was it perjorative? — flick of his head it was safe for me to exit into the shop. I did so gingerly, my eyes all the time glancing at him, as if seeking recognition. Not finding this, I walked past him, carefully not touching him (the thing I longed for the most). And he, overtaking me in an officious manner, marched straight to the door (but as if he was straightening a doily in the front window) so that as he leant back up he flicked, seemingly accidentally, the snib on the front door so it was open and I was free to go.

The sound of passing traffic rushed in the door.

He said to me — he had a pleasantly deep speaking voice, in fact it was the secret of his attraction for me; he had no idea how I had ached, through this first encounter, to hear the timbre of his voice — 'See you next week.' It was not a question.

Naturally, the following Tuesday I was in Mr Kernow's shop, my whole week running towards the moment in a chill, followed by a flush, of anticipation.

The doorbell had stopped its chimes. I was standing there, ready for Mr Kernow, full of a kind of dread at the powerlessness which had once more overcome me, yet he was nowhere to be seen. It occurred to me at that moment that each object in this room had been touched by people who were now dead. It was as if I had found myself alive within an Egyptian tomb, still breathing.

I did not know if Mrs Jolley was behind the brocade curtain. I was also gauchely uncertain about whether it would be right for me simply to walk through there. The shop itself was exposed, with floor to ceiling windows, to a busy road. I was aware that the constant traffic meant I was being observed. I did not know what Mr Kernow was doing.

When my hope, which had risen to such an exquisite point, had reached an almost unbearable pitch — I was about to go, retrace my footsteps out the door, find the air — abruptly, indeed, quite theatrically, Mr Kernow pulled aside the curtain and, seeming not even to see me, said in a terse voice, completely devoid of emotion again — although the deep vibrating timbre thrilled me into an automaton — 'Lock the door.' He did not use my name and this brutalisation of my personality actually pleased me. I wanted my existing self to drop off. I wanted to be told what to do, to be.

'Put the five minutes sign up.'

Inside the room, he wasted no time. He stripped me naked as I stood there in front of him and he turned me round, looking at me for a long considered moment, from different angles. I did not look at him, though this act, so cool and proprietorial, amused me. I could not help smiling. I felt like a horse, or a piece of stock he was considering buying. He took off his jacket. Then, with something like a groan — a groan of anguish, of want, of longing, perhaps mixed with a fear of what he was doing — he slumped to his knees and buried his face in my lap. I was so startled I involuntarily leapt back. He simply grabbed hold of my hips and pulled me, glutinously, towards him.

Soon he was making strange sounds, both encouraging me and at the same time letting out what sounded like stifled sobs, coughs which never fully emerged, cries which quivered through his body.

I was confused, though I was in no doubt that he was liking what he was doing. The harsh prickles of his chin — to me, a boy, shaving was a self-conscious act — suddenly made me laugh. So, in a moment of impulse I let my hands fall and my fingers touched, just lightly, his hair. The face which he instantly turned up to mine was frightening. I took my hands away, as if I had been stung by a wasp.

Instantly I looked away, dismissed. His expression was hurtful to me, who wanted above everything to hear on his lips some endearment. He simply went back to his task, this time with a rough, almost vengeful speed so that when I finally exploded, I felt pain bleeding out of me into him, and return from him into me. We stood like that, cupped together, for several long moments, motionless. These moments were as near to tenderness as we got; yet the tenderness was equally as much a fear of movement on my part, of not knowing what I might involve him in emotionally if I so much as moved. He released me gradually.

His feet were still wearing their immaculate, tooled brogues. Some of my semen had splattered across them. He was bending over, flushed, sweating, wiping this off with an unreadable expression on his face. Shudders of pleasure were still shaking my body as I stood there. It was like an earthquake whose main momentum had passed, and now aftershocks of pleasure passed through me. He said nothing, and moved round the darkened room, carefully avoiding piano stools, trays, cups and other objects in between owners, like me.

His face seemed not so much to have no expression as to have returned to a satisfying absence of feeling or emotion. He had not come himself, I knew this. All his passion had been spent on bringing me to consciousness about the various erotic responses of my body. In this way, his seduction was like an education to me — a boy whose body was a map full of names which had not yet been visited, and hence were still as mysterious as foreign places I had only read about, or seen in stilted photographs, inside an Arthur Mees Encyclopedia, where the reproduction was so imprecise as to further mystify, and render opaque.

He handed me a towel, which he had warmed by running under a hot tap. The sting of the heat, as it passed across my belly, brought tears to my eyes, yet they were tears of gratitude: I read in the careful modulation of the heat a concern for me, that I would not be hurt. I had seen him testing the degree of heat on a small patch of white flesh, on his wrist. Yet he said nothing. I dressed in something like shame. When he went on ignoring me, or rather, I imagine, our silence moved on seamlessly in companionable peace, as if words were dangerous things which might threaten an already ambiguous liaison, I said to him — he was standing sideways to me, so I caught only the downward slide of his nose and the distant glitter of his eyes (already I was memorising his face, to last me till our next encounter) — I said the only words I could think of: 'Thank you.'

Standing so near to him I felt and smelt his breath in my face. It was that almost bitter cigarette smell — he smoked unfiltered Gitanes — yet he was also standing just far enough apart from me so that I knew, above all, I must not reach forward to touch him. To touch him would break some unexpressed rule I was confident with time I would learn. He looked at me so our eyes met and for the first time I felt we were equals.

'You know this is dangerous,' he said.

I looked back into his eyes. In the grey I could see small yellow lights: topaz colour I thought they were, like splinters of a jewel, straws of incandescence suddenly evaporating as his iris grew and expanded in dimension until his whole pupil seemed an oscillating world of black. It was a lustrous dark into which I swam happily, my whole being dissolving into an ideal nothingness — the oblivion I had tasted only a few moments before.

'You do understand that?' he said.

Danger? I could not comprehend it, standing there almost shaking with the physical nearness of his body — a body I longed, above all, to feel and stroke, to touch and hold.

But he kept his distance from me, two small lines of a frown, scars of concern, cut into his forehead. At that moment I longed to slick with the pad of my tongue the bristling black hairs of his brow. I felt an almost sexual ache from my core: to lick his body all over. He made me feel both frightened of him, yet paradoxically and more powerfully, frightened *for* him. I wanted to protect him, yet I was younger. And this, I knew, was the danger.

That afternoon I simply nodded. And a sudden sadness, almost a foreboding, passed over me.

How many other boys had there been? I knew from the very politesse of his fingertips, the experience of his lips, the abrupt messages of his legs, that I was simply the boy who was in front of his eyes and before his body at that moment. And in my naivety, perhaps, I thought he longed above all for a continuous boy, one who would last through all time, all his time, anyway; and his age seemed to make his position to me more precarious, more delicate — more beseeching, so that I longed, passionately at that moment as we stood apart, looking into each other's eyes, to make myself into someone who would never arouse the furies of this unnamed danger, be that impossible thing: his eternal boy.

I did not understand this at that time. I could not see my

youth was a separable thing from my self, and that one would depart, evaporate, leave me behind while the other, a more cured companion, would be forced to move along, separate, carrying all its own burdens of experience and joy and the pain that is a necessary condition, it seems, of knowledge.

There was almost, I think, a flicker of boredom in his face as he turned away from me.

This too I read as an erotic signal: to have spent time with so many men or boys that what we had done was reduced to a routine occurrence appeared to me deeply sexual, as if in our one act we had compounded all the other junctions which had occurred in Mr Kernow's electric presence. Yet now I was going he treated me with a slight disdain, one I found both wounding and enticing.

I longed for him to grab hold of me, kiss me on the lips, say he was pleased with me, that my obedience had satisfied him. Instead I was left — and this was perhaps his intention — with the feeling that I had not yet gained his sexual approval: that I had to return to that shop for any number of times until I had broken through some kind of barrier with him. It was a point, even as he let me out the door without so much as a cursory glance — his attention was elsewhere, changing the positon of a Satsuma cup on a saucer — I was confident of reaching.

But so silent was he it was only at the last moment, in a voice reedy with lack of confidence and intent, I asked him — begged him, really — 'Shall I come back . . . again?'

There was the shadow of a smile across his lips.

'If you want.'

The imperative stayed with me.

The following Tuesday I undressed immediately I got into the room. I threw down my clothes, carelessly, across the blue brocade chair. I turned to Mr Kernow, excited, ready. But today something had happened. His glances at my body were almost sidelong, as if I had developed something undesirable in the week since we had seen each other. His actions, too, were mysterious.

He walked away from me and went and sat down. He took

out a cigarette and as if I no longer existed he lit it, drew in and sat there, smoking in absorbed silence. He did not look at me. I was painfully aware of my exposure, yet at the same time, somehow driven further, just by the degree to which I was exposed. I made no effort to cover myself. But when he continued to ignore me, I felt a kind of dismal anger overtake me, a feeling of being worthless and of failing even to keep his interest. He seemed to want me to go. Silently I began to dress, telling myself I would never return, and that this, unromantic and prosaic, was the end.

Yet he said to me before long, 'Why are you getting dressed?'

I looked at him silently, blushing with a confusion which I loathed, since it expressed my inexperience.

'But don't you want . . . ' I stammered, neither dressing nor even moving. I watched the cigarette smoke coil and unravel in the still atmosphere. It had all the beauty of an exquisite piece of Chinese calligraphy.

'Want . . . ?' he said to me and sat there, looking across the room at me. The traffic sound outside was muted.

'Come here,' he said. He put down his cigarette when I stood in front of him. My penis had immediately got stiff again, another source of humiliation to me: it was as if I had no control over this situation, least of all over my own body.

He flicked my penis lightly with his fingertips, so that it swayed. I immediately scissored down, not that it was precisely painful, but it left me so exposed.

'What is this?' he said, looking from my penis to my face, which was still red.

'My . . . penis,' I said at the last moment as he flicked it again, almost contemptuously. I had selected the most medical term I could locate.

'No,' he said to me, taking hold and gently beginning to massage it, so that momentarily I sensed my centre of consciousness losing focus. 'It is your cock. Anything other than —' and now his hand left me alone, his voice was disdainful, '*penis*.'

His eyes moved up towards my face and we looked at each other in silence. I felt incredibly hot, though I could not tell whether this was a blush at my exposure, or a deeper warmth that pulsed through my whole body and which really was a response to being talked to in such a way, which I saw as both adult and childish. In fact I was so naive I believed, up until that moment, the word he had just run off was peculiar to local boys and had no wider currency in the world. Now he was telling me it was part of a whole undercover world of sex, one which adults used as well as children.

He began, leisurely and with a complete control in rhythm and speed, in nuance and sudden, abrupt changes, to bring me to the point of orgasm; then, as suddenly, retreat into smaller, lighter intimacies, only to abandon them, smoke his cigarette, then continue to bring me to a new plateau of pleasure. But as he did so and I increasingly, wordlessly, ceded to him my self-control — in fact, any ownership of my own body — he began to recite into my face a sentence which sounded at first almost like invective, but which was a catalogue of words to express that part of myself over which he had such control.

'Cockprickdongdaggerdanglerfatjackknoblunchmuttongunpassion prickplungerprideandjoyjewelpurplebobskinflutestalkstickstiffssword tool.'

Now he was talking, almost chanting, and it was as if I had taken over his role of silence. Because I did not answer — in fact I had no idea whether he wanted any sounds from me — he repeated his sentence, shortening it, yet speaking with more intensity as if I were deaf or incapable of understanding. 'Danglerfatjackknoblunchmuttongun.' His hand increased its tempo.

I reached out, as if not so much to stop this tirade as to join it, and with both hands, grabbed hold of his forearm and, first of all raising his hand so I kissed his fingers feverishly, one by one, I put his fingers in my mouth, inside my lips, and felt their rough, cat's-tongue, texture. He stopped momentarily reciting those words which I found as disturbing as I found them exciting, then I took his hand and placed it back on my cock and I repeated to him the words which acted, I imagine, as an accelerant, because now, with teasing and aching slowness, he stroked me into orgasm.

Mr Kernow appeared satisfied. There was the trace of a smile on his face as he squatted, legs akimbo, as methodically, almost as if I were a horse or dog he had become fond of, he swabbed down my belly, thighs and cock. He did this slowly, his eyes only once travelling up to my face, at which point I was surprised, even shocked to find him looking at me intently, as if for the first time I was actually a person — individually me.

This frightened me, if anything. I had a sudden presentiment I was probably safer the more I was an anonymous or episodic boy, one of any number who gave him pleasure. But now, he appeared to recognise me; recognise he was tutoring me in his ways of pleasure, and I was a candidate as much as an emissary of youth, meeting his knowledge of the past in the present.

When I went to get dressed he took my clothes out of my hands. He smiled into my face; or rather it wasn't so much a smile as a kind of mirror which he held up into my own eyes, so briefly I saw myself as I might be to him. I was frightened. I saw my face was bright as it was hungry: I was exhausted but I felt a weird, overwhelming exhilaration — a kind of freedom which almost chilled me with its force. What might I not willingly do? What was worse, I felt a metallic visor of greed clamped upon my face. My lips were wide open, my eyes viscid. Yet I was eager — hungry for pleasure, but also, as importantly, hungry for self-knowledge, for experience of this new creature which was moment by moment emerging under his fingertips. And the strange thing is, although I felt he controlled me in every way, I was more than willing for this to be so. I sensed already I had a great power over him.

He told me to pull myself off.

Some strange impersonality now came over me, as if to protect me. I felt I could be most safe if I continued on, oddly enough, as cold and emotionless as he had been when he had first seduced me. Because I sensed, however inchoately, I had turned a corner and was proceeding to seduce him as well as I knew how: which in this case was to be hardly myself, or rather any self I had known up till then. I assumed a lascivious position in front of him and slowly, with occasional interventions from him, followed his orders.

He did not release me that afternoon until I had come three times.

His expression when he let me out the door was again blank, or if it possessed any shade of meaning, it was of subdued pleasure, distant, objective.

I spent the following week in a daze. I tried to re-order and make sense of what had happened. In one way, it was as if nothing had happened at all. The surface of my life continued along uninterrupted, but, if anything, this made my waking world distant, unreal, disturbing simply because it bore no relation to those sexual moments which had a jagged violence to them, a sharp reality. I slept badly, because my dreams had become so real.

When I walked along the busy thoroughfare on which Belgravia Antiques stood, I felt myself to be an artful masquerader. To everyone else I was simply an overgrown schoolboy, lacking enigma, walking home. But I now knew the joke of the circumstance, and that was that everyone else was a masquerader too. Everyone in clothes was actually a sexual being. Ordinary life involves endless pretence. I had a heightened sense of the mystery of other people's lives, just as my own had started to become less banal.

But at those moments approaching the shop, it was as if the space of my existence was narrowed down to how far I had to go to reach that door, then opening it, hearing the bell, I transformed into another person — a naked person, reduced, stripped back to what I actually was. I knew I looked the same as the boy who endlessly questioned his own image in the mirror. But I did not know, really, what I looked like to someone else. My self-image was so distant to me as to be a fantastical place I could only visit, and find, on Tuesdays. My visits were research. I felt for the first time in my life I was doing something for me, for the nebulous, unknown being which I was. And at those moments, waiting in a state of rapt becoming until I saw Mr Kernow again, I felt it was part of the power of his attraction that he alone had recognised this essence of my personality. The very decisiveness of his actions lulled me, seduced me. I felt chosen, rhapsodically chosen.

Yet that day, when I got there, Mr Kernow was nowhere to be seen. I assumed he was simply in the back of the shop. I pressed on the glass door, expecting it to give way and for me to have the comforting vision of the outside world reeling away on glass, sliding into a hurried likeness, beyond which I saw only space and air through which I would walk, diminishing the distance between my essential self and the masquerader who stayed outside, a hologram of my outer self, embellished on glass.

But the door did not give way. It took me several seconds to see the 'Closed for a Week' sign slashed across my face. I looked at my expression. I was laughing, I remember, a strange reaction. I could not have been more cruelly hurt, stung, if he had hit me. It is terrible. I would have liked that. Anything from him I wanted. I wanted to learn about him, about myself. I believed he knew things which I needed to survive, to live, to be a person. I was right there, I think.

But he had gone. He had dismissed me. This man out of nowhere had returned to whence he had come.

I walked by the shop every day for the rest of the week, my newly found sexual confidence successively ebbing until I felt my self had drained away and there was nothing left except resentment, fear and depression. On Monday afternoon, this mood instantly somersaulted when I saw a person in the shop and the door open. But evanescence changed swiftly to dismay when I saw it was only Mrs Jolley sitting there, head bent over some intricate work, ready to deal with the occasional 'punter', as my mother called them.

Like someone in a trance, I found myself walking towards the shop. I entered as nonchalantly as possible. Mrs Jolley was inspecting an embroidered kerchief.

'The work in this is simply extraordinary,' Mrs Jolley said, looking up at me and smiling, as if I had been standing there for hours instead of just walking in. Our conversations always seemed part of a long continuous one, each lacing up where the other left off.

'I often —' *Awften*, she said, using an English intonation: in those days everyone in the antique trade spoke with a conscious 'counties' accent, New Zealand speech being seen as inherently comic when it wasn't actually tragic — 'I often wonder what unfinished romances . . . lie behind needlework of this quality.'

She held the tapestry before her, meditatively. It was of inter-laced initials, surrounded by small birds, flowers and stars. It was exquisite. I looked into Mrs Jolley's lined, powdered face, with its short nose, moist as a Pekingese, and her perceptive, bulging eyes.

She glanced up at me and smiled. She had decided, from my masquerade, that I was 'a nice boy'. In my guise as such I looked round the shop for a long time, in a quandary about how to express my question.

Mrs Jolley had her eyes down on the kerchief.

'John has asked me to mend this dear old treasure,' she said slowly. 'But I don't know. Faded embroidery has its own *je ne sais quoi* — don't you think?' she paused and glanced, somewhat assessingly, I felt, at me. Was there a new meaning in her gaze? I reddened, seeing myself suddenly in a way I had not until then: as one of possibly a long number of boys who, numb as me, must have stood there and tried to frame questions about Mr Kernow's whereabouts.

'His family live down south, don't they?' I said somewhat brutishly. I was looking at the bottom of a tea cup, not seeing the label through a blur.

I heard the quaver in my own voice.

The stillness beside me forced me to look back at Mrs Jolley. She had laid the embroidery aside. She was looking at me direct-ly, but much as a doctor might look at a patient with clearly diagnosable symptoms.

'He will be back next Monday.'

There was a long silence of comprehension as she looked at me and read, I am sure, the relief which had flooded my features. My hand was shaking. I placed the cup down.

'It is so difficult,' Mrs Jolley took up, a little like a ball, I felt, being sent off from an accurate and experienced volley, 'to add something new to something old. Without the entire thing being compromised.' She held her own handiwork away from herself critically. 'I mean, it has to be done extraordinarily well.' Again the anglicised pronunciation, which had the effect of stopping me from speaking, because in doing so I would reproduce my second-rate New Zealandness.

'The new stitching has to meld so that to the naked eye —' her voice and my gaze quivered a little at that word, 'to the *casual* observer,' she amended herself graciously, 'they are, as it were — *indistinguishable.*'

I both did and did not understand: it was a warning, the warning perhaps of an old friend of Mr Kernow's. I had seen them, often paired together, at auctions, where they might even have passed for brother and sister, or for those completely not in the know, for husband and wife. This was, perhaps, their masquerade.

As if reading my mind, she turned back to her embroidery, flipped it over and said without looking at me, 'You must join John and me when we go out on our hunts, sometime. I sense you have the curse of the antiquarian in you,' her voice was pleasurably ironic. 'Your mother — ' she said, then she stopped. I knew she saw my mother as a vulgarian. 'I am sure she would delight in your knowledge of this esoteric area being — extended.'

She smiled somewhat vaguely in my direction, then took up humming to herself, a capricious tune. I looked at this unusual woman more closely. How could people like Mr Kernow exist without their natural allies? What was her story, I wondered to myself: this woman who lived in an apartment on her own in the middle of the city, without any sign of there being a husband: she had a collection of jazz records, art pottery, and often talked, gaily, of visiting hotels and her consequent hangovers.

I had glimpsed her once in the glamorously louche coffee bar, the Cadora, where I had seen her and Mr Kernow, wreathed in dense cigarette smoke, talking energetically to a person as unusual in our midst as a lunar traveller: a handsome blue-black African, with a golden earring. Was the antique trade, I began to wonder, simply a lingua franca for a whole underground group of people who lived lives other than those of us who were trapped forever in the world of prosaic everyday objects, ones which lacked any history and hence any mystery?

As I slipped out the door she murmured, 'Back on Monday, back on Monday,' much as a child might be placated, or a dog.

When I walked out of the school gates on Friday afternoon how-ever, my mood instantly catapulted: for there, two houses away, was Mr Kernow's sportscar; scarlet, brazen. I went numb with shock. For one long moment I did not know whether to go back inside the school, as if I had not seen him. But I had glimpsed his silhouette sitting, still and intent, within the car; seen him start as if in ricochet from my presence.

I began to walk, casually, just beyond a dawdle, towards him. Schoolboys all around me were talking about the type of car, its engine, make, year. The closer I got the more I could see of him. Just as the car surrounded him and became the expression of his personality — stylised, defiantly elegant in the brilliant sunlight of that suburb — so his Italian sunglasses gave him an exciting foreignness: in my eyes he had all the dissolute charm of Marcello Mastroianni, and I felt my life had lifted up into the unreality and unpredictableness of an Italian film of the sixties.

He switched the motor on. I did not hesitate. I suddenly walked towards the passenger door, pretending he was my 'uncle'. His action, in leaning across quickly and opening the door for me, completed this fiction. No sooner was I seated, and we had exchanged one momentary, searching — greeting, glance — than Mr Kernow's foot had lifted off the brake and pressed on the accelerator so we surged away from our surroundings, shak-ing off like brittle flakes the images of the houses, eyes, boys and bikes which had up till that moment held us imprisoned.

Soon the streets were empty of schoolboys. We had entered an anonymous world in which neither of us was particularly known. We had not spoken: it was as if we were both fed by the adrenalin which was gushing through our bodies. But now we were out of the danger zone my act crumpled and I felt a kind of naive awkwardness overtake me. I barely knew what to say to him, though I longed to ask him where he had been. Instinctively I knew this was the wrong question to ask of a man so quixotic.

Mr Kernow appeared to be driving somewhere with determi-nation. I watched his hands shift the gear lever, his feet, in brogues, operate the clutch and accelerator. He drove with per-fect precision, but with a military flair. For one moment I dallied with thoughts — pleasant thoughts — of being his sexual captive.

But gradually, when we paused at a red light in a distant suburb, I realised we were possibly going nowhere: or rather, our complete destination lay inside that car, between us.

'How have you been?'

His question was fired at me almost with antagonism.

I felt I had been asleep. I had been luxuriating in the radiance of his presence, its extreme comfort. I was relaxed, in a kind of sexual languor. Now I was awake, in the dangers of the present.

'OK,' I lied, and I was surprised to hear my voice registering as sulky. 'That was dangerous,' I heard my mouth — my mother's mouth, in a piece of weird ventriloquism — speak. I even heard the sour, down-turning disapprobation of my words.

He looked at me, and from behind the strange impersonality of his sunglasses his face relaxed into a sardonic, almost scornful smile.

'I know,' he said, and the lights at that moment changing, he accelerated so suddenly my head was thrown backwards as the car surged forward hungrily, gleefully, attempting to lose contact with gravity. We were speeding. The sensation was intoxicating, not frightening. I relaxed in my seat, giving myself up to the wilful sensations.

'Talk to me,' he said.

I was silent.

'What've you been doing?' He sounded vaguely testy.

I felt I had been doing nothing since I last saw him: all of it was empty, a blank, a long stretch of nothing. But again I found my mouth talking for me and I began to tell him about a film I had seen. It was a rerun of *Psycho* and I told him, artlessly, the plot line, even enlarging on the theme of the mysterious mother. I gabbled on enthusiastically, running one sentence into another: the truth is I was frightened to fall silent.

We were heading towards the Waitakeres. Soon we were surrounded by bush. Far below was the harbour like spilt liquid, and in the distance a white clutter, Auckland. The air felt thin. It had recently been raining: drops held on ferns, there was a dank, pleasing smell.

I had the odd sensation Mr Kernow was not listening to me, though occasionally he nodded or surprised me by asking what almost seemed a trick question. What was the name of the lead actress? Who wrote the music?

When he asked these questions he glanced over at me for a fraction too long, so I could tell he was registering my whole body. This confused me, because he was wearing sunglasses, and each time I glanced at him, seeking confirmation, I had returned — thrown in my face — my own image. I did not like it. In my mind's eye I saw myself as sophisticated. In his glasses, I saw only a schoolboy. I did not seem to fit the scenario. I did not find myself handsome, or desirable. Yet the moment he looked away, I felt absolutely convinced that I was attractive. I knew this by the erotic tension of his silence.

At a roundabout I suddenly reached across and took away Mr Kernow's sunglasses. He was so surprised he took his foot from the accelerator, looking at me. I let out a laugh and put his glasses on. Now my world had darkened to a different subtlety. His face seemed naked, with a small red mark on the ridge of his nose where the glasses had pressed. The car roared away, as if taking the glasses off him had freed him from some constraint.

We did not talk. We gave ourselves up together to the enjoyment of speed. The road was loose metal, and I was aware that if the car went into a spin, or a slide, it would be very difficult to maintain control. Dust foamed up around us. Hard rocks spat at the underbelly of the car. In one moment, when the car began to slide, I instinctively laid the palm of my hand, flat, upon his thigh. The car miraculously maintained its direction and I left my hand there, a lodestone.

We drove on, furiously. I felt the heat of his flesh through the thin layer of cloth. I felt the hardness of his thigh. I felt the length of his thigh muscles ridging and moving beneath the cloth as he subtly played the car. I had become thick with excitement. My hand slid up his thigh. He continued to look ahead. Perhaps this is what made me bolder. The sense that he was separated from what my hand was doing, and what his own body was revealing. I felt his hardness. I ran my fingers up and down, teasingly, just as he had first done to me. I unzipped him. He glanced at me. Looked back.

We had reached the top of the mountain range, on a stretch of road you could see up to a hundred metres ahead. The city was a miniature. Forgotten. Harbour a puddle. I began to stroke him, teasing him with my rhythms, just as he had taught me. Occasionally he groaned a little, and changed his position in his seat. My speed increased. Around us now the bush raced and I felt a sense of epiphany overtake me: we could die and I would be happy. Mr Kernow's face was as naked as I had ever seen it. He was smiling.

We were ricocheting round bends. Each time we came to a dangerous bend I slackened my grip, allowing Mr Kernow to return to some sensibility other than that of his flesh. But the moment we entered a smoother stretch my grip tightened, my rhythm took up. I felt, holding him, controlling his excitement, that nothing could hurt us: together we would engineer our way to safety.

So I controlled our descent down that smooth trajectory of roads until finally, in one long stretch, I lightly set to work to finish him off. Calculating the speed we were travelling at and the space before the coming bend, I brought him to orgasm. He let out a single warning cry and a second later a long victorious shout. He splattered all over his trousers. We sailed round the bend. My hand rose to gently guide the steering wheel: for appreciable moments it was me alone who drove his car. He was sitting there, splayed back, momentarily blissed out.

After a while he pulled the car over and ran it rockily under ferns. In silence he turned to me. He dragged me to him. It took only a moment.

We drove back to the city in companionable silence. He let me out in a busy street. He drove off without saying goodbye. Instead he left me with the most erotic word, for me, in the whole English language: *Tuesday*.

I went late to my appointment, as I saw it, on Tuesday. Deliberately I left it until a few minutes before the shop officially shut. I knew this could make my appearance at home irregular, if I stayed any time with Mr Kernow, but I decided that I would risk whatever problems this created.

I felt dread, oddly, as I went towards the door. The Open sign was still there, and inside I saw the figure of my lover, as I liked to think of him, head lowered, inspecting, I saw, when I stood by the door, hand frozen as I reached towards the doorhandle, the embroidery Mrs Jolley had been mending. He was inspecting this with such minute attention — he was famously particular as a dealer, refusing shoddy or second-rate work, a real epicure — that when I turned the handle it was he who started and laid aside the piece of embroidery slowly, his hand falling as if it had suddenly lost all power. But his eyes were looking into mine intently and there was something almost pleading in them.

'You came,' he said, and I knew he was grateful. We stood there uncertain how to go on. I sensed this meeting was the most important one we had yet had. Somehow we both knew more about each other, or at least I had begun, I felt, to get an insight into him. He did not move. He stood there looking at me as if it was the first time he had ever seen me totally, and his gaze moved over my body slowly, until our eyes once again, yet shyly almost, met.

He smiled. *He smiled*.

My power over him felt complete. Without saying another word I turned to the door and with a brazen casualness which I felt would be completely convincing to any passers-by outside, I flipped the Closed sign over and walked, as if I worked out the back, behind the curtain.

Behind the curtain.

Once in the shadowy dark, lit only by a single high window, I felt breathless with my daring. I leant against the brocade chair. My fingers felt nerveless. I did not undress.

He came in after several minutes. The length of this time seemed deliberately calculated to make me pass through a number of transitions or emotions. I felt certain he would not leave me there alone, even though this was, apparently, what he seemed to be doing: I longed to touch him, and to bury my tongue in his mouth, possessing him, or pulling him towards me so that we could merge again as we had done before. But his absence, his silence, seemed to point to the intensity of the decision-making process he was going through.

He pulled the brocade across. It seemed he had been standing there all the time, almost in the room, feeling for me, listening. He turned away from me and, carefully, with that nicety I recognised in him, rearranged the curtain so that there was not so much as a splinter of light entering the room. The traffic, the world outside, was muffled. The room was pleasurably dark.

He came and stood beside me. Again, we looked at each other, and I found myself smiling. He began to undress.

His undressing, like everything about him, was deliberate. I watched his fingertips calculate the undoing of the buttons. The small ivory disk as it slipped sideways through the carefully stitched hole. The sharp susurration of his singlet. The sound, slithering, of his shirt falling on to the arm of the chair. He slid his singlet over his head. It was like a theatrical curtain rising up, revealing for me the vulnerability of his chest with its valley and river of hair running down in a furrow, towards that juncture: his leather belt. He stood for the slightest moment without his shirt, so that I could see him. His eyes, dark, they looked, grazed against mine. I was aware of the sound of my own breath.

When he was certain I was captured, as it were, by my own glance, he leant towards the curtain. He twitched a dim wattage of light into the room, and stood deliberately within it, showering in its fusillade. I looked at his body, which I had never seen. My eyes felt like starving thieves, full of hunger.

Yet he stood there showing his body to me in a prosaic, unerotic light. It was as if he was saying: look, this is the body of a man aged forty-two, this is what you are making all this romance around. Look at it, see the way the chest muscles are starting to slip, read these lines, running in sharp scars, down under the arms. See the slight swell of a belly, and the jellied tensity of the body of an aging man. Look at the hair, and the way it is tufting all over my body: see my flesh and feel how it has been carried round, year after year, through any number of encounters and sagas, sadnesses and ecstasies.

He stood there, defiant, mute, in front of me: allowing me to inspect him.

'I knew a boy once,' he began to speak. His voice was thick. 'Somewhere else. Another town. I was working in an auction house then. He . . . he *thought* he loved me. He was like you.' His grey eyes mockingly saluted me. 'Sweet, nice. Naive.' I blinked. 'This boy was just about your age ... and I ... was ... unlucky enough, or ... lucky enough ... to be ... his starting point.'

He drew in a long breath. I sensed this telling was painful to him — and more possibly, would be painful to me. 'At first it was just sex. Good sex. Then ... he fell in love with me. I could tell. I could read it in his eyes. His face. I was ... frightened, at first, to love him back. What is the point?' A pause. I fought my inclination to speak. 'But what sense is there in living like that? So we loved each other. And we planned to leave the small town where we had met. Where I was living.'

There was silence a moment and outside, like a soft rain falling, I could hear the sound of cars passing and people walking. I listened to this for one moment then it fell out of focus.

' ... it was ridiculous,' he continued, undressing now, as if he were not thinking. His thick fingers unlatched his belt. 'I had grown too casual with ownership, you might say. One afternoon, in the municipal park. Surrounded by ferns. I lowered my head on to his shoulder. He leant his head back and I buried my tongue in his mouth. We thought we were alone ... It was intoxicating, that brief moment.

'There was a cicada down by my foot, I remember that. His tongue. I remember. His tongue was like a river I wanted to follow forever, to its source.' His voice was deliberately cool, as banal in its telling as possible, as if he desired, above all, to strip the facts of their emotion and thus to protect himself.

'Someone saw us. They took a photo. I was blackmailed. I had to leave town. Leave my job. Even him. His parents were told. His parents ... who had left him in a boys' home. I left that town. He was to follow.' He let out a short laugh here. 'We promised each other,' he said. 'We swore.'

He now began to unbuckle his belt. I was silent. His belt slid slowly through cloth loops. He reached down and pulled the zip of his fly open. Released, his pants began to slide down his legs, revealing his stocky, densely black-haired thighs. Briefly I lost a sense of what I should do — to look, to touch, to speak.

'What happened?' I tried to make my voice sound casual.

He was silent a moment, as if he had not heard. Then he

shrugged, but it was as if he were shrugging something off. 'Nothing,' he murmured, his voice reduced to its essence, stripped to a tonal darkness which seemed to me, at that moment, the essence of masculinity, of manhood, even in its shyness and unwillingness to express emotion. He leant down and casually stepped out of his underpants, so he stood in front of me, almost accidentally it seemed, naked.

'He killed himself,' he said to me, avoiding my glance, looking down at the floor in silence. He made that same, futile shrugging motion. Then he looked at me. 'I killed him,' he said softly, so softly I had to lean forward to hear him. Perhaps this was his aim. For one almost terrifying moment, he leant towards me and raised his eyes to look into mine. But before this had happened, my own mouth had betrayed me. My youth.

'What do you mean?' I cried out. 'You didn't kill him. You couldn't have.' He looked at me for one second of coruscating intensity: there was a bitter irony, even cynicism, in his glance as he looked into my face. I had the hallucination that he wasn't seeing me at that moment. He was seeing this other boy.

'He held the razor.' His voice was again deliberately banal. 'He bled to death. On his own. In that park . . . where we were photographed.' Again that shrug. 'Sure . . . '

I took my clothes off, unconscious almost of what I was doing. It happened so quickly, he seemed caught off guard. And when I was naked, there was the briefest pause in which we both rested in the rarity of the moment.

It was such a novel sensation to be naked with him. I felt a whole, almost impersonal, quality of discovery overcome me as the palms of my hands investigated the contours of his body. In my excitement I began to kiss him, almost frantically. Pulling my head away, we stopped there.

We looked at each other in one of those series of looks which seemed the most significant moments or stations in our friendship: they were like glances which grew fractionally closer each time, with a remorseless momentum inwards, a form of surgery almost, exploratory, removing barriers. Yet as I leant in towards him, preparing my face to receive his kiss — or to kiss him, if he so much as hesitated — his hands rose up and held my arms in a brace. He pulled me away from him.

I felt his eyes move over my face, almost cautiously. When he spoke there was a kind of carefulness in his words and I felt a distance grow and widen between us, even as we stayed there, not moving, silent.

'You know what we do together . . . doesn't mean anything . . .' he said to me carefully, ' . . . anything more than what we're doing now.'

My answer was to move towards him, to try and bury that questioning face, to blind it. However he pulled my face away from his, holding me by my face quite painfully. I felt the pressure of his hands on the sides of my face and for one moment, as the pressure increased, the thought crossed my mind that I did not actually know him at all and that he might actually be violent: if that were the only way to make me understand — comprehend the little, or in fact, how much, I meant to him.

'You don't get it, do you,' he said to me. His voice was thick. '*You really don't get it at all.*' He said this so quietly it was barely a whisper.

'Yes — ' I said to him, in a low voice. 'Yes . . . I do get it.'

When he went on looking at me, in silence — in disbelief — I repeated my words — 'I do' — in a lower voice then murmured the words again, and again, a prayer, a purr, my supplication, 'I do, John . . . I do . . . I do.'

He seemed as if he was on the point, not of being convinced, but at least persuaded out of the darkest recesses of the mood which had overtaken him.

'I . . . love you,' I whispered.

This was the worst thing I could have said.

He let out a short, derisory laugh. He hit me sharply, on my backside.

Our faces were very close together — he could see the tears start out in my eyes and he hit me again, harder. I looked at him. Into his grey eyes. He seemed to be staring right into me. He hit me harder still, but with a slow processional rhythm which allowed me to see he was not so much out of control as leasing out his power, suggesting what might await me if I continued on with this lunacy — the lunacy of love. He paused, drawing his hand back. '*You — don't — love — me,*' he whispered in my ear, and his voice was curved and carved with whatever had happened to him during his life.

I cannot explain this. I felt an incredible and wonderful safety at that moment. I did not fear danger. I felt he was expressing, on the contrary, the depth and intensity of his love. No matter how he might try to hide it, or choose to express it.

'What you *love* —' he whispered to me, as if what he was saying was so essential only I should hear it, 'is —' he pulled me towards him, so there was only a fraction of space between us, but a space nonetheless. His fingers were digging into my flesh. He pulled me into him, violently.

The pain was sharp, and I heard myself crying out. I heard my own voice, as if it were a stranger's, because my own voice was not saying any words at all, but making these small noises which sounded as if I was enjoying whatever power he had over me as much as being hurt by it. I felt this person, whoever it was, had to be expressed — it was as if some part of me was being born — and his power was his recognition of this in me, and his mastery over this transformation of self.

'This is what you like doing.'

And his finger, dry, slid into my pucker.

Gradually, his full, dry finger was inside me and I felt the pores on his skin, the irradiating pattern of them, and more distantly, the pull and lull and throb, like a tide, of his heart, and the blood in his body pumping through, and then back through his finger and into me.

His face filled my entire vision; I saw an angry eye, an animal's eye, like a fish on a hook, an eye which accuses you when the body, or heart, is dead. Yet if his eye had looked into me, my eye, in equal part, had looked back, into him. And I too had seen.

He lowered his hands then, slowly.

'Don't love me,' he said in a flat voice, as if to prove, simply by saying it, that it was an obvious, proved point.

'No —' my own voice surprised me with its disembodied strength. I felt for the first time in my life — so this is what it is to be adult. 'No. I do not love you.' And yet it was as if, by saying these words, I had proved the exact opposite.

An almost overpowering feeling of sadness ran through me: a quake. Perhaps he felt it too. He went over to the basin and he simply stood with his back to me. He turned the tap on; the water seemed an expression of his feelings. I went and stood behind him. In the mirror, a small elegant mirror with a flaw in it where a piece of mould was caught, like a trapped moth in glass, I saw his face: and for the first time I saw Mr Kernow — John — as another human being. Not an adult. Not as someone older who could teach me essential things about myself. But someone human like myself: confused, uncertain, torn.

Perhaps this should have been disillusioning, the moment in which I turned and left him. Instead I wanted perversely to stay. I could not stand that face in the mirror, the way his face, always so intact and firm — chiselled and elegant was how I saw it — was now distended, eyes red, pockets of flesh dragging under them, his mouth half-open with pain. I forced him round to face me and slowly, very slowly and silently, so that the sound of my tongue on his skin was the only sound, I found my tongue moving all over his face.

I held his face between my hands. His eyes were lowered. Taking the initiative in a way which surprised and even shocked me, yet I felt only an exhilaration at the discovery of this new self within me, I placed my lips against his and pressed against them, so that, at first inert, almost stilled with shock, he began to respond and soon I was pushing him against the handbasin as my mouth and tongue searched him out.

I did not want to talk. I did not want words. I only wanted whatever it was we could work out together, eliminating the space between our two bodies. He cried out as my teeth, amateurishly, grated against his skin. But I kept on going until I felt the strain, and fight, and stiffness ebb out of his body, and he began, just lightly, to moan.

Now we began to struggle, like two humans within a sack, struggling to be made free.

It was an almost unspeakable relief to have entered that zone in which the only question is the arrangement of limb to limb, and of answering symmetry, and then the remorseless drive towards convergence. For me, at that age, still half-animal as it seemed, it was as if I were being made human, as if in reverting to that most basic of all instincts and motions, I was reaching out towards a realisation of my self, that inchoate form located inside my flesh. I wanted him in me, inside me; I possessed him as much as he took me and I felt he gave me some quality of humanness simply by making me realise the animal which I was.

The pleasuring he gave me was long, intense, and with many gradations in pitch, motion, intensity, depth and even feeling. I felt he was both angry with me and protective of me. I felt at moments he hated me even while he was making love to me, and I felt he was loving me even while he was hardly even mentally, it seemed, beside me. It was an endurance test and it was as if he wanted to make sure, at its end, after he had come and I finally came, that there was almost nothing of my old self left. Or as if my old self was simply that spurt of liquid, now growing cold, which he was leisurely smearing, back and forth, forth and back, slowly, abstractly, on my chest.

He cradled me for a while, and breathed in my ear. We held still like this. I could smell him. I could smell me. In the zone of our smells lay a minute arena: seconds ticking away the hour.

Suddenly, as if he were swallowing back a hiccough too enormous to be suppressed, he burst into tears. This was profoundly shocking to me. He turned his face away from me, as if ashamed. His weeping was hot and deep and passionate. I lifted his arms which were like deadweights and placed them around me. I crawled into his body, straddled my own arms around him and sticky from tears and visceral juices, I stuck myself to him.

I held his face between my hands. I kissed his tears away. That moment when he looked up at me. That moment.

Warrior of tears, geisha boy of fear, alone in our lake, drifting.

After a time he got up and lit a candle.

How many times, I wondered, as I watched the practised efficiency of his naked body as he moved round the room. But the fact was I was thrilled by the thought of his experience, and I only longed, in one sudden gust, to have the shell of my innocence, or rather, inexperience, removed, taken from me so that I could, it seemed, have my own intelligence, sexual intelligence; be human.

He washed me down, we dressed and then he did an unprece-
dented act, brought on, I think, by the breakthrough we had
made in our friendship. He drove me home (at least, that is, to
the corner of the street). As we passed under streetlight to streetlight, liquid dark swirling around us, I saw his face being made
and remade, formed, undone and then made again, so I had a
sense which was pleasant to me of knowing him and seeing him
in various guises: I believed, quite unreally, that I knew him.

He dropped me off, looking at the last moment with piercing
intensity into my face. There was a trace of concern on his features, that double slash about his brow, though whether it was
for my physical comfort — I was rejoicing in the warmth of my
arse — or his own safety I could not tell. Already he was Mr
Kernow again, and his dismissal of me was without irony, I felt.
I was already a stranger, released back into that other world.

'See you next week.' There was the light lull of a pause. He
looked at me: then he suddenly smiled, as if he had recognised
me: 'Frosty Boy.'

I was halfway out of the car. I paused and looked back at him,
uncertain I had heard correctly.

'You know,' he murmured. 'The ice cream. *Often licked, never
beaten.*'

He was smiling. Then his face assumed a serious demeanour,
as if unseen through all the windows were scrutinising eyes and
ears.

'See you later. Frosty Boy.'

He spoke as if he were saying the most mundane of sentences,
behind which only I could read an excess of tenderness.

This was the endearment I had been searching for so long.

The rest of my story is unimportant.

*Did we stay together long? Were we happy? Did he abandon me for
a younger boy? Did I find someone my own age? Was I seduced? Did
I seduce him?*

That is not part of this story.

Letter to a Young Man

Darling Boy

Do not become cynical. Cynicism is too easy in the world we inhabit and it coats your nerves. It destroys the very thing you need to keep clean and alive: enjoyment in the contradictions of life, the way it can suddenly change about. One day you may be the belle of the ball in your imagination. The next day you are Cinderella's ugly sister cramming your feet into a shoe which will never fit. But this change is to be welcomed. It is a sign that your life is moving.

Do not worry. Life will come. But you must go out and meet it, a smile on your face, with an open, welcoming expression. Don't forget this: men don't want sex — or not only sex, which after all can be reduced to the essence of pantomime. Men want a sense of connection, of fission, fusion — a momentary delay in the inevitable, implacable pouring forth of time. Men want the enjoyment in the utter particularity of a moment only you and he have made together.

So do not appear to search, or be haunted by the paranoia of the search, because then you have succumbed to the roulette in our world — a roulette we all succumb to in moments when we lose our nerve. Our lives become waiting.

But in this time of waiting, convert it to enjoyment. Talk to the man next to you. He may not be Apollo or Ganymede. Instead he may be Baudelaire and have an extraordinary wit. Develop the gymnastics of dialogue. This is every bit as useful as hours spent lifting weights. Better. It will last longer. You may entertain, even when you are eighty.

A good talker will amuse. But accept this: if you cannot be a good talker, you may yet be that other thing, equally as golden — the listener. Listen to the tales of other men. They may occasionally appal you, but then you are learning about human behaviour. Do not frown or look dismissive when someone is hopelessly drunk or drugged and making a fool of themselves. Step swiftly out of the way. Catch them as they fall, then detach yourself if you wish no further commerce. This is the essence of being a man: of being a human.

And do not look askance. Remember this: at some stage in your life, this will be you. Do not be appalled. You have no idea of the horrors and unhappiness which wait in the wings. But there is no fate, no heroism in this. Once again, the hugeness of it will make you. It is in this that you may discover yourself. To be afraid is only to be human. To live perpetually in fear, however, and succumb to it is to accept less. This is cowardly.

Develop your body. You are at an age when musculature comes easily. This is the thing you possess most fragrantly at the moment, the raiment of youth. And because of the nature of the transactions of the world, the tiredness of its commerce, charm, physical charm opens doors. We believe in its freshness. But do not seek to exploit your youth. This makes you, instantly, into a very old person, impersonating a youth. It may make you rich, but it ages you before your time. Allow time to perform its own tricks. They are cruel enough in their inventiveness.

Dear and darling boy, how can I say this to you?

I know you will not listen.

Listen to the whisper of your own feelings. It is this which will tell you that an affair has reached its climax — and all affairs, if they are anything, have at least several climaxes — but it is this whisper, insistent, unstoppable, which will finally tell you the affair — no matter how good it was (how sexual) — is over.

You must heed this small inner voice, because, painful as it may be in its repercussions, this news is basically good. It means you are free again — free to be lonely, to consult your own feelings — but free of course to begin to fall in love again. All life may be seen as preparation for these fits of intoxication.

This brings me to my next point: sex, or more precisely: how do you work out a pattern, or patter, in life which allows you to remain emotionally alive but also open to the reverberations of sex.

The sexual barter is necessarily, on one level, cold and calculated — moving only according to the ruthless calculus of attraction. Perhaps this is all the more reason for manners, manners of warmth.

But remember this: there is always someone for everybody. It is one of the mysteries of the globe. There is no deformity someone won't find attractive. More cheerfully, you are neither as beautiful as you appear in certain lights — nor as ugly.

But most importantly, you have that light weight, freight, burden and blessing — youth. It appears endless but it doesn't last as long as you think, and then you enter, like a train sliding into a station, maturity. Oh the melancholy edge of the longer vista, the view. Of knowing more yet it not meaning anything. The failure of the previous generation is always absolute.

This cheerful information came from a toilet wall: *Young men grow older every day*.

On cruising. Occasionally it is necessary to escape from your body. Or rather, perhaps, it is essential to escape *into* your body and take refuge in all the mute messages it can give you. This awards you clairvoyance of the senses. You gain a knowledge which comes from an utterly intuitive response to another body, or a person's looks or, even surprisingly, a memory of a body. Who is it you are seeking if not yourself? Or is it an escape from yourself? Really it is a deepened knowledge of yourself gained through intimacy with other people's bodies.

You must work out exactly what attracts you. It can be surprising. It can educate you about yourself. In one sense, it is a mirror. But better than a mirror, it is another human being — flesh.

Do not forget the other person is just that, no matter how epochal the union, or the sex: they are always finally another person and it is only a matter of time before they return to their island of self. Say goodbye with good grace. Then, when it is the time for men to say goodbye to you, some of the fragrance of your own farewells will linger, sweeten the descent.

On getting fucked. There are two ways of getting fucked in life but only one way to enjoy it: that is, to surrender. Make it a joyful salute.

It is impossible not to hurt.

To be young is to believe that one is born with a destiny which time will fulfil. That is to say, it is only a matter of time before this destiny is revealed. Just what this destiny may be, time defines. And for how long that takes ...

I have written this because, when I was a young man, no such words existed — and I was lost.

Confidence Trick

It was simply that a rail strike was about to happen. Otherwise I would never have sat beside him. I had just been to Cannes and when I first slumped into my seat, grateful to be getting out of an endless rondelay of parties, run on a glut of champagne, I had no way of knowing I was about to fall sick and be utterly dependent upon my travelling companion.

He introduced himself to me as Eugene.

He could have been a beautiful young man, I saw that at a glance, but some internal worry had changed what could be fine into an almost perverse, even profane ugliness. An air of obsession pervaded his person as much as his clothes which seemed to express eternal pessimism about the weather. He was the kind of person who walked or biked alone about Europe. I sensed perhaps all his possessions had been refined to a single grimy knapsack.

I had with me several scripts I had been given to read, but my attention was wandering, pale as those tendrils which escape from darkness and meander, thin and yellow, seeking the light.

Perhaps I was seeking diversion, which I had had before on trains, with beautiful young men: perhaps I wanted the oblivion of an adventure. But perhaps too the fact was I was already sick, without being quite aware of how deeply. So I accepted his hand, shook it, murmured my own name, safe in the knowledge he would never recognise it. I glanced past him to my own image in the window — there we were, two profiles sharply different: his own, tense with the uncertainties of youth, and mine, that of a gambler by instinct, overweight, jowly, puffed with alcohol, faintly liverish.

He asked me if I was connected with film, because I had got on the train in Cannes. Some sixth sense of self-preservation made me lie: I had been visiting friends in Antibes, I said.

He closed the book he was reading thankfully, as if he had been too intensely caught up in it (it was Bresson's *Notes on Cinematography*) and he smiled at me. He began by telling me he hated the world of film as much as he loved, passionately, the art of cinema.

I asked him how he could live with this contradiction. It was fine, I suggested, for those who simply file into the dark and believe, by watching what is on the screen, that they have participated in the process (which they have, I hastened to add, wary that in our crowded carriage there were punters present who might finally hear their irrelevance to the cinematic process), but to someone who earned their living by the process . . . to hate what you did was not a happy state of affairs to find yourself in.

'I am imprisoned,' he said, in the somewhat darkened tones, I felt, of a Bressonian dialogue, 'by both my love and my hate. Shall I tell you how my prison sentence began?'

As I was beginning to grow a little alarmed at the intensity of my companion I simply nodded, lay my head back against the headrest and directed my glance out the window, to the far point of an horizon in ceaseless motion.

'It was at the time of a boom,' he said. 'An absurd time, a time of waste. When I think of the opportunities which were offered then! People could have made films which enquired into the very wellsprings of human nature. Instead, what did we get? Waste! Stupidity! Ugliness! It makes me almost physically sick to think of it.'

He paused to look out the window. I had a feeling of bitterness in him, an introspection which was not only highly unusual for someone working in film, but one which probably made his work more difficult. For film people often have a kind of knockabout toughness, no doubt a combination of being prepared for any eventuality and an open disposition to exploit anyone at any time, for anything, and to be surprised if this is turned down. Eternal opportunists — or is it perhaps that friendlier description, the eternal optimist, to my mind a more suspect customer than the true survivor of the species, the pragmatic pessimist.

Yet this young man, who I sensed was older than he first appeared, was a pessimist who lacked, totally, the kind of pragmatism necessary to survive successfully in an industry which is equally a circus to whatever is framed, intensely, under an emotional microscope.

Indeed, although I was beginning to feel physically sick with the first intimations of food poisoning, I felt he possessed another, more profound sickness, an affliction of the nerves, a kind of tubercular intensity. Like a dim cousin of Dostoevsky he was the kind of person, to be frank, I usually make fun of behind their backs. Because I find myself to be a pragmatic pessimist (what else can a fifth rewriter be?) I see myself as a swabber-down of the deck of a sinking ship. What does it matter? I am at least near the lifeboats. And I can swim. This young man, I sensed, may have read every manual on swimming styles, yet at his first introduction to water he might panic. On the other hand, he is equally likely to be the person who pulls five people out of raging surf, with superhuman strength, fuelled by idealism alone.

But enough of my own thoughts, which I realise, looking back, were already febrile with the sickness which was to make me so dependent on my travelling companion. In fact I cannot, with any reliability, testify to the truth of what he was telling me. At times I seemed to have fallen into some reverie myself, experiencing his own adventures as if I were the unfortunate hero. Not that there was anything remotely heroic or Odyssean in his tale.

'My story begins the day I obtained a job to do research on a film called *Enigma*. You will never have heard of *Enigma*,' he hastened to add with a somewhat unpleasant laugh. 'It played for a fortnight in our home town. It went to some festivals in towns you won't know. If you heard of the countries, you'd be doing well.' A bitter cough of a laugh. 'Now it exists in the graveyard of afternoon television.'

I sensed he was getting enjoyment from this part of his recitation. His face had lit up with an almost diabolical glee. In fact, in this mode I have to say he was particularly attractive: the venom gave his face a kind of energy which was otherwise lacking, an energy which no longer came from creativity, unfortunately, but which was animated by revenge.

'It was a film about — oh for heaven's sake,' he hurried his tale along, 'it hardly matters. Implausibility meets necessity. All that matters is the story ends on an airfield, amid a tearful farewell. A homage is another word,' he said tersely, 'for lack of original thought.

'Yet I fought to work on it. That was my mistake. My initial humiliation was such that I had already gone further than I ever thought I would: I was used to living almost on nothing, writing small essays on erudite aspects of silent cinema. I lived for the dark which blossomed inside cinemas. The poetry of the screen was inside my very head. Now I was lining up in an office, and instantly it was as if the alchemy within my system had altered. I lied. I said I had worked on other films. They knew that I hadn't. But they respected the fact I wanted the job so much I was ready to lie. Besides, they had an endless amount of money to invest.

'Yet on the first day something happened which should have warned me. You know how there are portents which you read very clearly, looking back. The first assistant director, called Hemus, came on the set and within an hour he humiliated a young man called Quentin. I can't recall what he had done wrong. Something quite trivial. But Hemus abused Quentin so vehemently everyone could hear. The place went silent. Electric. There was a real rupture of ugliness in Hemus's voice. It was like tasting bile. Nobody said anything.

'When it was over I went over to Quentin and said to him it was horrible to hear someone spoken to like that. I meant it was demeaning to everyone to witness a human being stripped of his dignity. He looked at me and smiled with white lips and said he intended to be an assistant director one day. And that, he said, looking me in the eyes so intensely I had to look away, was exactly how he intended to behave. In fact he looked forward to doing it.

'I avoided him after that. But I think I understood something then — something I didn't want to know, but which was inherent in being there, working in that place.

'I took my job seriously. Of course. I had been trained at

university to do footnotes. Attribution was always important. So when the costume department, for example, said Scene 34 (a cocktail party on a train: American officers "entertain" local women), my mission was to locate the correct uniforms, down to badges, insignia, hats and buttons. I worked away conscientiously and after two weeks' intense research, presented over thirty pages of notes to the wardrobe department. The designer glanced at them then laid them down, unread. She said: "But we don't want to be tied down by realism. The real 1940s," she said to me, "are simply not cinematic enough."

'I watched her place the sheaf of handwritten notes on a shelf, just above the cotton, beside the crowns where the hats would be made. The notes stayed there, the length of the production, gathering dust . . .

'I realised I had a meaningless job. No matter how well I did it, its basis was flawed. Perhaps someone else could have ridden this out and enjoyed the absurdity of the situation. I admit —' he spoke this so passionately, that I found my half-closed eyes opening to glance over at him. He appeared to be sweating, facing some personal tribunal. Guilt is a most unattractive emotion, I remember airily thinking — me, the author of rewrites. 'I should have resigned immediately, that is what my instinct said to me; but the fact is I had got used to the money. I liked the freedom it purchased.'

I looked away from him. I was having trouble concentrating. In fact I was trying to rack my brains for what I might have eaten in the last twenty-four hours. Naturally I had avoided fish from such a polluted coast. Perhaps my increasing nausea simply came from cumulative overindulgence itself, so that like a goose gorged to make foie gras, I was ripe for the harvesting; otherwise, I risked being poisoned internally.

The young man's voice had taken on a quality as remorseless as the speed of the train.

'I found I couldn't stop working there. Then, as if to make my quandary into a joke, there was "the hiccough". It was pay-day, I remember. I went to the bank, to draw some money out.

'When I got to the counter, the woman behind it, who knew me quite well by this time — a Polynesian woman, very neat and

104

expressionless beyond a series of polite attenuations of response, behind which lay whatever moods or resentments I don't know, fed my withdrawal in and then quietly, so nobody else could hear, returned the book to me and as if she were telling me something of benefit to me, she said: "Your account is overdrawn. These cheques have been returned." It was my voice which alerted everyone around me to my distress. "It can't be so!" I remember crying out, snatching the book back from her. She looked at me with an expressionless face.

'I went back to the studio. Hemus had become very friendly. "A problem with the finances," he said, smiling at each one of us as if we were his personal friends. "Everything will be fine. Just a slight hiccough." His smile grew broader. "By five o'clock this evening," he said, "we will know whether any of us has a job."'

Eugene's face was so close to mine that, for a moment all his features appeared disconnected: or rather, the connection was his earnestness, and beneath it a coiled dark despair, a memory of collaboration, perhaps.

I had begun to realise I was actually very sick. I had no control over myself, my skin felt chill. I remember thinking: just sit here, and let it wash over you. It will be alright. Above all, I knew I had to retain consciousness. And simply by listening, and following his story, I would retain, at least, some mode of survival.

'I mean, I guess,' he said to me passionately, 'I hadn't realised the film business is so closely allied to a confidence trick. I guess all art is, in a way. You say something exists, then you call on people to believe it.

'We gathered at the studio. The producer never turned up. By ten o'clock it was clear the film was over. I remember phones ringing all over the building. First one, then another, as news spread out round the town. I got very drunk. I felt I had been duped and went home, pleased to be released back into my own, admittedly limited, life.

'The phone went at six o'clock the next morning. It was Hemus. He said the money had, at the last moment, come through. The film was on. And I was late for work.'

There was a long moment of silence here, as if his story had come to an end. But I sensed it had not, and, feeling more dependent each long second on the presence of another human, I forced my eyes open and said to him, in a voice which sounded curiously like his own: 'But that is not the end, is it? You refused to go back to work?'

'Oh no,' he said and laughed with bitter glee. 'I got up. I dressed. I went back to work. I was so glad to be back, don't you see?' he spoke at the same pitch of earnestness.

'Please!' I cried out suddenly. I had risen to my feet. The movement of the train overcame me. I pitched from seat to seat, wrenched open the door and ran into the toilet. I was violently ill. It amazed me the volume of what poured out. I felt my entire insides were running through me. When it was over, I found myself looking at a stranger in the fluorescent-lit mirror. I looked at myself for a long time — it felt long — and it was one of those quintessential moments in life where you ask yourself: what has brought you here? What processes of fate and life, what accidental cross-sections, have placed you in such a position of vulnerability that you feel more wretched than you have ever felt?

I saw how I had aged and lost whatever good looks were incidental to my youth. My skin had lost its lustre and sagged, and my eyes were dull, like those of a sick animal. My breath stank. I felt a kind of disgust for myself, which was far more than physical. How long could I continue conning everyone — before my own lack of self-truth became evident? Or was my inner ugliness really just some recognition of the fact that I had decided to come to terms with my appetites, my own mediocrity, and simply push for the highest selling price?

Was this what success meant? This was my own private confidence trick, perhaps. And now, for the first time, I recognised it.

It was a moment of truth in that mirror.

I washed my face twice, three times, and returned slowly, like an old man, to my seat. My companion glanced up at me, concern on his features. He had a bottle of mineral water open.

'Please,' he said. 'Take mine. Please!' he added, placing it carefully in my hand. 'I'm sorry,' he said, 'I had no idea you weren't feeling well. I would hardly have kept on my inconsequential tale . . .'

'No — please —' I said, taking the bottle away from my lips. The water felt like a physical weight falling down my body, inside my chest. 'If you don't mind talking. Please continue. It takes my mind off . . . '

His book, unseen, had fallen to the dirty floor. My companion looked at me, frowning.

'It is just something I ate . . . ' I murmured, resting my head back against the seat. I was feeling one of those momentary respites which follow evacuation. A weird lucidity overcame me. I had begun to feel that unless my companion's story was completed, I would gain no rest. Or was it, perhaps, I had begun to associate the unhappiness of my state with his story itself?

I cannot tell you the morbid fear which possessed me: the feeling that if I lost consciousness, I would lose whatever control I might have over myself and that travelling as I was in a foreign part of the world, even with a companion who seemed trustworthy in the extreme — I knew it was just this kind of person who might turn out to be a thief, artful in his presentation of injured innocence, luring me on all the time with his tales of unfortunate existence. I might wake up somewhere, soiled, despoiled, robbed of my identity, or worse, his papers substituted for mine.

'Please continue,' I murmured. 'Please . . . I beg of you.'

'There is really nothing more. Except my final day. I mean, the day the absurdity of my situation expressed itself.

'It was a beautiful morning, one of those pure fresh days we have at our end of the world. We were to assemble, just after dawn, at an airfield on the outskirts of town. I was among the first to get there. It seemed beautiful to be alive that morning.

'We set up quickly. The guarantor was due on the set at any moment. You see, the film was essentially in a state of bankruptcy. This man would turn up on the set and watch, to see who could be made redundant.

'You can imagine the pantomimes of labour this led to. It was as though there were two plays occurring: one in front of the camera, and another, more compelling because our livelihoods depended apon it, behind the lens. A terrible artificiality had overcome everything.

'The guarantor, a disturbingly negligible man, as if one of the tricks of his trade was to fade into walls, always turned up at an unanticipated moment. He was, after all, interested in the play, not in the setting up of the curtain. And sure enough, I looked around behind me. The guarantor stood a certain distance away — watching.

'Yet it was at this moment, when the official drama commenced, I became aware of a small, occluded drama. We were all waiting for the director to call action. Everyone around him was standing absolutely still. The actress was poised on her most prescient emotion. Yet the director refused to speak. Hemus went up to speak to the director. Then Hemus started walking away very quickly. I happened to be in his direct path. He called me to him. He told me the director had lost a contact lens. He was blind without it.

'I cannot tell you the intensity with which I inspected every blade of grass. On my hands and knees, I expressed the happiness of at last finding a usefulness. My back was aching and my knees felt chilled by the time I accepted I had failed. I could not find the lens.

'Hemus whispered to me I was to go into town, to the director's optician, and obtain a replacement. In the meantime he would create a diversion by rehearsing the following shot. There would be no film in the camera. The star actress was bundled like a hostage towards the next set-up; the guarantor withdrew to make an enigmatic telephone call to New York.

'I drove like a demon into town. Those twenty-five kilometres passed as if in a dream. At long last I was useful. My existence had a purpose.

'In fact I arrived in town so early that it was a shock to realise the shops had not opened yet. Like a man possessed I paced the streets, waiting for the optician to open. Can't they understand, I cried out to myself, how important this is! Without a lens, a director cannot see. And without a director, a film cannot function. Hundreds of jobs are dependent upon my action: my speed. Thousands upon thousands of dollars. How is it nobody can understand! Open these doors! Open them!

'This is how far,' Eugene said to me with a small bitter laugh,

'I had travelled. Finally, an optician's assistant — a pretty receptionist type, with long false nails and a carefully rehearsed smile — bent down and opened the glass door. Because I was the first of the day, perhaps, her smile was most honest. "Can I help you?" she said.

'I explained, possibly too tersely, because I was so intent upon getting the job done well, what my mission was.

' "You'll have to wait for Mr Hearne. He doesn't start work till 9.30," she said. She walked away from me, behind a screen. I saw a buzzer on the desk. I reached forward and put my finger on it. When she did not appear immediately, I simply pressed the buzzer harder and longer. Its angry sound, like a wasp caught in a jam jar, resonated round the glass and terrazzo room. When she appeared — quite a while into my buzzing — her face was impassive. "Can I be of assistance?" she said to me icily.

' "Look, I don't think you understand!" I yelled. I felt my insides fill up with this enormous pressure. It was as if, coming through my mouth, was the entire force of all those people standing waiting around on an airfield, actors on the precipice of no longer pretending and hence no longer serving any purpose. As if the whole confidence trick was on the point of evaporating, and it was up to me, as a con artist, to keep it alive. At the same time — and I couldn't stop it and that was what was so horrible — I felt my voice change into Hemus's voice.

' "*This is film!*" I yelled at her. "*Film!* There are hundreds of people standing around, waiting for a single contact lens. It belongs to the director! If he cannot see, nothing can happen. Dollars are ticking by even while you stand there! Get the optician! This is important!"

'Her expression was pasted on to her face — distaste, disquiet too, as if I were a lunatic who might leap behind the counter, push her aside, or into a glass window, then rifle all the shelves, flinging them on to the floor, till I found the correct contact lens. And the fact is, I was poised to jump.

'Mr Hearne, the optician, came out. He was a man who looked like he spent a lot of his spare time fishing in the harbour; he had that pleasantly grizzled, almost philosophical look of someone well suited to his job and happy, in so far as one can be continuously, with the world as he found it. He did not like what he saw. What was worse, I saw myself through his eyes, and I did not like what I saw either.

'At that moment I realised what I had become.'

My companion fell silent. For an unendurable space, in which I felt myself falling into a void of unconsciousness, we listened to the susurration of wheels on track.

'My mission was utterly futile in any case. The film went on shooting without me. After I left the director remembered he had a spare pair of glasses in his pocket. They were even surprised to see me back. I was made redundant that afternoon.' He let out a laugh. 'I was deprived even of making that decision.'

'It sounds,' I said, from behind closed eyes, 'like, as you might say, the end of your prison sentence.'

'And you are free?' I thought I heard him murmur, but I could not be sure.

He let out a long, slow breath. It was as if he had delivered himself of some essential message. He seemed calmer somehow. With indefinable relief, I saw we were nearing the outskirts of Paris. While I knew it would be an ordeal getting to a hotel, my nightmare was coming to an end.

As the train drew to a halt I suddenly felt a resurgence of my consciousness. It was as if in stopping, I was locating gravity again. A wave of relief passed through me. Whereas before I had been chill, now I felt warm.

My companion was standing up, stretching.

'Can I help you with your luggage?' he said. He seemed to have found a curious peacefulness with the delivery of his confession. It was as if two divergent images of himself had merged together to find a sharper focus.

He smiled at me.

'How are you feeling?' he asked me companionably, if not intimately. But now, sensing I was about to be released into the freedom of an hospitable city, I rebutted this intimacy by a quick smile and a handshake. He stood beside me for a moment, frowning a little as if he were uncertain about what course of action to take. But my handshake had decided it. I wanted to get away from him. If there is one thing I have learnt, it is that failure is contagious.

'I could help you to a taxi,' he murmured. 'Perhaps to your hotel . . . ?'

It was curious, his face seemed almost rhapsodic and he appeared, briefly, enticingly beautiful. I wondered if I was making a mistake in not attempting to seduce him. Yet I felt reduced by the sickness which had passed through me and though I knew I was getting better, I needed, more desperately than the consolations of his body, the pleasures of a good night's sleep: that sweet oblivion. Besides, I felt old and compromised, wise and ugly.

As he turned to go, I asked him, 'But maybe I can find out where you are? You're staying in Paris for long?'

'Oh, let's leave it,' he said with a smile. 'We might just meet up.'

He turned to me and smiled that pure abstract smile which had first attracted me to him: the smile which indicated we had met somewhere else and that in some future moment, when my head was not so clouded with illness, I would recognise it.

With infinite care he packed his Bresson book into his knapsack then, smile still hanging on his lips enticingly, he put his knapsack over his shoulders and came close to my face. He murmured the word: 'ricordi'.

All around us travellers were merging into one another, losing whatever intimacies and connections that had been made on the train, breaking apart into atoms of anonymity.

Everyone is finding their own way, I thought, tracing their own route which in turn becomes the pattern which describes them.

I watched him disappear amid the heads of the people in the vast dark echoing station. And I stood there, suddenly wondering what I had lost.

Transiberian

They waited till the coffee was brought and the sweet dishes taken away. Alan had lit another cigarette and was playing with the stem of his glass, filled with riesling as gilded as apple cider. Around them, voices of happy diners rose. Perhaps it was this camouflage of content which gave them courage. It eased their passage to that essential point: the reason they sat there together, Thyssen and Alan and Ben, expectant.

'You haven't talked about how the Transiberian went,' said Ben. His experience was that people were often embarrassed to bring up the subject of recent death, thinking silence was more sensitive, whereas he himself found it impossible not to talk of it: bear witness, as it were, to what was still a living reality, persistent, undeniable, even companionable — as if the fourth person present at the table, at that very moment, merely unseen, was Bradley.

Alan shifted slightly uncomfortably on his chair. He shot his lover a warning glance.

'If you want to talk about it, that is.'

Thyssen looked up from a long way away, then laughed, as if in surprise at finding himself there, in that warm room, people all around him eating and drinking and enjoying life. Against the restaurant window night pressed glamorous as anthracite.

'It was something Bradley always wanted,' Thyssen said simply. 'So we did it.'

There was a caught moment. Alan and Ben's eyes met, grazed past each other then settled on Thyssen who had lowered his eyes again, looking into his glass, which he inspected with a strange smile of recollection playing on his face.

Ben and Alan waited.

'I was so worried about whether it was the right thing to do,'

Ben felt like he was pressing. 'I saw some footage of the Transiberian Express on television, and it showed these carriages practically collapsing under the weight of Chinese going into Russia. To sell just about anything. Gym shoes, golf balls, plastic raincoats — anything they could barter.'

Thyssen, he observed, was in a state of almost restless ecstasy, febrile, alive, haunted, happy all at once, mixed up, churning. Thyssen did not look up. It was as if he wished, for as long a time as possible, to keep certain visions refracted within his own eyes. Whether he was reviewing what had happened then, or excluding what was happening now, Ben did not know.

'It looked like the train stopped at every tinpot station,' Ben went on, his nervousness making him unusually loquacious. 'Everyone got off and laid blankets on the ground. In the middle of nowhere! People were cooking in the middle of the passageways. Whole families in what had been private carriages. Holding roosters, bound-up goats. I kept thinking of you with Bradley ... '

Thyssen looked up at Ben quickly, checking something deeper than the expression on Ben's face.

' ... my idea of a nightmare,' Ben tailed off. He quickly lifted his glass feeling the need to hide his face, get drunk; or if not actually drunk, to have his feelings blurred and softened, to have the ache eased, find oblivion.

'It worked out quite well,' said Thyssen. His eyes returned to the bowl of his glass. 'Bradley actually liked the company. We had two Australian sisters in our compartment. Karen and Susan. We sort of took over the space and barricaded ourselves in. After a few days everyone accepted it was ours, so we set ourselves up. Like everyone else.'

With Thyssen's eyes downcast, Ben had a good chance to look at him. Aged barely twenty-four, Thyssen was a handsome young man in an excitingly dissolute way. He had long black hair, like an Indian brave, thought Ben, pushed simply back off his face so when he spoke, his hair fell forward, masking his expression, giving him an odd, even childlike look of inwardness, self-absorption. This innocent expression alternated with bravura tosses of the head when his hair went flying back, a glittering curtain. He was aware other men, and women too,

113

were watching him. Ben remembered for a moment, with a pang of something like loss — or was it purely a sense of age, and time passing? — when his own hair had fallen heavy and soft against his lower back, naked.

He reached for a cigarette.

Thyssen had quickly raised his head, a surprise raid, and his shining brown eyes passed penetratingly, in a passage almost of mockery, between Alan and Ben. Ben's face was obscured behind his glass; Alan was breathing out a long, contemplative shaft of smoke. Thyssen saw he was questioning his own image in the mirror opposite. As Ben looked up, Thyssen swiftly masked his gaze.

'Have I told you the story of the plunger?' Thyssen laughed, as if to himself. Or perhaps to someone physically not there.

'No.' Alan and Ben spoke together.

'Bradley took along his own little battery plunger. So he could heat up water to make his own tea. He was really proud of it. You'd think he practically invented it. The way he guarded it. No one else was allowed to use it. Which is unusual when you consider, actually, how generous Bradley is.'

Alan noted the present tense.

'Isn't it strange,' Ben broke in, 'how you can never get a really satisfying cup of tea away from home? What is it, do you think? The water? The tea?' Enthusiastically, almost like a dog at long last given a bone, he explored this cul-de-sac. 'I can never work it out. Can you?' He looked from Alan to Thyssen, both of whom were staring at him as if he were a stranger. 'It's like I never feel I've properly arrived home till I'm sitting in my own kitchen, having made my first pot of tea. I think it's our water . . . ' he tailed off, eyes switching back to Thyssen whom he saw was looking at him intently, small lines of humour — or was it mockery? — round his lips.

His lips, Ben suddenly noticed with the sharp perception of a person caught off guard, had the appearance of having been kissed hard and brutally, possibly only an hour before. He quickly looked away.

Thyssen, Alan saw, was regarding Ben much as a foreigner might regard the natives of a country whom he had once found intelligible but now found merely amusing. He rejected this perception quickly.

'Well,' Thyssen said, looking away from Ben and swallowing his own laughter which yet kept bubbling up his throat as if inside him were an endless supply of aerated energy. But his face as quickly looked as if his laughter had peaked and he might, as soon, break down crying. Alan had a sudden vision of what Thyssen would look like when he sobbed. It was not dissimilar to a sexual vision.

'Bradley was in the middle of laying down the law,' Thyssen was speaking quickly now, his eyes looking into an abstract space which indicated only his voice and his physical presence were in that restaurant, sitting between two of Bradley's oldest friends who in turn were looking at him transfixed.

'He was raving on about AZT and how it is so difficult to get other medicines in New Zealand. He was planning a surprise raid on Parliament. Person to person. With a minister he'd met in a sauna once. He forgot he had the plunger in his hand.

'He was using it like a conductor with an orchestra. Suddenly he got too carried away and it went flying through the window.' Alan and Ben both witnessed the plunger disappear out the window. Alan saw a quick glint of metal. Ben saw dust — a mosquito swarm of brown specks, engulfing. 'So — ' and here the bubbles in Thyssen's laughter took up, moving the train along, 'Bradley jumps up and pulls the emergency chord. The whole train slows down and screeches to a halt.'

'Oh no,' Ben covered his eyes with his hands. He groaned. A couple, a man and woman at the next table, looked over at them, then registering something invisible to the three men, returned to the pact of each other's eyes.

Ben slid his hands off his face. He had been listening to the silence on the train, ticking. 'Go on,' he said. The sound had at last died away.

'We all just sat there, looking at each other in totally dumbfounded silence. Karen and Susan looked at me. I looked back at them. And I just shrugged, I couldn't help it. I was laughing. Bradley is saying, "Open the door, come on, we've got to get out there, find it." I'm saying: "Well, hold on, it's not quite as simple as that." "I can't wait," Bradley says . . . '

Ben heard a train door open and footsteps coming closer down the corridor. The footsteps paused.

'A guard came in and Bradley jumped up off his seat. He's like a jack-in-the-box. The guard can't understand a word. The guard looks at him in silence a moment. "I have to have it," Bradley keeps saying. "I can't live without it." '

Momentarily the eyes of the guard look not so much at what Bradley is saying, but at the huge Adam's apple painfully bobbing, like an obstruction which can't ever be swallowed; the occluded pupil of Bradley's left eye. His breathing rattles, like stiff brown wrapping paper in the wind. The desert wind. At night. Thyssen sees and hears and knows this.

' "I must find it," Bradley says.

'The guard just looks at Bradley and scratches his head and looks at me. The whole train is waiting.'

'But why didn't you . . . ' Alan broke in.

Ben signalled with his eyes for his lover to shut up. The two exchanged a look of mute antagonism, in which Alan's eyes remained slightly longer on Ben's face.

Ben said: 'Go on, please.'

Alan reached impulsively for Ben's glass and took a large mouthful of the wine.

'Everyone is waiting to see what's going to happen. You can hear people talking excitedly up and down the train. The guard takes his hat off and wipes his bald head where the hat has pressed down. He has a dirty handkerchief. He pats his head all over, very carefully, as if he's considering. We wait as that handkerchief travels slowly, intimately over a space which starts to feel like the whole of Russia. Finally, as if he's thinking of something else entirely, he nods.

'Bradley doesn't wait another second. He has this sort of wild energy, he's shaking with it. As he's running across the sand his feet sink in, he falls over sideways and lies there. Everyone is looking out, they don't know whether to laugh or to cry or to shout, whether it's some kind of entertainment.' *But they can see*, thinks Ben, *everyone can see, it's almost an animal sense, every living person can see, he's not much longer for this world so this gives him some kind of protection.* 'And he is out there, and it isn't long before other doors open and people start piling out, to stretch their legs, and breathe some fresh air. To feel the ground not moving under their feet.

'I think it's good they can't speak English because otherwise they mightn't like the idea they're being held up over a convenience to make a cup of English Breakfast Tea ... '

'But why make a problem about the train being halted?' broke in Alan, heatedly. He shot his lover a glance. 'When the time of arrival has lost all meaning? I mean, with all the delays ... '

Thyssen's brown eyes grazed past Alan to Ben's eyes which he saw were fixed on his own. Ben's eyes slid down to his lips; lingered, like the second before a kiss.

'The guard finally comes outside too,' Thyssen's lips said, 'and he looks at his watch and he looks at Bradley then he looks at his watch. He walks away slowly and goes and stands in the shade of the train. He takes out of his pocket a piece of meat, wrapped in coarse newspaper, he unfolds this carefully, pushes the cap to the back of his head, and with the minute delicacy of a large man, begins to eat.

'He eats, intently, all the meat off the bone, then he dusts his uniform down with his handkerchief, folds the paper back up neatly into squares and puts it back into his pocket. He comes back and he has this look of wariness on his face — as if he's frightened something fragile in his hands might break. He gets to us, and looks at us. He watches us for a long time, in silence. There is the sound of children playing. There is wind, a distant wind, sweeping, it feels like, all over the steppes.'

Ben hears this. In the restaurant. Even though it is warm, he shivers.

'The guard looks from Bradley to me, and shrugs. There is weariness in this shrug, an apology, even a hint of tenderness — the tenderness of a man, maybe, who has no power.

'The guard says something which is as sad as the note of a balalaika. He shrugs and trudges off back to the train. He has got everyone else back on board. It is like the holiday is over. The door shuts.

'Bradley and I are left out there alone. He is sitting down, his

117

legs stretched out in front of him — like a child playing in a sandpit. He looks in the direction of the guard and speaks to me in this soothing, childlike voice — the voice of one to whom all things are reasonable. "You know I can't go on without my plunger. I need it to make my tea." '

Ben thinks of Bradley. He can see Bradley capably making tea for four people in a shaking compartment: making it his role, his duty almost, which he would do with all the urbanity of a hostess used to entertaining any number, and quality, of guests. He had a certain sarcastic energy, Bradley: the huge energy that some old women in particular have: a kind of agitated intelligence, incisive, bawdy, almost reckless. He would make the tea, and laugh at himself while doing it. Ben saw Bradley now coming to terms with losing the tea-maker.

'It was incredible,' said Thyssen, his face alight as if he were seeing it. 'You felt like you were on top of the world. Or nearer the sky, or heaven, or whatever you want to call it. The middle of nothing, maybe.

'So we wait. The whole Transiberian train waits. While we have our domestic.'

He lifted his glass and looked into it, shaking the contents from side to side so the wine rose and slipped down, glaucous. It suddenly appeared he might cry.

Ben can see sand blowing over a train track, speck by speck. He can see lashes, webbed with sand. He can see tears.

'In the end,' Thyssen shrugged and smiled, 'I persuaded him back on. Cursing me all the way. I was every effing bastard that ever lived. I helped him back on. And . . . the train took off . . . '

The couple at the next table rose soundlessly to go.

Ben looked up, as if pulling his eyes away from a departing train as it rocked away, a tiny black speck in the distance, only the lines of the track like two black hairs curving back towards him, growing wider and wider then splitting apart where he stood. He watched the train disappear. And he realised he had been left behind and it was he who felt alone, utterly. He listened to the wind, and the sound of the train dying away in the distance, till there was silence. Now this silence crowded round him. His eyes were wild.

'You did get the flowers we sent? To London. And were they white? I *particularly* asked for white flowers. Roses.'

'Yes,' said Thyssen as if he were consciously straining to look at a detail on a map which he had already folded up and put away, in his pocket. This detail was of a small piece of metal, glittering in the sand. 'Yes.' The shimmer went out. 'They were white,' he said, after a pause, conclusively. 'Roses. At least two dozen. Beautiful. Even scented.'

'We always deal with the same florist,' said Alan with the satisfaction of a housewife finding a particular cut of meat. 'She treats flowers like I do. *Seriously*. No carnations, I always say. Horrible things that last forever. For a funeral, they're so depressing . . . ' His voice tailed off into silence.

Ben moved the position of his glass on the table top, a little away from Alan. The pattern of the empty glass played across his fingers. Thyssen watched this hologram in silence.

Bradley for a chimerical moment sat as a fourth at the table. He looked at Alan but mostly at Ben, who he could see was sweating. Ben wiped his brow.

There was a pause at this point, in which the three men lifted their heads up, simultaneously, under the pressure of the same font of thought. Each of them looked slightly beyond the other two present, into a long middle distance: each listening to the last echo of that train as it finally departed. As this silence fell and expanded its web, their eyes changed the perspective, or depth of the distance at which they were looking. They looked back at each other, at the fleshy actualities of their faces. In this stood their history, their flaws and minute, finite fame: their histories. Ben and Thyssen smiled shyly at each other. Alan looked down.

The restaurant, as if by magic, had emptied.

In the kitchen, a large Niuean grandmother wiped clean a bench, face omniscient as a judge. A waiter was flicking out the next day's tablecloths.

Bradley, with one searching last look at each of them, disappeared.

Adieu.
There are many ways of saying goodbye.

Different Landscapes

The scars had not yet healed. Each morning she looked at her face searchingly, with the pitiless eyes of one who has gazed on the same territory for over sixty years. She required a steady hand to put on her make-up. And now, with her face having been remade — skin scraped back and lifted over the same old bones — she gazed at the unknown continent of self, marvelling at how sins could garner, mollusc-like, new camouflage.

She was wounded, she knew that. But at least the scars were self-inflicted, aimed at betterment. A wedding ring removed, after all, leaves a patch of white, vaguely scurfy. The surgeon's scalpel had left its own trail, crosshatching of stitches, sutures of flesh neatly folded. The mirror told her she looked more like someone plunged headfirst through a windscreen than the triumphant implementer of her own make-over. She had undergone, she knew, less a surgical operation than an act of personal transcendence.

She was living now under an assumed name in a different town, with a changed face. Out in the living room, sprawled on a settee, stoned to a point of insensibility, was the young man, Bobby, aged twenty-nine. Her son.

He had come to keep her company. Do her shopping. Sit with her while she spun out the hours, watching television, flicking through women's magazines, sometimes simply sitting still and staring out the window, marvelling at the metamorphosis of her condition: banana palms on the Gold Coast rather than the neighbour's tiled roof in Sydney, sprinklers as diadems rather than pavement.

The air-conditioning hummed away, panacea for her pains, each hour another stigma as she spanned the time between loss of consciousness when she underwent the knife and that marvellous moment when her bruising reduced, her wounds healed, she could burst out that door — into *life*.

It was three weeks now since she had written the carefully considered note. 'Please don't look for me, Arnold, I have left you. There are dinners in the freezer for the first week. Good luck. Edwina.' She had finished her job, collected her first week of the pension. It was all planned. She disappeared into the private hospital. She lost her name there. She tried not to think of Arnold in their apartment, pitifully missing her, strangling her with his need. He couldn't cook. He couldn't even drive.

Do the wounds ever heal, she mused, staring in the mirror. Through neglect, like a callous? Through the attrition of time, like a darkened toenail hardening, then falling off? But the scar remains, the subtle eruption in the pattern of pores, deep in the flesh.

'Are you all right, Mum?'

'Darling . . . ?'

She came out of the bathroom putting on her sunglasses, so that for a moment she appeared a kind of imitation Joan Collins. 'Don't you think it's time we had a coffee?'

Bobby, bored almost to the point of unreason, put down his novel. Balzac, a subject on which she could never question him, and perhaps this was its secret. He looked up at her. He saw a thin, intense woman brazenly searching for her new life — again! But he also saw the woman he had known forever, by touch, sight, smell, shape. She had always had this whipper-snapper greyhound sleekness; that and her regal tallness were her chief attributes. The deeply hennaed hair had given way to blonde with time (or change in movie fashions, as Lana Turner, platinum, surpassed red-haired Rita Hayworth).

His mother's hair was still brilliantly blonde. Bobby had made the mistake, in greeting her, of saying cavalierly (carefully not looking into her slashed face), 'Hey! Who is this? Marilyn Monroe?' Finding a spot, somewhere on her neck, to kiss.

She, wincing with pain even as she spoke, said indignantly but not without a note of triumph, 'Marilyn? I'm not that old! *Madonna!*'

Perpetually young, eternally old, that was his mother to

Bobby. For how long, he wondered, had it seemed that he was the older? Helping her with her make-up, acolyte around the mirror. Mother hurrying up to go out, to meet the man of her dreams. Bobby had pictured him quite differently. He favoured someone frankly masculine, with hints of Steve Reeves. In fact as a moony adolescent he imagined himself choosing his mother's lover. His first meeting with the real Arnold had been a shock, strident with the tension of three quite different people pretending they were looking at the same scenery: it took time to realise, all along, they had been looking at different landscapes.

Now his mother came out and sat down by him, half petulantly, on the edge of the sofa. She removed her sunglasses. She looked down at him, his oyster-coloured eyes, his gangly untidiness, as if no appointment was ever important enough. Fred's jug ears.

'Well?' she said, half expectantly turning to him.

He had raised his book, almost as a defence. He sighed. The moment now was leaden. They paused, looking into and slightly beyond each other, towards a receding point. The fact was they had covered every possible route of conversation, ambushing any stragglers and ruthlessly dealing with whatever was left: indoor plants, movies, diets, favourite television programmes of the past. Bit by bit, they had covered every piece of terra cognita. Now there remained only that scary territory — the essential.

'Are you going to keep me company? Or?' she charged him, with a vaguely flirtatious smile — keeping herself in practice was how she saw it. 'Or are you going to bury yourself in that boring book and leave me stranded here, in silence?'

Bobby was tempted to say, if she was stranded she was herself responsible: but he saw the familiar eddy of an argument there and preferred to move beyond that shoal. He only wanted peace, after all. Or rather, he wanted to help his mother, but in a way which afforded him as little discomfort as possible. He had not seen her in eight years.

'What would you like to talk about?'

Her long fingernails, perfectly manicured, reached for the remote. She flicked on a soap which returned an image of actors, togged up in grand emotion. The sound came on —

'You don't even care how I feel!'

Edwina flicked the sound off, reducing them to masques of motion.

She sighed, toying with her glasses. Metronome.

'Well then,' she said in the disappointed voice of a spoiled child. Yet she was smiling, and in this lay her charm. But then her smile faltered.

'Tom,' she said, struggling for a moment as if she found the simple word difficult. 'You never really talk about him. Was he sick for long?'

Bobby looked at her frankly. He wanted to laugh. She had no idea how surreal she appeared to someone stoned. Impulsively, as if to deflect his gaze by whatever means, she reached for her nail polish.

Edwina had stupendous nails of extreme unreality. Her colour of the day was called *Sassy Red*. She took up her cosmetic art, momentarily intent.

It was a sign, almost, Bobby thought, of how far she had penetrated the blizzard of boredom that she had finally reached this unknown station — one she had never talked about before. Even though she had sent flowers, and a crimped, awkward note. (Feeling for you at this time. Love always — Yr Mother). The flowers were tight buds of baby roses, pink.

'Did I tell you — ' she said, breaking in while Bobby gathered together his dispersed thoughts. She was speaking with her usual volatile nervousness, almost recklessness. She raised her eyes briefly to look into her son's. And then, as quickly, shielded from him her fear before the unknown.

'Did I tell you what I'm thinking of — when I get the new place? I'd like those new bunched up curtains, "festoon" I think they're called. Probably pink. I like pink, don't you? Susan Renouf's got them. Maybe,' she said inspirationally, 'when I, when we're out-and-about' — her synonym for her face having healed — 'we could go down town and shop — '

She paused, rounding off a particularly difficult whirl on her nail.

Glanced up, tense.

'Don't tell me if you don't want to,' she said.

Bobby stirred in his seat, sat up. Vivid emotions, feelings were running wild, in streaks, all through him.

He had had a sudden vision of Tom.

Up till that moment, in a different place, surrounded by people and buildings and streets he had never seen before, he had been enjoying a sabbatical from grief. Now it all came back, mixed up and confused — the last image of Tom lying skeletal, reduced (like some sauce to its essence, as Tom might have said; bag of bones, guts, a leather hide for flesh). And behind this image, ganged up, impatient as people to enter a wild party, images of Tom as he had been when Bobby first met him, when they had just become lovers. A small and indiscreet smile. A thick forefinger. An Adam's apple bobbing, thirstily, just below his hirsute shaving line. Not much.

Bobby himself felt as anaesthetised as his mother on her painkillers. In fact, up till this moment, they had shared a weird, underwater sensibility of mute pain. And each had respected — so it seemed — the other's grief.

But now his mother was mending.

She looked down at him again, feeling her own inward moment: Bobby looked so eerily like his father, Fred, her first husband — the one she still felt some sadness for, and hatred. For one moment she felt all that she had left behind — Fred, now suffering what was politely called Alzheimer's, but which she knew was alcoholism in its last, most bitter rages; and now a second husband, Arnold. All lost. All left.

'Darling, did Tom suffer much? They say it's a terrible death.'

Bobby croaked out a gagged laugh. 'Tell me what's not? And I'll sign on.'

She looked at him now, startled.

'I wanted to ask you . . . ' She was almost breathless.

He observed his mother's face — the yellowing bruises, the terrible nicks. It was only with him she would allow herself to be so naked: to let her guard down. Now she was asking him to do likewise.

'You can tell me,' she said, stopping work on her nails.

'Tell you what?'

His tone was queerly belligerent. He didn't want it to be like this. Besides, he needed the territory of his own life, his own ego, to survive. Memories of his unsteady childhood, rocked by his parents' divorce, flooded back to him. The morning he and his mother tiptoed out. Unlocking the door soundlessly. The taxi in the street at dawn. His mother's silence as they drove away, interrupted by her first shaky match and the conflagration at the end of her Virginia Slims as she dragged the nicotine down into her lungs. 'I need to breathe, I need to live.' Another drag. He discovered he had forgotten his favourite Abba record, personally signed. He asked if they could go back. His mother had looked at him, sighed. They had to understand each other's weaknesses. The taxi had circled back. He had crept into the house.

His memory was of edging along on the wire of his father's breath. Occasionally it appeared his father had stopped breathing. Bobby froze. Then his father's breath broke out, and Bobby stole on through what had been, till that moment, the family house. The suspense of — would he wake? Or more precisely, that deeper question: would he ever awaken now, his poor father, isolated, asleep, unaware of the silent erosion of his masculinity? His harassed shout would greet an empty house. Shivering, imagining his father's rage, Bobby had crept out of the house, out of his life. His mother waiting in the back of the taxi, biting back her tears — or was it simply cigarette smoke?

Now again, in a different place, she waited.

'Bobby,' she said, almost breathless. 'Help me. Please. You're not making it any easier.'

The air-conditioning hummed.

'Are you . . . ?'

'You mean,' he said almost brutally. She flinched. 'You mean do I have AIDS too?'

'Bobby, I am your mother. You don't have to speak to me like that.'

He looked around the room. Its emptiness, its barrenness. He thought of the ten days he had spent with her. The fight on the second day over instant coffee. I hate it, he had yelled. I can't stand its taste. It makes me sick. And then realised they were arguing, not so much over coffee, as approaches to life. Her economy and saving up for something better: his preferring to luxuriate in the present — even if he couldn't afford it. On his disc jockey's salary, as she put it. (He worked in a public library, in the music section.) And to think he had come here to help her! So he thought.

Now they accepted, almost ludicrously, separate brews made with ostentatious preparation.

'I only want to know . . . ' How that completely false question echoed through his youth. I only want to know . . . who you were with last night, was it a man or a woman, are you taking drugs, you're not involved with transvestites are you? You are careful? The questions flowed and gushed and filled up the narrow tube of mother-son relations, then swiftly overflowed. They seemed intrusive, guiding — as if she knew better! From the mess of her life. She seemed to forget he had seen her keening with unhappiness. Or perhaps it was because he had seen her like this, she sought to return the favour.

'Do I have AIDS?'

He seemed, she thought, to savour the brutality of that word. A word which haunted her every time she picked up a paper, or watched the news, to the extent that she tensed, headachey, with each bulletin. Arnold beside her creaking in knowing silence.

'We weren't lovers for the last six years,' Bobby said in a suddenly tired voice.

She looked at him, startled by the accelerating revision she had to make of life. He looked away from her, casual, almost impertinent in his power. He smiled at her wryly. 'Not that this necessarily means . . . ' She was almost beside herself with her lack of knowledge, her loss of equilibrium in the seasickness of it all.

'But I'm not,' he said quickly. Saving her. 'I've been tested. I'm free.'

It was odd, she thought, how he used that adjective — free. He was free from what? The obvious things, of course, as she misunderstood them: premature death, a life of invalidism, social shame. But no, she felt, he meant something different.

She was free of course. Free for the first time in over twenty-five years. And it was terrible: she did not know whether she actually liked it. Would her new face be a passport to another life? She was still, she knew in her bones, a woman of sixty. But if she could pass for fifty-three? Her son was young enough to let her get away with this. But then what exactly did she want? A new partner. Another man. But weren't all men somehow issued in the same edition as Fred and Arnold — on first meeting full of charm, on fuller acquaintance a known theorem of set tastes, hit parameters.

'Oh darling, poor Tom. I used to think of you and him and how horrible it must be for you going up to the hospital all the time . . .'

'There were crowds of friends. He used to get sick of them. He was bitter about dying so young. He needed time to think.'

Bobby looked beyond his mother's tribalised face to the court-yard where a palm frittered, nervous as a cat. It blurred.

'He hated everything at the end. Even me. It wasn't easy.'

'He seemed such a nice young man,' she ventured slowly, ten-tatively edging on to a bridge of friendship, sympathy.

'You only ever met him once.'

'I liked him,' she said, 'well, the little I saw of him. You were so cold,' she murmured, remembering the time Tom and he had come to Sydney, for Mardi Gras. They had 'fitted in' Arnold and herself for a lunch. 'He booked us that table. He knew all the waiters. He made a fuss. For my birthday. Remember?'

Bobby could remember a lunch in which alcohol had cast a momentary gloss over the gaps — the views of people looking at different landscapes. Tom that day had been especially good. He had known for three months. He had not let people know yet. No symptoms had appeared. It would affect his work. He knew it would. Then he would be poor. Or what is worse about having no money — subject to the vagaries of other people's sympathy. But for that lunch he had rallied wonderfully, brought all his restaurateur's arts to bear. It was only by subtle eye movements he had indicated to Bobby what he thought of Bobby's step-father's shoes (a wonderful homage to the seventies, he had called them later). Arnold's dandruff-speckled jacket that Tom, with his wicked tongue, christened 'traindriver's mink'. The waiters around them, gay to a man, had erected round Edwina and Arnold, unseen, a mobile of sardonic glances. After all, everyone had excruciatingly exposing family somewhere.

Edwina's memories of the lunch were of a warm glow of fandom. She had felt for the first time close to the stylish young man who lived with her son. (For god's sake, Arnold, you were on ships. You must know a little bit about it, she had threatened Arnold when he had made some curmudgeonly remarks, half lost in his wardrobe grumbling about backache.) She had even, in her mind, constructed a fantasy whereby they could all go — two couples! — on a bus-trip and view the heartland of Australia — Ayer's Rock! This wobbly mirage crashed down when the two boys disappeared, waving and smiling, as she and Arnold were ushered, half tiddly as she called it, into a taxi. Tom had somehow even engineered to pay for it in advance. Her last view was in the rear vision mirror: the two young men disappearing in that weird contrary sway by which, the more her eyes followed them, the further they receded. Her final glimpse was of Tom waving to someone he knew across the road. Or was it at her? She had waved back.

The lunch had been a thing to boast about to her friends at work. If she didn't exactly reveal the gender of her son's inamorato, what did this small slip conceal? Yet when Tom had got sick — well, he had gone into hospital and died, it seemed with frightening haste — she had had no one to tell. To talk to. She had found some odd scruple about sharing it with Arnold. By that stage, besides, she was carefully saving up grudges that might expel her from her marriage. She also felt some odd tenderness, as if she wished to keep her view of that particular landscape to herself.

She rose up quickly from her chair. She felt restless, a desire to live, to see new things. What was she doing here, in this room? When her face had healed and Bobby had gone back, she would — her vision faltered slightly here, but she felt she would go out and see different parts of life. She hungered now to see, to feel, to understand new things.

She looked down at her son. His face was cast back down the tunnel of remembrance, as if at the furthest end he caught a flickering figment. Like reflection of a distant rain, feelings moved down his face.

'Sweetboy,' she said to him quietly, lingering before him. Her old name for him.

He almost jumped.

'Darling, when my face is right, let's go out and get a different look for my new place. You'll help me, won't you? I know you and Tom —' she felt a small subliminal bleep of warmth, to be mentioning him — and if we do not mention the dead they surely die, inch by inch, of unoccupied sound and space — 'you and Tom have such good ideas on colour and décor . . . '

'*Have?*'

Bobby looked up at her as if, for a moment, he had trouble separating the double image of his lover and his mother, and fixing who exactly she was. She looked so fearfully damaged, so fragile in her new invention. She was starting out again, and he, he was still saying goodbye to someone who, even though he had not been his lover for more than six years, still remained an indelible mark, and he was finding it hard, very hard, to accept, to cover the groundwork which went into saying goodbye.

Perhaps this was the secret then, of both of them coming together, in this foreign, almost lunar landscape, to share these moments together — to heal slightly the wounds internal and external.

Edwina glanced down again at her son. What did that odd smile mean, more grimace than laugh?

'Queers have some use, don't they? Even if it's only advising on décor.'

'I didn't mean . . . ' she said. She felt like crying. 'I don't mean that. *I don't.* I mean — I would value — I *do* value your — *our* time together. *Companionship.*'

She looked at him in silence. She had said it. *I need you*.

Her mind returned, hesitatingly, to a vision of Arnold alone in their apartment. He needed her too. But was *need* enough? It was a basic human hunger, as necessary, no, more necessary than sex, as primeval as the relationship between mother and child. Yet it could be a kind of eating disease, a devouring of the flesh. If you did not mediate the other person's needs with your desires. Arnold. Fred. Just as with Tom, just as with Bobby perhaps — goodbye.

She was getting near the moment when she could move out that door, into different landscapes, ones she had never quite known — or not known for long, and then as a younger woman. Who knew what perils lurked there? It would be hard. But she had once been able to manoeuvre through them. Besides, how did they measure up to stitches being whipped out of your face? She went now towards the door and, turning back towards her son, she saw he had returned to his book — or perhaps he was simply sitting there, gazing not so much downwards, as inwards, saying his own farewells. So this was their symmetry, was it? Not one to be found in words, but dwelling in mutual silences.

She pushed the door open a little. Immediately warm wet air rushed in and ran over her face. She closed her eyes.

She knew the world out there was fecund with germs, full of dangerous, ticking insects. Snakes even slithered, unseen, through the grass. But now, on the Gold Coast, it was sunset. In a distant apartment block, a party had started up. It appeared a beautiful landscape and she lingered there momentarily, crushing her lids shut so that — through tears, it was true — she seemed to be viewing paradise.

A Colour Known as White

Snow everywhere, whiteness and chill. It was difficult to tell where you were but there was a lake, a large lake, a lake as large as Alaska it seemed. It was Antarctica, it was unknown, unnamed, nobody lived near there or went near there, except once a man had wandered off course and perished there, his body still frozen under the ice, perfectly kept, a time capsule down to the golden watch with a repeater chime given him by his honeymoon wife, who had engraved her initials in swirling, romantic Edwardian script on the back. And it was a fact that even after this man had died, the sweetly lyric chime of his expensive timepiece, bought one late autumn day in Regent Street, London, towards three o'clock in the afternoon, when outside the plate glass windows a violet twilight had fallen and men and women leant into a cutting wind as they walked past the glass, holding on for dear life to the parcels they had purchased: yes, this small bell beneath the ice continued to chime long after the lost explorer had drawn his last breath. Long after the snow had fallen, petal after petal, whitening his dark dot of a shape until finally there was no more of him left, just a vast frozen whiteness, a place without a name, an area without identifiable characteristics, an illimitable stretch of whiteness near a frozen lake, they said, almost the size, it seemed, of Alaska, though — and this was where it was so anonymous — it was actually that largely unknown continent to the south.

She had seen this through half-closed lids as she woke in the morning. It was a sensation of coldness, piercing yet comforting too. She felt the nature of the embrace of the snow, the way it had held the dying body of the man as first it numbed him then softly killed him, killed him softly and slowly. Beside her, the man slept on his side of the bed. She heard his troubled breathing as he continued on in his dreamless sleep. She had been visited, she knew, by a man she had not seen or touched for over fifty years.

It had been one of those absurd situations when, as a lass of seventeen working in a flourmill, she had been driven to meet him. She had chosen him. She had picked him out. She waited for him to finish and ignoring the other girls, even the men, she had boldly presented herself to him and suggested that she walk home with him. He had been startled, his large handsome face like a sculpture, she thought, a snowy white marble face she had glimpsed in the Mechanics Library — Jove or Antinous, one of those gods she never knew much about except they had beautiful bodies and their jewels were hidden by a figleaf. Her mother had encouraged her to call them jewels. That evening, because it was evening when they finished, she walked home with him slowly, his large handsome body covered by his clothes: he was from Finland, he could hardly speak English, and the English which he did speak was a joke combination he had picked up from his working mates. His first sentence to her was both charming and obscene: 'Boy I am tired as a fucking dog.'

Her first impulse was to be angry. A working woman like herself, especially aged seventeen, could not afford to let herself be talked to like this: it was a simple enough way to begin that slide that ended in pubs and street corners and Salvation Army barracks, and worse. She had looked at him sharply. He had turned his pale, icy blue eyes to hers, perhaps attracted by the quality of her silence. She had searched his eyes. It was then, she told herself afterwards, she had decided she would marry him and have children by him and perhaps, if she were lucky, live with him and love him forever — till she died.

His eyes were that colour of an early autumn sky in late morning, that time before the sun can give any heat, before the blue either deepened or grew more yellow: it was a pure blue, as if you were simply looking at a representation of space, of air densified to such a point it became shaded, tinted, to a pure azure. And this was, she decided, what she liked so much about him, what she loved; it was not only the largeness of his body — he stood, naked in his socks, at six foot two — it was not the unwieldly, almost childish uncoordination of his limbs, his propensity to knock things over or spill glasses of water, or damage her dress when he tried to undress her — it was the sense she got of vast space — of an unknowingness — of a vast continent somewhere away from this city she was born in and lived in and worked in: she loved to know, she *needed* to know that somewhere else, over the sea, or in his case, inside his eyes — there was a place both vaster and more expansive than the world she inhabited.

It had not been easy. Her family was narrow-minded, aggressively religious. They all worked in the flourmill, her father, mother, her two sisters. Besides N was a foreigner who could hardly even speak English — a man who was a joke to his workmates, someone who seemed even to have hearing difficulties, so his vagueness seemed as much a part of him as his joke English. Why not marry someone who prayed in their chapel, her sister had said, proud of her fiancé whose father was a grocer: her fiancé who had managed to get one step away from manual labour and was a clerk in a shoe factory the other side of the city. But no, Elsa had made up her mind. Stubborn as a mule, her mother said pursing her lips together, ever since that time she had refused to come with them to the firm's picnic. She preferred to sit alone, inside a dark library, reading. She was that perverse. Mother and daughter had argued about it bitterly, so nobody except her younger sister came to the wedding. ('At least I know what I want,' Elsa had said to her mother. '*Want*!?' cried her mother. 'Whoever taught you to follow what you *want*?')

She was pregnant soon enough, after they had had their tight little wedding ceremony at the registry office. It had been at the end of summer, she remembered, and when they emerged into the street the wind had hit them hard, like a blow which knocked the breath out of your body. It was a southerly, a wind straight from the ice continent, she had said, and they had both run, numb and laughing, to the hotel dining room where they had a lukewarm meal of roast lamb and cabbage and baked potatoes, icecream and baked apple. She had sat at the table running the reddened palms of her fingers over the damask table cloth again and again, thinking as she looked down at the snowy whiteness of his flesh which she would soon be touching: the way the flour

133

from the mill still seemed to powder his skin, so touching him was like sliding in a dream across some ballroom floor and she would soon, forever, be caught in the slow waltz of his life.

His foreignness, her own abandonment by her family, meant they felt a double isolation. They had spent their honeymoon night in a second-class hotel on Karangahape Road, in a room with highly patterned wallpaper, an imported ewer like a swan and a lithograph of an old Queen Victoria. The bed looked like it had been the recipient of a thousand other lovers. Not that this mattered to N and Elsa. Elsa had discovered a form of communication which lay beyond language. Their love-making, motivated as it was by a deep passion for each other, was a revelation to Elsa: her only experience before this was a clumsy boy whose technique was as crude as his conversation was duplicitous. N was patient, tender and elusive. She felt the following morning as if their night together had vindicated her choice, for she had chosen him, she had no doubt of it.

The first child was a boy and her family came around, to the extent they officiated like prison officers allowing out the captives, at the child's baptism. But Elsa would have none of these patronising airs and soon enough the slightly false jollity of a family occasion evaporated. Besides, the child had looked more like the father so her family had felt slightly misled, though quite what they would have expected, she did not know. Now N became melancholy; perhaps she was spending too much time with the baby, but she felt alone. N's moods became as long and dark as, she suspected, the winter nights in his own country. She knew now he came from a small town where the mud and wood were not unlike the conditions in the backwoods of her own country. So he had not come from a vast ice continent, as she had romantically imagined.

It was two weeks after the birth of her second child. A clerk from the mill came to see her. He took his cap off as he came in the door and she knew it was bad news. She picked up her first child and held him to her, too tight. He struggled but she suddenly needed the warmth. At that moment everything had whitened out about her, she had lost all sense of sound and for one moment, one very long and eternal moment of suspension, she found herself walking in a snowstorm, a blizzard whose snowflakes fell on her face, whitening and wetting. When she returned from this snowstorm she found they were tears running down her cheeks and the man was sitting on a bentwood chair, his cap on his knees, and he was saying he was sorry. It was the zoo tram. It was coming down Victoria Street, it had a lot of momentum because of the hill. N wasn't looking. He didn't appear to hear it. He looked like he was dreaming. He had walked straight into it.

She went up to the hospital and sat inside the white corridors and her child cried because her milk had dried up. N died soon after. She never saw his scarlet blood. She saw his face, white.

The Northern Roller Mills Company took up a collection for her. Everyone forgot he was a foreigner and, besides, it does the heart good to help another. Indeed, the giving became quite competitive, and finally a bleary photograph was produced in the evening paper of the owner, who lived in a splendid two-storey wooden mansion in a part of the city which was never clouded with coal smoke, giving a cheque for one hundred and seventy-four pounds to her. Beside her skirts in the photo were the faces of her two children, one looking up with suspicion at this strange man talking to his mother.

What could she do? She had two small children, the younger already ill, a family which still refused to know her. 'Lie in your own bed,' her mother had said. For days she felt hunger, numbness, unhappiness. In the shock of his death, she had had no time to accustom herself to this new world. She had walked through it all, a stranger to herself. There was no money for a tombstone, that went without saying.

In the next room, in the boarding house, was a decent enough man, different in every way from N. Perhaps it was this difference which finally persuaded her to accept his proposal — though the way he worded it, it lacked that elemental air of romance. He said that humans need company and together they could 'walk down life's path'. He was a sailor in the merchant navy and, she reasoned, he would often be away. He seemed to like the children: that is, he had no particular objection to them and in 1933, in the depths of the Depression, a woman with two children could not make too many objections.

She found, after her first night with him, that the walk down the path together had various sidepaths. He was a tireless sexual performer whose acrobatics lacked, however, any grace or finesse. It had been a shock to her, this invasion of her person, this insistent demand. She told herself his interest might slacken with time. But the sad fact was his sexual appetite never altered: it had all the impact of a train bearing down on her. She submitted to it and found that the way she could best survive was to think of other things, which she proceeded to do. The pattern of light which had come in the glass windows at the chapel, mottling the white paint. The twirl of wool on a sock she had been darning. The colour of bread still warm from the dairy. She never, at these moments, thought of N. It seemed, in fact, as if the purpose of these feats of sexual endurance was to drive any thought of N out of her head. She lay and looked at the dirty white ceiling of their room in the boarding house.

So the paleness inside N's eyes, a sky which had seemed to arch over her entire life, first of all faded: then it died.

Her second husband, Alfred, was quite successful, it seemed. Her family had come now to accept him into their fold. He was like them, he even liked them. The children too were eager to join the tribe of her family and Harald, the one who looked like N, was particularly eager to deny any foreignness. He had attacked her vitriolically, with all the angst of a child, when she had said he was half Finnish. 'I don't want to be different,' he had said, raining blows on her legs.

'They are my children now,' Alfred had said to her later as he undressed for bed. They even took his surname.

She had changed. Of course she would change. At times it seemed impossible to her she had ever been that young woman who had stood by the gate, waiting for a young man she had chosen. Sometimes she seemed to see him in a far distance, standing like a dot, wandering. A kind of numbness overtook her, a dislocation between her earlier life and her present. There was a lost connection, like two selves divided, one moving along having given up all hope of ever meeting with the other, plodding on out of sheer necessity, just as she had heard people had to do in a snowstorm. After all, she could not simply die by with-holding her own breath and she was so demoralised that the thought of taking her own life demanded too much energy. This is the story of many unhappy people who spend their lives impersonating ordinarily happy people.

The children got older. Alfred continued with his time away at sea. Now when he returned, she felt a sense of shock because in his absence something drifted back into her mind and it was N's eyes, their shade of blue, and she found herself thinking of him, of what might have been. She found, in fact, she disliked her husband quite intensely and their relationship became that of many couples: exiled to live together till their foreseeable deaths, but actual strangers to each other's emotions, feelings, likes and dislikes. Or rather, it could be said, both were fully conversant with each other's worst points which either could enlarge upon.

One day while Alfred was away at sea, on one of his last absences, she did a surprising thing. She caught a bus and went to look at the grave of N. She knew exactly where it was, almost without consciously thinking of where it was placed in the ceme-tery. It was as she had pictured it, unseen over all that time, in her head. As if she were walking under the sky of his eye. There it was, a small patch of kikuyu, indented where the earth had sunken. She stood there and she looked at the sky, at the rough grass, and she felt nothing except a sense of disbelief that there, down below just a few feet of clay, lay the one man she had loved, the one person, in fact, she had loved more than anyone else in life. It was raining far out to sea and the harbour looked silver, like a vast silver tray buffed in certain parts, flecked with forgotten bits of paper, specks of white.

The following day she went into town. It was a day of early autumn and the leaves from the plane trees swept past the plate-glass windows down Symonds Street. Outside, people leant into the wind and the air turned the faded violet of an old and for-gotten postage stamp from some mandate of the British Empire. It was almost three o'clock. She had decided that out of her own pension money she would spend her nest-egg, saved for the proverbial rainy day. She would buy a proper tombstone for N.

The shop assistant had the gravity of an undertaker. He

flicked the pages over and she looked at patterns and prices. She chose again, but this time it was his tombstone, the marker of his existence. And now, for the first time in over twenty years, she said out loud, to another person, his full name. She said his years. And she said that she wished certain words to be engraved on the granite: Together Soon.

A shiver, not of cold but of recognition, of presentiment, of being suddenly accompanied where before she had moved alone, overtook her. She looked now at the shop assistant, a short shy man with a red neck and hands which indicated he did a lot of cleaning. She looked at him with her eyes but also with N's eyes. This was a moment she would remember for a long time afterwards.

That night she went to sleep quickly, deeply in the way you sometimes climb into dreams as a thirsty animal might guzzle water. Almost immediately, it seemed, she had arrived at a place she knew distinctly, even though she had never been there before: she felt a shock of pleasure, of eagerness. It was a vast white area, it was snowing too, a kind of pale whiting-out and she looked around and she didn't know what she was doing there. She was trying to find something, locate something; and then, as she walked across the ice she heard far below her — as if she had at last found the point, located the essential dot, the cross on the map, the heart — she heard far below, down through the ice, the soft sweet chime of coincidence — the coincidence which happens to all people when they find a person with whom they fit — and in that space of white, for one brief second she uncovered him, perfectly lying there as if he was simply asleep. She held him and she looked at him and then the dot was whitened out, and in that solitary moment of the infinite she heard the sweet chime finish, and she became the colour known as white.

Profane Lesson

When I woke up that morning, I could remember hardly anything. I lay very still and then, my eyes closed, felt out with my fingers to the other side of the bed. There had been a shape there. There was still his smell. A kind of husked smell, like something shelled. I did not like it. I opened my eyes into a bloom of black, a soft webbed moss of it, a blotter almost, with an oblong leaching in diamonds, hundreds and thousands, sprinkles and sparks of small brilliants. Gradually I saw a thin curtain like a paper floating on the surface of water, detached from whatever it had once been joined to. This is me, I felt. I lay very still, listening.

Down below the small dog I had never seen skittered across the marble floor, its unmanicured nails rasping. That ancient woman, the mother of the soignée madame who often stands down by the street door. Sometimes when I go downstairs to the door, the old mother is there. She is almost blind: she has that sensate listening aspect of a person dependent on their hearing; perhaps smell, too. Could she smell the men on me?

She was always extremely gracious, charming in a sort of imaginative drawing-room kind of way, so that even though she was almost bald, with thin hanks of hair roping round her head — the concave surfaces of her toothless face were like an animated skull — she managed to bob her head, as if to acknowledge my imagined bow. 'Have a pleasurable evening, monsieur,' she would murmur. Leaning all her force on her walker-frame, her weight planted in two very old cloth slippers, the toes of which had been eaten away by the slightly monstrous growth of her toenails. The shame of her middle-aged daughter. 'Oh, Maman.' The swift click shut of the door. 'Pardon, monsieur.'

I lie there. Beneath me, the swift frilling of my orifice, a happy grinning arsehole. As if I am only distantly connected to this

139

other mouth, it takes me a while to smile, in the darkened bedroom. A face, now I see a face. It is like looking up through water. His face is about a foot away from mine, flushed, the centrifugal pull of gravity dragging his eyebags down, making his lips pendulous. I look into his eyes, which are slightly glazed, as if reversed and looking inside his head; as if they have travelled down his body to that junction in which all his pleasure is happening. I can hear the sound, a moist slither, followed by the sharp bang of the frame of his hips. I too am concentrated elsewhere, not in my mind. My pleasure is something which needs constant stroking. So we both exist there, in a nether world of preposterous positions, our sensibilities located other than in our heads — the relief of this! — the prosaic perfection of this method of exit and entrance. We communicate by whispers, murmurs, leaf-falls of words which dwindle down from a shaking tree — 'You OK?' There is a pause for a few moments, a few motions. 'Yes. You?' 'Yes. Please. Thank you. Yes.'

The phone went. It was his son's music teacher. He was puffing audibly. The conversation was long, detailed. He must practise more. 'But he is improving?' asks the proud father. 'I try to keep him at it. He likes it but . . . '

I have no idea why I like getting spanked. A man asked me once: 'Were you spanked as a child?' I said I couldn't remember. It's just that: I like it. It is good to lease out the permission of one's control. It is a pleasure. Anyway, I say, laughing, all of life is pretty much S & M, when you think about it. He doesn't reply. I have told him I work for a real estate agent, and my name is Paul. When I first met him, I murmured, by mistake, my real name — Cary. He was momentarily confused. I said Cary was my surname, quickly, with a monosyllabic terseness which often goes with sex. At least at the beginning: then come names and jobs, addresses and telephone numbers and problems and the ordinary boredom of the minutiae of life.

I often want to say: I want only the abstract of sexual pleasure. I understand now those men who give themselves up, literally in the end, to pleasure: who live for fucking. There is a kind of satisfaction in this. Perhaps the satisfaction of ending control of your brain. But there are problems with this, too. Obviously.

140

'Why are you laughing?' he asked me. Because I like it. Because I'm happy. Because right now, I didn't tell him, it is because I am free. He is discovering what I like, moving his hands over my body as if he is blind, discovering my psyche by my responses. 'Yes. Hard. I like it hard.' The ideal: a grunt of yeses, rising into a pant, then a moan, then a gasp: then just ululations, sounds which defy language but which, once you have heard them, or better still utter them, are completely descriptive. An escape, an exit, a perfect state of non-being: through the body, if that isn't a conflict.

Later he says to me: 'The walls here are very thin. Come into the other room.' The other room has no bed. We fuck on the floor, on the chairs, on the carpet, leaning against the wall. But the walls are thin, the walls are always thin, and everyone in the world is always subconsciously listening for sounds of pleasure.

I suspect the old toothless madame downstairs is like this. I imagine her sitting in the room down below us, directly below, her face raised to the roof, as if to receive beautiful raindrops. I imagine her listening, and nodding, and smiling. Her daughter, though: I can imagine the pain in her face, if she heard. The disgust. 'They are animals! Animals!' She who takes her small dog down on to the street, with its overgrown nails blunt from scurrying over marble: she who stands by the dog, tethered to its leash, and waits patiently, murmuring small endearments, eyes decorously averted until the proper moment when she can check: the object on which she showers all her confused love tenses its hind-quarters, shivering all over its pelt, and extrudes a small, black, noxious smelling piece of shit; at which point she murmurs, feeling the peacefulness of an orgasm: 'Good boy, Rufus, sweet boy, Rufus. Mummy really loves you. Good boy. Good boy.' Then, her nose lifted appreciatively into the air, with all the happiness of an act complete, she walks along with her dog, along a prescribed path, littered with the ordure of a thousand other trapped little dogs, before she completes her circuit and returns to her apartment, where, unlocking the door, she finds her mother — is she asleep? — her heart jumps a joyful beat, yet one full of unspecified terror, the anguish of future loneliness. 'Maman,' she murmurs, to fracture the image, the mirage of her mother, head thrown back, toothless jaws wide open as the elderly maman, with a facial expression of almost grotesque pleasure, lowers the surface of her face from the ceiling at which she has been staring, transfixed, blinded, returned to other rooms in which she herself has been murmuring endearments, enticements, and she turns her blind face to her daughter, the intruder, and, with complete seriousness, calls her daughter 'Georges', the name of the manager of her husband's perfume business.

And the daughter, coming in the door, shaking off all the smells of the street, the exhaust fumes, the just-baked pastries, the odour of cigarettes and one thousand breaths coming from other humans who have all come out of doors to walk up and down, with their dogs, their children, their lonelinesses and their memories and longing for love and sex and the sweet short oblivion which comes from good sex — this daughter now closes the door. The dog skitters in, towards the old lady, then, at the last moment, as if smelling some scent its nostrils do not appreciate, it skirts in a wide arc round the old lady whose hand has slipped down to touch the bristly blood-running warmth of a dog, a living thing, and her hand having been lowered now lies there, motionless, too much effort to raise it again until her daughter comes towards her, undoing her scarf, blotting out the light, as she unshakes all the smells of the outside world, the living world, in sprinkles of scent and stink all around her. 'Maman, darling, you have missed me?' she asks in the petulant voice of the fond infant, as her mother adjusts her gaze quickly, a crafty, devious expression falling down her face like a curtain dropped from the top of a proscenium arch, to offer an abrupt change of scene; and as her daughter lowers her chaste, long-unkissed lips — lips which only ever welcome food into them, or graze past her dog's salivating snozzle — her mother crushes her eyes shut, and listens as upstairs, across the ceiling, she hears the sound of footsteps, reaching down from a bed, walking slowly across the floor, moving towards the bathroom, where she hears, presently, the sound of water trickling down the pipes, and distantly, so far away it is as if she herself is imagining it, she hears a voice singing to itself, and she recognises the voice . . .

He was one of those men who liked to jump up the moment after an orgasm and reach for a towel. Half asleep, momentarily sinking gratefully into a world in which consciousness first narrows then dims, then becomes opaque, I was abruptly awoken by a cat's cold paws — a cat which has been outside in a frosty night — padding over my thighs. He had thrown a towel on to me, incidentally covering my penis, as if that no longer had any use: as if the sexualisation of my body had to cease, its function having been realised in orgasm. Occasionally, and this was better, he would wipe me down, turning me over like a mother cat, so that when I was still almost asleep, he took the responsibility of cleaning me down, and as he did so, taking a proprietorial look at the state of my orifice, gazing at it scientifically, even sliding a forefinger, now cold, rough as a cat's tongue, into my pucker, which, naturally, eased itself open gratefully. 'You're insatiable,' he says to me, laughing. He playfully slaps my thighs.

Or he does not jump, athletically, off the bed, to get a cool towel. He stays there, clamped round me in a statuary of stilled orgasm. Juice runs everywhere, swiftly cold, as if to express the fact that all the choreography which led towards it has now reached its optimum expression: he runs his thick fingers through it, then, sliding his slippery hands round to my arse, he kneads my arsecheeks, massaging feeling back into them. I become viscous, like a newly born baby. In fact, in all our processes, there are many points at which one reaches an ideal pre-born state; perhaps this is the ideal and immaculate secret of this profane lesson.

The hands speak a lesson, the eyes murmur a word, the lips can be silent and those parts of us which are made to connect, and intrude, obtrude, are the clumsiest of all, yet in some ways the ones which can give the greatest physical pleasure. But, all said and done, a perfect meal is a more selfish pleasure, but not one lower by so many degrees than that of the sexual act.

'What do you do?' he asks me. We are both naked at this point, sitting on a perfectly bourgeois sofa on which a towel has been placed to protect the midnight blue velvet.

What do I do? Haven't we just been discovering it? This is

what I do. I undress in front of you, as you undress in front of me. We come together, two men reduced to flesh: we try and find pleasure. We work to create oblivion. We are careful of each other, while attributing sought-after pain. Hopefully we coalesce, then fall apart. We wash, or don't wash. We dress, and dressed in the clothes we have individually bought before we ever knew of each other, we move off, in our costumes, our habitats of unreality, and thread our way through the labyrinth which on these days, this particular day, opens into doors, halls, shortcuts, lanes, alleyways, highways, by-routes, trammeled paths, untouched walkways: in fact, on this day, simply by walking we create a new path, in which all is discovery.

The water now runs down the pipes, washing away whatever remains of him, his smell, his juices, his sweat, saliva, touch of his hands, he disappears down the small brilliantly metallic eye, whirling.

'Good evening, monsieur, I trust you have had an entertaining day.'

'Good evening, madame, the night looks propitious.'

Parlez-vous Français, Monsieur?

When his name was announced it had the eerie weightlessness, yet the predestination, of a message in a dream. It was all the more curious, too, because his name was sandwiched in between a long — to him — incomprehensible announcement in an entirely foreign language. Yet there his name was, embedded, flying out into the vast auditorium, towards the suddenly moist audience, which at that very moment rippled alive, then roared into a tumult of applause.

It was as if a vast breath had come towards him and picked him up bodily, filled him with all the energy of those unseen people around him, behind him as he rose, yes, through a dream, fingers nervously, distantly feeling for the buttons on his dinner jacket, smoothing down his trousers in order that they might hang properly: so that he might approach the simulacrum he had rehearsed, secretly, in front of the hotel mirror.

He hurried, as if to catch up with his physical body, which was racing, it felt like racing, towards the platform. There was an almost abstract physicality of sensation. The thud of the leather of his shoe as it hit the scarlet carpet. The singe of the arc light on him, irradiating the edges of his body with blue fire. Faces turned towards him, smiling.

Around him now he felt a suspension of breath. He was aware of a kind of surreal silence, almost as if he were within a bubble, tender, viscous, which held him enclosed and safe until he hit that deck of prominence, of fame.

Ahead of him, up a flight of stairs, waiting under the blaze of light essential for the nimbus of live television, the star. From his distance, as he approached, she appeared doll-like, small, hardly human.

A normally impassive guard, the one who had barred him

from the door when he first arrived, now nodded at him, extruding a smile that said, 'Hurry up! Time here has another meaning.'

His dream unfolded. Now he was climbing in towards the light. The light felt physical, curtains which he parted, climbing through to find himself in that essential arena: the stage.

He walked now in slow motion, diminishing the space between himself and the woman he had seen in films made before he was born. She was a legend, with her drawling voice and imprecise lipstick, her mocking sexual allure. The legend looked at him sharply. Her hands swiftly reached out and placed him before a microphone. Her push was surprisingly powerful, brusque almost. Her thumbs seemed urgent to mould his clay. Her lips were parted in a ritualistic smile.

He stared now into a silent auditorium. He could see nothing. Rather, he could see, shining powerfully into his skull, a curved line of lights strobing his innermost being. He felt rather than saw a sigh move through this dark animal known as *audience*. He had felt its power during the festival, its molten ability to change. One moment applauding wildly on its feet, another time sullen, reverting to the rumble of disapproval. He had known the dread of this.

He must open his mouth.

Later he would try and re-rehearse what he had said. Was it — I am deeply grateful to be honoured at this most sublime of festivals? Was it that he, a boy from an unimaginably distant place, from a country quite often left off maps, was unprepared for such a public immolation? Or was it that he felt bedazzled to be where he always knew he would, one day, be? Yes, it was his appointment.

Or was it a mistake?

A voice in that incomprehensible language yelled out from behind the lights. Its tone was threatening. The legendary star let out a small, involuntary creak. He could not understand. Immediately he assumed the camouflage of a diffident winner. He was modest, polite, charming: the very picture of a well-rehearsed New Zealander. Almost too quickly, yes, he wanted to hold back, to leave his hand a fraction too long in the legend's dry grasp, but already she was glancing down at her notes to prepare for the next prizewinner. Too soon his moment evaporated.

He was being led away, to the next stage of his canonisation.

Down below the stage, a fury of flashbulbs ignited. Behind him, on the wall, his own shadow grew, multiplied, shrank, to be reissued more mightily, a Disney configuration of shapes, all attached to him, a short and endearingly modest figure, half raising his prize in deprecation.

Hubert Winchester forgot and forgave in that second all the agony and doubt.

Yet he sensed danger. 'You have no idea . . . ' He heard, like a whisper, the dry laconic tone of the American. He was at a meeting. It was a seduction, really. It did not matter that it was he and another man. Gender had become indiscriminate. They were seated, suitably anonymous — it made them more like spies — in an expensive café, right on the Croisette. Beyond the barriers, a tightly packed crowd pushed past. Was it because they were excluded the passers-by seemed so dejected? The passers-by sweated in their humanness. Their feet ached in too-tight shoes. Their clothes bit under the armpits. The acid of boredom, of longing, corroded every glance they made. (Yet these people changed, chameleon-like, into an audience!)

'You have no idea . . . '

Hubert had forcibly taken his eyes from these people. (Was it his own anxiety which made them appear so ghoulish?) He turned and looked at the man talking to him in a low caressing whisper. A Bel Air agent, he was small, fine-boned as a jeweller. His grandfather had escaped a pogrom in Russia. Now the agent lived in a mansion, behind a high electrified fence. He talked, it seemed, with deliberate quietness so Hubert had to lean in closer.

'In several days' time,' the agent was saying with slow emphasis, 'your life will change. Forever. You have no idea —' he paused to laugh to himself. 'You have no idea what lies ahead.'

When Hubert did not reply, (sometimes it was better to play the New Zealand naive, more politic), the man took up again, glancing at him with mute contemplation. 'Perhaps it's better that you don't.' And Hubert's eyes turned to watch a particularly ancient madame, wrapped in a rug, being wheeled along by her flinching daughter. To be in public, the daughter seemed to be saying, is to die a little bit. It is as if I am wheeling along an older version of myself. My life is already over. And my life, thought Hubert, is just beginning.

Remember that image, he thought.

'You have no plans in September? Will you be available to tour America?'

Again that low insistent voice, the voice in a dream: 'Not less than twenty cities, not more than sixty.'

'Are you ready . . . '

The voice faded, fried, in the bright burning light.

The audience, behind the lights, let out a communal breath, a sigh, it seemed, of longing.

A ventriloquised woman, in a long black gown, came towards him. She beckoned him with outstretched arm, more like a banner really, directing him towards a bank of seats. Up ahead, world-famous celebrities. Their faces were a blur of pleasantry, welcoming him with a serene sense of objective distance to their club. It did not matter, really, their practised smiles seemed to say. We have been here before you. We will be here after you. But welcome.

A line-up of Taiwanese actors looked baffled, washed to that isle of fame by the flood of an equally incomprehensible language. An old and toothless man, epitome of a village storyteller, nodded companionably to him. Cackled.

Hubert sank down on the surprisingly hard plastic seat. His award felt sharp against the pad of his fingertips. Beside him, a once-great beauty.

Time had changed her into a pigeon-plump housewife. Soignée. Her naked arm, beside him, gave off a surprising heat. She was breathing peacefully, rhythmically. Hubert ordered himself to breath more deeply. He had almost forgotten, so airless was this dream.

On his other side, a great contemporary star. Her pendant earrings flashed blue carats in the floodlight. She sat with all the cool hauteur of an American princess. He watched, fascinated, the swing of a slipper from her pedicured toe. It was hypnotic,

148

this exquisite boredom.

'Your life will never be the same again.'

He was inside the barriers, down the stairs, on the beach. Two guards had taken his invitation away. It was as if, at the last moment, they were expecting an imposter. They had glanced from his name to his face, critically. Hubert sweated. He felt so insecure, at that second, he might have broken down, produced his passport, argued.

Wordlessly they passed on his invitation to a young lady, seated beneath a beach umbrella. She checked his name off. The guards nodded brusquely. He could enter.

It was past four in the morning. All night long, a concatenation of parties had been exploding, a kind of electrical sequence of haphazard chance, people flowing from one event to another, flushed along on a wave of alcohol, searching all the time for the quintessential party: the one where the most powerful were, where the essential contact could be made.

As the hour was advanced, the air was frenetic. The chances were evaporating, the possibilities fading: or growing more desperate. It was schmooze-time, in Hades, under the twinkling stars which were wired bulbs anyway, attached to septic barbs. Every human, at a certain point, turned whore.

Hubert Winchester was no different. He was simply looking for the seller at the right price. As he moved through the knots of negotiation, fleshly or temporal, faces casually turned to glance at him. Was he someone important? Was it safe to ignore him? He pretended not to see them.

He made the sand. On the horizon the tycoons' yachts were moored. Lights shimmered off them, glamorous as tiaras. A single tipsy woman wavered there, alone. A ballgown, bare feet. Holding her shoes.

'You know all the best parties happen out there.' Her voice oozed cigarettes, alcohol and a not entirely unenjoyable cynicism. 'You haven't really made it till you're invited aboard. That's where the stars, the producers, really party.'

Her face, when she turned it to him, was burned brown, weathered into an undeniable personality. She was chic, he could see that: around fifty-five.

'I like to think —' her accent had an expensive perfume: not entirely convincing as American, it hinted at Basel, or Geneva. 'I think, you know, those boats are flats made out of cardboard. They are held up by wooden struts. A single worker labours to provide the smoke, which comes out of a fake chimney,' she said in a flat-broke voice. She waved a hand at the yachts, far across the water. 'But we all want to get aboard. No? Desperately. Are we not the modern boat people?'

Hubert retraced his steps to a canopy. The air was almost dank with promise. On the sand a feu d'artifice was sparkling. The brilliance lit everyone to a harsh, unflattering chiaroscuro: you suddenly saw lines, and sag; the metallic gleam in certain eyes. The bargaining had reached that moment of silence. The touts, tarts, toffs, the agents, the actors, the directors looking for work; the fat men, the thin procuresses: everyone froze in mid-negotiation.

It was then he saw the faces.

They were up on the promenade. He had seen them mutely waiting outside of theatres, just as they lingered for hours on end before the brightly lit doors of hotels. Red velvet ropes kept them at bay. These people, the forever uninvited, came from miles around — from factories and shops, in buses and cars. Daily, nightly, like creatures of hell, in a purgatory of fame, they wandered up and down the Croisette, searching for the famous.

Now they had stopped. They had paused to look down. And there they stood, silent and unmoving as witnesses at a fatal accident.

There was something deeply unsettling about the fixed attention of that crowd. It was not envy. It was not pleasure. It was remembrance — people in the act of remembering each person there, their consumption of food and wine: the weighing of their lives upon some more subtle account.

Was what they were doing worth it? On what basis did it gain its high renown? The actor circulating through the crowd had dandruff on the back of his jacket. The great contemporary star had a bad complexion by firework. Her skin looked vaguely grey, a Reynolds painting when the tar had surfaced. A frantic tic revealed her cocaine addiction.

These moments now were his last.

'You have no idea what lies ahead. Perhaps it's better that you don't.'

From where he was sitting, high on the stage, he could see an archipelago of lights swarming towards him, brilliant and blinding.

There was no shadow, he noted, on live television. It called for synthesis, coming from all directions so everyone around him appeared suspended in ether, unreal, pickled, pricked, hair-edged and rimmed with an undertaker's brilliance.

It had all the unreality of a live occasion.

At that moment a figure hurtled up from the dark body of the audience. He climbed on to the stage. The legendary star staggered back slightly, regained her step and vacuum-sealed the second with her unshakeable equilibrium. Hubert, along with all the stars, leant out slightly.

The audience held its breath.

The guard slid his eyes down, significantly, to his watch. His fingers tapped the glass. He smiled.

Hubert looked away swiftly.

Hubert could not understand. He could not, literally, understand the language. But he could sense the ripples of interest emanating from the man behind the microphone and then flowing directly towards *him*.

The guard flexed his strangler's fingers.

Hubert sat there, a false quiescent smile plastered on his face, both accommodating and alert to possible dangers which lay in changed meaning.

Startled, he found the American princess was looking directly at him. It was a rueful contemplation, as if he were a purchase she had, at the last moment, decided not to make.

When his eyes connected with hers, and his face lit up with the concupiscence of a fan, the great woman removed her glance with surgical precision.

He glanced down at the trophy. His name was not written on it. Was it all, then, a mistake?

Such was the sophistication and cruelty of the occasion they would not deign to tell him. They would simply pretend he no longer existed. That he had never existed. That air pertained to where a person once was.

The last thing he remembered, before the guard summarily ejected him, was the great star turning to him and awarding him a single, enigmatic smile. 'Parlez-vous français, monsieur?' she murmured. And her tone was incredulous.

What is Paris Like?

He awoke in a small chambre in Paris. This was a surprise. When he had closed his eyes, or rather, when he was last conscious, he had been driving down a long straight road, bordered on either side by black water. It was night. Full moon. All the houses were in darkness, apart from one window made of three panes of glass. He had felt a thrill of recognition. Inside he saw someone standing by an open door, a man talking over his shoulder. He was carrying a cup. It looked like he was going off to bed. There was also a standard lamp, with a lampshade somehow reminiscent of the American West. It was his home town, and he was not so much looking for someone as searching for something. Something lost. He felt he was actually finding it. So he had gone on driving until there was complete darkness.

In the light coming in through the curtains, the ceiling appeared to be nicotine-orange, shiny as false teeth, curved over like the last ripple of wave, down to the dado. There was wallpaper of an indeterminate blue-green stipple. There was a picture of the Virgin, with a blank face. The man beside him stirred. This startled him, his glance shot away from his surroundings — yes, Paris. He looked at the man.

He was aged in his late fifties, with thin fine hair quivering on his scalp like bird feathers. The skin on his face was mottled, red and veined where bristles of a black-grey beard were beginning to show through. His lashes were a stippled grey-white. This man was still asleep. In his sleep he had reached out a claiming arm, which fell against Andrew, pinning him down, against the wallpaper. Andrew listened to the man's breathing. He dreaded him waking up. Looking up at the ceiling, he wondered how many people had lain in the room, looking up at the same square, trying to work out a plan of exit.

To slip out of the bed, unnoticed. To try to slide out from under the man's arm, even though his arm was skinny, skinny as an old chicken, Andrew thought, looking down at it. This might be difficult, without the man waking up. Besides, could he take his clothes out and dress in the corridor? But was it his room?

He tried to remember the previous night. His head felt thick, kapok. There was no reason. Feeling down under the bedclothes his fingertips registered the flaky dryness of semen on the left side of his belly. This made him feel vaguely sick, yet, at the same time as if he had somehow paid his due. One day this will be you, he thought, looking across the landscape of the older man's face which was lost in a vacancy of sleep. This will be you.

There was a smell of old buildings, of dreams trapped in between walls, a sponge of memories, sweat, yearnings. There was the sound of car horns, and the subdued sibilance of passers-by, three floors below. He could not quite understand the language. He felt the nausea of a hangover which he always associated with petrol fumes. It had been a full moon. 'I don't mind if I do.' 'Let's not waste time.' 'You are direct.' 'That . . . no . . . there.' 'What is your name?' 'What does it matter?' 'I like to know.' 'John,' he lied. 'John.' 'That is a good name, John.' He did not ask the man his name. He wanted him to be nameless. He wanted him to be kind. He wanted him to be cruel. He wanted to be kind. He could not help but feel cruel. The man when he had come had let out a small cry — le petit mort — and slumped down on to John's body, the body of the man not called John. Later the man had said to him, before falling asleep, 'Your body is so comfortable. So warm.'

Andrew had fallen asleep himself.

He was driving down the dark road, at full moon. He passed the house he had lived in as a child. There were lights on, his old bedroom. He kept on driving. He drove past the house of his best friend from childhood. He knew her mother still lived there. The mother's light was on in the bedroom, and a bright fluorescent light, so reminiscent of surgeries and hospitals, burnt in the living room. He had not known whether anyone was home, or whether it was a careful ploy to deflect burglars. He remembered then that there had always been a fear of burglars and madmen because of the lunatic asylum a mile up the road. And because, at their end of the road, there was only the road running into the sea, and at night it was dark, and still, and waiting . . .

When he woke up there was a hot layering of skin, sticky, sweating, pressed against him. The weight was dead, as if the person beside him was in deep sleep. He had almost none of the bed, he had been pushed to the very side, on the hump of a strut.

Perhaps, he thought, this was why, during the night, he had dreamt he was up on a mansard roof, poised to fall down four storeys if he so much as moved. He had lain there, stiff with fear, hearing the moments move by, uncertain of how he would get himself out of this predicament.

He lifted his head up, spade-end of pain in his neck, and looked at the boy in bed with him. He was black, or rather, his colour was of faded mahogany, all over, shining on his chest, on the slopes of his inner thighs, on the plumpness of his forearms. His face was turned away, violently contrapuntal, carrying with it the grand mythic sweep of a baroque painting. In sleep, he appeared to be looking away, beyond the frame of the painting, directing a metaphoric message to someone elsewhere: someone outside the room; perhaps the man he was in bed with.

Andrew lifted his hand up and slowly, carefully, so as not to wake him, placed the pads of his fingers, then his palm, on the boy's chest. The boy had small, inverted nipples, shy nipples, Andrew called them to himself and separated wisps of black hair running down the funnel of his diaphram. The breathing was deep, regular.

His body was incredibly hot. Now the boy swung his head towards him in one almost feverish sweep, so a hot, acrid breath erupted from his lips and splayed all over Andrew's cheeks, and lips, and forehead: almost up his nose, tickling. The boy's lashes were lowered. In his sleep, he murmured a few words, then, inside his throat, there was a quick series of clicks and lickings, which finally erupted into a cough. Instantly his eyes opened wide: glossy black irises surrounded by a junket-yellow pool, fragmented by little lightnings of blood. There was a small sack of pus in the corner of his left eye.

For one moment the two men looked at each other in silence.

Out the window was a smell of pastry and coffee. He saw himself as an old man in the globe of the boy's eyes — an old man the boy had found himself in bed with, waking beside him, in surprise. 'I shouldn't have slept. That's not good,' the boy's voice said thickly. Andrew felt the voice vibrating in his diaphragm, between his pronounced ribs, down by his belly. He slid his hand off the boy's chest. The boy's cock was hard.

They looked at each other in silence. Andrew smiled, then laughed. The boy laughed also, but questioningly. 'Why do you laugh? Are you a madman?' Andrew felt down and placed his hand on the boy's cock, which was like a small and cheeky banana, a lady's finger, thought Andrew running his fingertips lightly up and down the vein which ran down, then round towards the florist's spray of his pubic hair. The boy yawned, stretched. When he did this the bed, which was frail, swung on its legs — it had small brown porcelain wheels gouged into old linoleum. It was as if their world was in earthquake.

The smell of the boy was of earth, and sweat, and perhaps, just lightly, a flail of ordure. Perhaps this was how a man in Paris came to smell of the earth? He carried it within him, composting. Andrew efficiently began to pull the boy off. The boy turned his face, sharp and direct, to Andrew, his mouth, a deep bay, wide open. He had widely spaced teeth, an Easter Island of a mouth, thought Andrew to himself, as his hand moved rhythmically then abruptly altered its pattern so the boy groaned a little, an ululation at the back of his throat. Andrew felt the boy's soft warm lips reach out for his mouth, then thieve love from his lips, thieve feeling, thieve all the fragrances from his part of the world: pull the moon, the full pale moon from out of the water.

They kissed in frantic silence. The bed shivered like a nervous animal. The boy's juice, like coconut water, thought Andrew, shot out, then backwards, as in slow motion, on to the side of Andrew's hand. Now the boy lay there, laughing, laughing, laughing. The bed shook and outside the window came again the sibilance of voices, of people walking off to work.

He was in a chambre, in a town called Paris. He was waking up. There was a body in the bed beside him. 'But I love you.' It was a mistake. I only wanted to spend the night with a body beside me. I don't want love. Of course not. He was waking up. The boy wasn't very good anyway. He was untutored in the ways of giving pleasure. He was only used to taking pleasure — to being pleasured. For all his young beauty, he was essentially lacking. As for the old man, the older man, he was greedy in his discovery of pleasure; he could not believe he was being allowed so much pleasure. But this did not make him graceful. He acted with ugliness. He, Andrew, had lain there, thinking this will one day be me. Be kind.

But it was the arm lying across his chest. The arm of a sleeping man. Andrew was not asleep. He was lying there, trying to work it out. If there was anything to work out. But then it came back to him, in bitter-sweet sharp chill fragments: this is what it used to be like. His bedroom, himself, a boy. He would lie there, and look up at the ceiling.

'One day,' his brother said, 'we will escape. You and me. We will go and live together in Paris.' Then he described Paris, lying there, both of us looking up at the ceiling, his hand lying on my chest, just down by my diaphragm. He did not kiss me. I kissed him. I kissed him feverishly, all over his body. I loved him wildly. 'Take me to Paris. Please take me with you. You will take me to Paris? But tell me,' I said, 'what will Paris be like?'

'There are chandeliers ablaze,' he said, 'and women wear jewels and the curtains are red velvet, and there is a grand staircase which is so vast you go up the first hundred steps, reach a level where you dawdle, so everyone can see you in your best.' '— what will I be wearing?' 'Black,' he said. 'I will show you the picture later.' 'Like in the Saturday *Evening Post*?' I said, 'Like in the Cadillac ads? Where there is a man and a woman, painted, they are getting out of a car, in front of a mansion, ablaze with lights. There is a full moon.' 'Yes,' he said. 'A full moon.' I was lying on my back, looking up at the dark ceiling, on which there was a pattern, like a scattered fan, of venetian blinds. 'Go on,' I said. 'We are going up the staircase.' His hand moved along my body. I arched myself, stiff, quivering, humming bird. I loved it. I loved him. 'You will show me Paris?'

I felt pity for him sleeping, my brother. He never looked more defenceless, more murderable, perhaps, than when he lay beside me asleep. I did not know whether I loved him or hated him, or whether I loved to hate him or hated to love him. But he was there, beside me, when I awoke, both an old man and a young boy; just as I was that young boy and old man.

And I was waking up in a chambre, in a town called Paris. There was someone asleep beside me and I had to remember, I had to remember . . .

The Happy Cadaver

Even the guidebooks — index of the anodyne — described it as 'faintly sinister'.

Visitors are advised, the guidebook continued, *to avoid attracting attention to themselves either by their behaviour or their way of dress, to refrain from night-time strolls and, in particular, to be on the alert at all times.*

He could, with effort, restrain himself from 'night-time strolls'. But how, Eric Westbrook wondered, could he, a gay man, avoid attracting attention to himself? His 'way of dress' in his own country would be considered, perhaps, a little too emphatic, colours a bit too carefully orchestrated with key aspects — thick leather belt, shaven shortness of his hair — sending signals to those interested in reading them. But, in this city, *this* particular circle of hell, it wasn't simply a 'way of dress', he knew, which caused people to look sharply at him — or worse, turn away from him as if his very existence offended them.

Already within twenty yards of leaving the hotel, a man had turned and spat with contemptuous accuracy right by Eric's feet. The day before a woman, a mother, had come very close to his face as if she bore a personal message, then her expression pincered into disgust, almost as if she were, involuntarily, going to vomit at the sight of him.

Eric now knew this was not to be an exception. He caught himself returned with astonishing clarity to the paranoid world of his childhood, when to be sexually different was to be extraordinarily obvious, almost an amusement for a majority so complacent in its selected paranoias.

But he was not a child, he told himself angrily — he was nearing what would be the midway section of *other* people's lives: and his knowledge of himself and the world was gained at considerable cost. For men of his age and type there had been no established learning: that was, he told himself ironically, beyond those provided by psychiatric hospitals, prisons and the occasional morgue.

This was, he knew, to be paranoid himself: but this city of gargoyles, tortured saints — proud possessor indeed, of seventeen (how joyously particular) thorns, thirteen pieces of the Cross, a sponge, flails and even, it was passionately believed, a liquefying phial of the blood of Christ — was not exactly unacquainted with the tinctures of the curdled mood.

Yet with what quixotic fervour had Eric and his two friends — Tim, an Australian of unshakeable self-possession and Guiseppe, his Italian ex-lover, a languid man from the North — chosen to stay within the heart of the old, decaying, *sinister* city.

Each carried the *snobbisme* that they were not so much tourists, perhaps, as cultivated men intent upon experiencing 'the spirit of place'; yet the Sunday of their arrival was enough to shake Eric. The taxi-driver had almost killed them taking them the wrong way up a one-way street not far from the station. Their night-time stroll — Guiseppe said in his charmingly enpebbled English, 'Please not to stray far from another' — had revealed a miniature view of hell: an alley cut deep into ancient slums, shop windows behind steel shutters. The sky, high above the streetlights, had the look of flesh several days after a beating.

Eric's immediate response, on returning to their spartan hotel, was to lie down on his bed and close his eyes. It was, in a way, his idea of nightmare. He had been paranoid — that word again — about even going away. He had fought a mounting feeling of panic as he was driven out to Auckland's airport that he wanted to do one single thing: to turn around and stay at home. But this would have meant hiding from his friends and acquaintances, all of whom viewed his departure as the beginning of the one true joy which lies in departing from New Zealand's shores: a rest from its repetitions, a holiday from its isolation. It would be as if he were trying to elude the 'time of his life'.

Perhaps he was. Eric, at the age of thirty-nine, had now to face the fact that in a foreign city, this positively sinister place, he might have to call a doctor, face the horror of an unknown hospital. A complaint he had almost managed to shake off only days before his departure had returned, like an avenging angel, to haunt him.

It was an intolerable itch which had begun approximately two months before: a small squadron of upraised pores which became, soon enough, a squabbling storm of pain, an armada of acute irritation. Before long he was reduced to something akin to an animal: lying in bed at three in the morning, ripping the heads off sores with septic fingernails, trying to claim some relief. Then, as a refinement of his torture, there was the scratchy irritability of flesh forming a scab: worse still, anything which attacked his equilibrium sent him off, uncontrollably, on to a mission — hopeless as it always turned out, self-defeating, lacerating in its very futility — to soothe the ache, the itch.

Uncontrollable was of the essence. Eric was faced, immediately and close up, with the reality that he had a nervous condition he could not control. Doctors in New Zealand had offered balms, lotions, ointments, all as useless as they were expensive. (Indeed in the expense lay the inverse potential of salvation.) And now he was here, participating in his own worse nightmare: to be in a foreign land and ill.

He had worked it out at home before he left what was so peculiarly threatening about this thought: to be ill in a foreign country was simply to experience in advance the reality of all illness, which is to be homeless.

It was to be in a permanent foreign land — one where the language used is barely comprehensible, or at least where words seem to match, only clumsily, what they stand to represent. Worse still, you had to adjust to customs you barely comprehend in a place which you never can be, you never actually want to be, at home. It was to be in permanent exile from the world you knew. You were a refugee before you even knew it. A refugee in your own world too, perhaps.

Yet was he really ill? If he could only calm his nerves — evade the uneasiness which held him in its grip — he might escape back to that once-known, fondly remembered homeland: *health*.

Yet he was not in search of medicine that afternoon as he made his way down the Via Duomo. Eric had quietly got out of his bed towards the end of the siesta hour on their second day in the city. He had left Tim and Guiseppe dozing in their room, blind softly tapping against the window.

He was driven out of their room, restlessly searching for nothing so salving as a miracle. Rather he sought to solve all his earthly problems by an eminently materialist quest: a pair of Italian shoes.

He knew he must return to his own country with a few selected totems which signal the returning tourist. Not to do so would be viewed as almost scandalous: as if all those kept at home, entrapped in the two small islands — no strangers to paranoia themselves — were being denied the news of exactly what people were wearing, eating, saying in that miraculous world which lay beyond New Zealand's three international airports.

Eric now took his *passigata* past the ancient duomo, looking in shop windows. He carefully manoeuvred himself around passers-by, avoiding ostensible eye-contact, rejecting, seemingly invisibly, the many intense stares which passed over his body, sought an entrance through his eyes, as if to snare out and hook, like an obdurate oyster, the moist matter of his soul.

Instead he concentrated on the saving safety of leather objects. The shoes were displayed in ranks, their prices discreetly placed by their toes. Yet even as he stood there, the soothing practicality of his quest lost its focus.

He could not precisely name the feeling which overcame him at these times, yet all the time it was as if he were waiting: everything seemed a preparation yet, simultaneously, nothing was enough. If anything this trip, as everyone in New Zealand called it, this voyage into the outer world, served only to exasperate his problem. Behind every destination lay another appointment, so everything seemed slightly out of focus, as if his eyes were always and nervously straining to something beyond. His smiles felt false, his attention flickering, his logic obtuse in its connections. The fact was he was already listening, with an almost manic intensity, to the silence within his own body.

Almost on impulse, to escape this introspection, he entered the shoe shop he had halted by.

Immediately an elderly gentleman, petitioner to a quattrocento court, came forward with crossed palms.

Eric, who possessed no Italian, mimed the shoes he had seen: they were supple plaited shoes of a kind one could safely not expect to find in his own country. The shop owner — his proprietorial hauteur was such that he could only own the shop — now mimed his own appreciation of true good taste. He ushered Eric to a low-backed chair set against 1960s mirrors. Eric sank back, murmuring, like a curtsey, a self-conscious *grazie*.

To travel, Eric now knew, was to be stripped of all your assets: you were simply what you were, in flesh, or, perhaps, that more indefinable thing, the spirit. Was it an accident, then, he had come to a country so loaded with the detritus of spirit when he felt almost spiritually fractured, in need of integration? Yet how could he hope to find solace in a religion so offensive in its hatred for his type? Not so long ago — that is, in the margin of this place, several centuries — he might have been burnt, broken on the wheel, crucified.

Comforting, then, to be alive, even in *this* haunted present.

As if in answer to his prayers, the shop owner came back with a pair of shoes. No, the shoes did not quite fit. Now Eric became subsumed into the shop-owner's drama: that he should make a sale; and in fact the flattery of the shop owner's attention —after the outright affrontery of the street — was curiously relaxing.

The shop owner turned and, with the dismissive gesture of a great theatre director to a bit player, sent a boy along the road to another shop. Eric waited now, paused. And perhaps because waiting had become almost his natural state — a kind of anxious anticipation, or foreboding, underlying every event — he oddly, even luxuriantly, relaxed into this lacuna.

He looked at the other customers. In the women's section, a dowdy middle-aged mama was crouched beside her daughter aged no more than nine. The child was dressed as an infanta in white. All around them lay an army of shoeboxes, all in disarray, routed in the quest for the perfect bridesmaid slipper. A grandmother, a more withered version of the mother, gazed on while a shop assistant crouched down in genuflection at the infanta's tiny feet.

The child, Eric could see, was making the most of her brief regnum of power. Her legs swung to and fro, brow petulant with the perfect vision of the golden slipper, no doubt, that would take her away from all of *this*. Yet Eric wondered at her chances of evading the fate of her mother and grandmother, women visibly soured by life, beatings probably, premature deaths, men indifferent to them; no wonder these people clung to superstition, as a compensating, even avenging, faith.

Eric caught his own image in the mirror opposite: or rather, his image betrayed him. Yes, looking at his smooth unfurrowed face, there was privilege in its softness. He was not visibly ravaged by any unhappiness: his unease was internal. He was simply looking on, almost a spy.

As if in answer to his self-doubt — did he really exist beside these people? — a man outside the door casually cantilevered his hips towards Eric. Behind the cheap cloth of his trousers, the man, possibly a gypsy, displayed a hand, frottaging a not-inconsiderable erection. The man's eyes hungrily fed off Eric's homosexual face. This was as much a part of the paranoia of the place, Eric now knew: the flagrant tumescence of the men.

Only the day before as he and Tim and Guiseppe went up in the funicular, a beautiful youth had engaged his attention. As they ascended — suitably upwards, as if only in a heavenly sphere this youth could exist — the young man had turned himself towards Eric, and under the eyes of everyone in the compartment — these people who saw everything — the youth had begun to leisurely, silkenly, squeeze his erection. All the while his grape-green eyes never left Eric's face.

Thoughts had sped through Eric's head: to spend an afternoon, even an hour — or let's get basic, several hectic minutes — with a boy so beautiful (he had an atypical colouring of honeyed skin, dusky gilt hair, the eyes of peeled grapes) would be, well, heaven. Yet was he, Eric, even capable of the magic which was sex, when he was so full of indecision? Finally, abruptly, the youth had broken off the gaze, the tenure of which had, as much as the wires pulling the funicular upwards, kept Eric's mood in ascension.

The funicular had lurched to a stop. The youth turned and walked away. Was it some small compensation that he who had appeared so perfect stationary — or ascending — walked away unevenly: he had a club foot. Even so, he did not turn back.

'*Si, si,*' Eric said to a pair of shoes which matched, approximately, the shape of his foot. Ah, the happy curve of an act completed. Now, almost bowing, in a flutter of money exchanging hands, the transaction complete, Eric walked out of the shop with his totem. He awaited, wryly, that de-escalation of mood which followed the efflorescence — or was it defloration? — which was purchase. In his room he would discover, perhaps, the leather was not quite so: perhaps the heels were packed with cardboard. There was any number of deceits for those people passing forever through: among the permanent inhabitants in the panaroma of life, a tourist.

As he turned back towards the hotel, Eric's eye, elated by the victory which goes with any sort of possession, happened to snag on the typography of an English-speaking newspaper. He hurried into the shop — really only a booth, maintained by a severely sceptical woman who eyed his money now, intently, as if he were a bona fide counterfeiter. Eric felt at this now-familiar affront a rush of irritation. Involuntarily, yet as if it physically expressed his emotion, he sneezed. The woman shrank back angrily, crossed herself, and handed him the paper, a chill dismissal.

Outside the shop, the paper in his hand, Eric felt an unreasonable anticipation of pleasure overtake him. He would celebrate his good luck — his return to the world of language, and the logic which lay inside language — with an espresso, an aperitif.

He turned and went instinctively to the small coffee place where he had seen, the day before, an astonishing male beauty. This, too, would restore him.

As he made his way towards it — the streets growing busier as the sietsa hour fell further behind — he thought to himself, amusingly, of Tim, Guiseppe and himself going, the day before, into one of those religious shops which specialise in items to ward off evil spirits. They had settled on some votives — small silver objects reproducing part of the anatomy which requires God's healing intervention. Eric had chosen a leg as gratifyingly shapely as an All Black's; Guiseppe had fallen for the Grecian profile of an eye and a nose: Tim who always went the whole hog sexually, went for an entire body, in toto.

A perfectly hypocritical madame had encased their purchases in whispering tissue-paper. Outside Eric and Tim had screamed with laughter as they walked away, imagining how the woman would think they were men with very extreme illnesses to placate, whereas their hidden humour was that the objects were purely decorative: interesting totems to prove they had been to that particular place. The votives would end up sitting on a bookshelf, dusty and forgotten.

The coffee place had several men standing by the zinc counter. A woman sat behind her cash register, bored as a magistate facing a daily line-up of recidivists. The male beauty had his arms in suds, washing cups and glasses, an act which piquantly feminised him. Eric's eyes magnetically found the young man who, withdrawing his ruddy forearms, marble-white above the elbow, pulled off an espresso for Eric. On impulse, Eric added an aperitif.

'Grazie, grazie.'

Eric took the coffee, the aperitif, and leant a discreet viewing distance away on a counter. He looked once more, appreciatively, at the young man. His face was Egyptian in cast, like those entombed replicas gáudily painted — eyes outlined not with kohl but lashes, with lips made for love, for kissing and sucking and teeth for biting. Eric quickly looked away.

He opened the paper with gusto; even the biscuity aroma of the pages he enjoyed. He caught up, speed-reading, the latest world news, the usual combination of catastrophe and calumny, then his eye, almost automatically, as if selecting the one true item of personal importance, found the celebrated capital letters.

In a profound silence during which Eric lost his presence in that city, in that coffee place, before that male beauty, he read the simple statement which had appeared a decade ago, that exact day in a New York paper.

An unknown cancer had appeared. Forty-one homosexual men had already died. It was possibly contagious.

He reached for his aperitif — an ouzo. He drank it numbly.

Suddenly it tasted too sweet, too intense. What exactly, after all, was he celebrating? He looked up speedily. The male beauty was holding up to the light a glass, the cleanliness of which appeared suspect. Outside the clatter of horns battered the air.

Eric returned to the few lines and as he re-read, as if to find in them some further intelligence, an awareness settled in him — the reality of what these few lines conveyed.

It was that date, he knew, that the fateful diaspora had begun.

He sighed heavily and thought of what it had meant in his own life: friends he had not appreciated were so particular until they were wrenched, like garden plants too early, from his life. Then the disease crept closer, robbing his heart of his best friend, Perrin, infiltrating his existence until it became an unavoidable, a central reality: a prism, as it were, to gaze upon a world.

Manners, over time, dictated that not too much was made of it. With so many people ill, it was grossly self-indulgent — risking even exhibitionism — to make much of the disease. The deflective language of the theatre was deployed: characteristic terms such as 'scene-hogging', 'spotlight hugging', 'prima donna swansongs' marked painful, humiliating demises.

In such simple ways the enormity had been reduced. The stark phrase 'having health problems' signifed the advent. From here the stigmata varied in their elliptical progress: a 'seizure', 'in hospital', 'on morphine' and finally — usually, thankfully — dead. Thankful because out of pain — thankful, too, because the difficult business of being a witness was over.

But what about when you were the witness to your own — not death exactly — but the presence? There were as few rules here as there had been in the wilderness days of sex: to follow your instinct, to try and have courage in your convictions, your choice. What did that mean exactly when you awoke in the morning with unanswerable questions: what have I done with my life? To be more precise: what am I doing with my future?

Future, an interesting concept, that.

Eric laid the paper down.

Oh, irony, his saving grace, his god, almost — could it desert him now when he needed it most? Yet how could its deflective nature, its silver armour save him from such sharp and piercing shafts of self-doubt? It could not, it would not. Yet really, when he thought of it, closing the paper thoughtfully, was there not a certain mordant irony in the fact that he found himself, at this moment, now, on such a personally historic anniversary, in the very city which had suffered a plague so terrible that at its end so many were dead there had not been enough living left to bury them?

He suddenly thought of the night before. Guiseppe, Tim and he were returning from dinner. The rubbish, in a nearby alley, was being collected. Eric could hear the threshing truck yet there was another sound his ears could decipher. He listened acutely. It was the scream of a cat in pain or abject terror. The truck's roar drew closer. The cat's terror rose in syncopation. A cat-lover himself, Eric knew instinctively what was happening.

Sitting in the café, newsprint moist against his fingerpads, the exact tune of the cat's torture returned to Eric.

Sometimes it seemed to him the echo of this scream pervaded the entire universe. It underlaid everything, it was a basic note. At times, of festivity, of amour, this note was overlaid, forgotten. But then, at other moments — the silent moments, in the immobility which is doubt — or, again, in moments of great violence, this sound returned. It filled all space as if it were the one true essence of existence: chaos.

Eric hurriedly left the café, nodding at the young man who nodded back, as automatically as a dancestep in the waltz of living.

He walked home to his hotel among Caravaggio's saints and executioners.

Tim had the way, he mused as he walked along: there were few agues that marijuana, booze and a raunchy sense of humour could not cure; and what could not be cured was faced with a blatant bray of black humour not indivisible from courage. Tim had lost more friends than other people had family. And Guiseppe, Tim's ex-lover, was a charmingly vague man, as imprisoned perhaps in his own language as Eric was by his own lack of Italian; yet there was peace between them, no linguistic war.

Yes, Tim had the right idea. Every daily dilemma narrowed down to a choice of restaurant, then of dishes, a particularity of wine, and those moments after a meal, having eaten slightly too much, definitely drunken too well: to a sense of well-being as rejuvenative as good sex, yet somehow infinitely easier to obtain and of course, in this world now, this fin de siècle present — a century running out of monstrosities with which to haunt itself — much safer.

Eric passed on the street an ancient metal skull on which a few pinched blossoms had already wilted. This living with death, this fond familiarity, even fatalism, was a reality for these people. They, their cynicism intact, had survived.

It was not good enough, he told himself, firmly: he simply must adjust his mood.

As if in answer to his prayer he remembered something he had seen the day before. He had come across a crowd of people clapping. Over their heads he saw a cascade of fireworks: like toitoi feathers dipped in emerald, ruby and gold they painted the air, fading even as others appeared. He had always loved fireworks, their evanescence. The fragility of their beauty comforted him.

He stopped to watch in the cold wind, then moved on.

But the yowl of that cat apprehending its own death returned, now, to haunt him. Why was it he in particular who heard it, while neither Guiseppe nor Tim appeared to? Was it that it tuned into his own frequency, as it were, of paranoia: which was that he might, in a more hauntingly real sense of the cliché, see the city and die? Or was it that his mood at present constrained him only to hear the descant notes: to view, mordantly, blackly, everything he was seeing on his voyage? And did this not mean, precisely, that he saw everything blackly? He must find — not the courage for optimism, that was foolhardy — but must locate at least an appetite for life. It was the essence, after all, of being a good tourist.

'Ciao bello!'

Tim pulled him into his embrace, and Eric let his thin frame lean into the large, comfortably fat form of his friend. Tim's stomach ground companionably into Eric's penis, as if by the rotation of his belly, its content, Eric might share in his happiness.

Guiseppe smiled and waved an elegant semaphore with a cigarette. He was lying down, reading *Vanity Fair*.

This, *this* was real now, this room with two friends, with whom he could share his thoughts.

He was suddenly tired. He eased his shoes off, and recounted, in as amusing a way as possible, the man outside the shoe shop, his proud display of an erection. Lastly, and self-deprecatingly, he produced his newly bought shoes.

Tim immediately said he had seen the shoes for half the price in another city.

To compensate for Eric's natural national disability ('the Pacific's True Boat People', 'Irish of the Pacific'), Tim poured him a glass of an exquisitely fresh rosé wine.

It tasted, on Eric's tongue, momentarily, of strawberries and mountain water, of ice and watermelon.

Eric let it enter his body, easing, cooling, numbing, soothing. His particular ache, for one moment, lessened.

Now Tim, who enjoyed being naked, stood there stripped for a shower. Eric, who had missed being Tim's lover more by accident than design, averted his eyes, caught Guiseppe's drowsy gaze and they exchanged a momentary jag, a snippet of shared amusement. How good it was to share a fondness about a mutual friend's peccadilloes!

Tim removed his magnificence and, for one moment, his psychological presence occupied the room, as if his rotund physical shape were indented on air.

Water splayed on to concrete.

Eric had instinctively not alluded to the epochal anniversary in the paper. An event so major in all their lives was better left to after dinner, perhaps, when satisfied appetite could better combat what would inevitably attempt to spread a pall.

A pleasant silence fell in the room. Guiseppe turned a page. Tim, from the bathroom, took up his anthem, all the more personal for being tunelessly defiant: '*I'm going to live forever! I'm going to learn how to fly!*'

'Those fireworks I saw yesterday,' Eric said slowly to Guiseppe, having deliberately saved the best, most private part of his thought for someone less proprietorial of pleasure than Tim.

His question was carefully un-elliptical.

'I wonder what the fireworks were for?'

'Oh, the fireworks,' said Guiseppe, thoughtfully, listening abstractly to Tim's watery ode to joy, 'that day was . . . I t'ink' — he could never quite manage that hurdle of the esoteric, that particular consonant which divided the world into the English-speaking and the forever-foreign, the aspirant 'h' — Guiseppe paused, searching his English inventory for the correct word, 'the Day of 'appy Cadaver, I t'ink.'

Eric said nothing for a moment.

Then a shout, a flag of irony, escaped his lips.

And Eric Westmore, a good tourist for the first time that day, began to laugh.

Hills Like Green Velvet

It was the fourth counter we had been to that day. I like to count things like that, it helps. Two steps. Three hours. Forty minutes by that railway clock over there, fly specks on its face. I keep trying to notice things, it helps me feel I still have some control. Otherwise it all begins to wash over you. Before you know it, you are sinking. Lost. Like Nerma who one minute was standing there, walking between the house and back wall. Next minute she was lying in a ball, air caught in her throat, blood foaming out. She was still holding on to a clothes peg. Some things notice you. You cease to watch them. You become caught by them. Memory's captive.

I am waiting here with my children, Anesa aged three, Braco aged five. His birthday was last week. We celebrated it with hats cut out of newspaper and a bar of Toblerone. I queued five hours for that, and in the end I did something I thought I would never do for a chocolate bar. But it is like that here. Bit by bit, all the rules of human behaviour change. Soon you find yourself watching things which once would have made you sick. Then you find yourself doing them. I had sex with a stranger for that chocolate bar. It didn't even seem shocking.

We went into a house. It still had the front door, though the walls beside it had been completely shot away. That curious smell of masonry, wood opened to the rain. All the odours of a lifetime: cooking, people sweating when they sleep, the first coal put on the fire in the morning. I think of things like that. Just in front of my eyes was old pink wallpaper, the colour of boiled sweets. I realised we were in what had been someone's bedroom. There was the faded patch where a cross had been. A Christian's house. In the background, mortar fire. You get so used to it, you only notice when it stops. Nearer. Closer. Danger.

I hardly looked at him. Him, I tried not to notice. He was someone else's father, someone else's husband. The sex we had was brief, urgent, pathetic. When he came, I was surprised to find him crying. I looked at him then. He had tobacco stains on his teeth. I think he hated me looking at him. He reached up and turned my face away. It was the only time he touched me during the sex. It didn't even seem particularly degrading. I was thinking of the chocolate bar.

After a while I noticed a small boy of about eight looking at us. When the stranger left, the boy came over with a stick. It was only when he was prodding it into me I realised what he was trying to do. I was going to hit him. I surprised myself. Instead I bent down over him and pulled him into me and hugged him so tight he began to cough a deep, racking cough. He was utterly limp in my grasp. So thin — I could feel his shoulderblades, sharp, tense.

He began to struggle as if I was trying to suffocate him. Perhaps I was. Then he saw the chocolate. He grabbed it almost before I realised what was happening. He was calling me dreadful names. A child using those words. Hurtful. But I heard my own voice using the same words back. Horrible words — demeaning. The boy began to keen, snot mixed with his tears. He was hysterical. But I had to have the chocolate bar back. I got hold of his fingers and one by one I prised them open. He was looking at me, his face very close to mine. We had fallen over by this time. We were lying in the debris, mud, wet carpet, rubble.

When the chocolate bar fell out, he went limp, and it was like a shade had fallen down over his eyes. He stopped crying then and lay very still. Because we had been fighting I was still holding on to him. I relaxed then and snatched up the chocolate bar and we just looked at each other, in complete silence. There was a long pause between mortar fire. It was like we were waiting for it. And sure enough, quite near, there was the thud of its impact, biting into the earth. We are still alive. A small piece of masonry, high up, falls. I pull my clothes down and dust the earth off the back of my jacket.

Why should I care what I look like? You have to keep something intact. It is like each day I wash my face. I always find water. Even after we were taken away from the village. That day. I keep remembering all of this. I keep thinking: I must remember. When you start to allow it to fade, then it is a dangerous time. A dangerous time for your mind. Not long then till you forget who you are. I am Mikira O, I say. I lived at a village forty kilometres from X——. I am thirty-eight years old. For fourteen years I was a librarian at Z——. It does not matter that this library no longer exists. People who were our neighbours, they burnt it down. My father had said in the days before the war they were fascists. But at that stage I had said, let the past be the past. We must live in the present. Now I understand there is no present.

We are waiting at the fourth counter of the day. My children and I are waiting for exit visas, so we can cross the border between one town and another. Where we can enter a place which is, if nothing else, away from this sound of mortar fire. It is strange what it does for you, that constant sound. I saw a church burn down last week. I saw a woman shot in the street. Her bag fell open. Potatoes rolled out. I waited for the gunfire to stop, then I went and gathered the potatoes. The potatoes were freshly dug, earth still clinging to them.

I gave the chocolate bar to Braco. The other women had gathered round. H was causing trouble by saying I had exchanged it for favours with soldiers. One of the older woman told her to shut up, that she was a stupid cow. I was afraid it might be a brawl. We have had brawls here, but I soon realised we were all too tired. I am tired every day. I am tired in my dreams. I arrive home. The door is wide open. I say to myself: did I forget to lock it? But then I see there is no carpet, no furniture, nothing but a phone book, spine broken, its pages blowing in the wind. It is winter, though when I left the house several hours ago, it was summer. Then I see four men carrying away my bed, my television set. I call out to them to stop. But my legs don't carry me down to them. They look at me. I see they are from the town on the other side.

I start running then, through the house, away. I run and find the children. That is all I want. All over the village, people are carrying things from houses. It is as if the innards of everything have come out. Wash basins. Sewing machines. A record player.

A dream. A nightmare. I am frightened I will never find the children. The school is empty. Doors open everywhere, which says there is nothing left to take. Nothing.

I am not even shocked the children are nowhere to be seen. I think of those times my mother had told me about. We were taken to the woods. They gave the younger ones a shovel. They were forced to dig a shallow grave. Then, when they had dug their own grave, they were shot, so they fell neatly into the pits. The women of the village had been taken out to watch this. My mother had seen it with her own eyes. She said to me: and what is so terrible is you realise you would do anything. You would do anything to survive. And that is terrible, she said, because it makes you into an animal. Not a human. An animal. But, she said, war is like that. Everyone changes into an animal. It is the end of civilisation.

I think of myself with that man in the bedroom, by the patch of wallpaper where there had once been a cross. I think of H who is visited every night in her room by the soldiers, a queue of them, one after the other. I was a virgin until I met my husband. He had very soft palms on his hand, which was unusual because he was a worker in a car assembly factory. I could have married someone in the Party. I was educated. But the palms of his hands persuaded me the Party did not matter. He was not particularly skilled at love-making, despite his reputation in the village. I think I taught him to take his time — that we had all the time in the world, and that was the best time to take. He had an angular body and small neat buttocks, and long feet, with toes like something out of a cathedral. His eyes were like windows in a church. But the ball of his hand. I will never forget that. I won't forget.

The children no longer ask. We found each other in a big empty dining room where the lights no longer worked. It was an abandoned hotel. We were so glad to see each other that we just hung on to each other, and cried. It wasn't joy, that is the saddest thing: they were desperate tears, bitter tears, the kind of tears a child has during a tantrum. Everything is wrong, nothing is right and you will never see your father again. Everything is alright, we will survive all this and your father has taken a long journey to where he will meet up with us again in the end. He is watching us now even though we cannot see him. He has no eyes. His eyes were taken out. They needed his eyes for science. He has eyes which see forever. His eyes are now in another person. And that person is looking at us now, except you don't recognise him; and he can even see you, and me, and Braco, sitting in this abandoned hotel dining room, under a chandelier with the bulbs shot out. Which one is he, asks Anesa, looking around at the soldiers. Which one? I tell her not to look at the soldiers. The soldiers are nervous. The soldiers are exhausted. But which one, mama? Which one? She looks around the room.

Lies. He has gone forever, apart from the touch of the ball of his palm, the softest flickering in the world, like a pulse of blood through your wrist. He put the ball of his palm against the back of my neck. He rubbed the base of my spine when I was tired, and we were in bed, and the room was dark. He traced down my body, past that spot which makes me laugh. Made me laugh. I try to remember all this. I must remember. I must. Without remembrance, we are all dead. It is the only difference between us and animals. The ball of his palm. That is the only difference.

We are waiting here in a railway office. The queue does not move forward. Ahead of us is a small bag. It is made of brown vinyl. It is so old it is splitting. I don't know what's in it. It belongs to the old lady squatting over there on the dirty lino, her back pressed up against the wall. She had been standing for two hours. I thought she might fall. She had told me she had walked all morning to get there. I could tell by the tone of her voice she was not used to queuing. Occasionally you still meet someone who was a bourgeois. Once we were trained to humiliate them. But I said to her to sit down. I would mark her place. She reminds me of my grandmother, although my grandmother never got out of the fields. So this elderly woman who I do not know at all becomes my own grandmother.

The people who arrived later did not like this. Everyone should queue, they said. Otherwise it isn't fair on any of us. I laughed at that. Someone said I'm glad she finds something funny. I said it was the word 'fair'. I couldn't help it. It set me off. Anesa tugged on my skirt. H, she said, worried. She is frightened I might get like H. Queer in the head. Anesa often sits and looks at H, fascinated. H yells at her: what are you looking at? Haven't you ever seen a crazy woman before? H who has a child in her womb implanted by one of any number of soldiers who systematically raped her. The devil inside me, H says, tapping her stomach, grinning. Anesa cries. And H cries too. It is bedlam there sometimes, in the abandoned dining room, the old posters still hanging on the walls, faded. Fly to beautiful B——. Come Relax by the lovely A—— coast.

This is the old woman's story. She had parted from her husband at the end of the last war. He had simply disappeared. A train, he was going to the next village. He never came back. Then she got postcards. Never signed. Cairo. Cape Town. Melbourne. Then from some place called New Zealand. All in his handwriting.

She says he lives there now. He has cancer of the bowel. He is waiting for her. If she can only get out. It is very beautiful and very peaceful, she tells me. It is at the end of the world. There is nothing beyond it. It is behind God's shoulder, she says to me, nodding. The hills are covered in green velvet and everyone has a sheep. How can you be unhappy in a place like that? she asks. The sheep can always eat. And you can kill the sheep if you get hungry. She says to me she is going there. She only has to get out of this town.

A distant cousin is waiting for her in the next town. He walked across borders in the last war. Last war, great war, we all talk like this. Yet this war, it has no name yet, because we are living in it. In the middle of it. She has already purchased her ticket. It simply needs to be franked. I haven't heard of tickets before. I suddenly think: I have been queuing all this time and probably I will get to the counter and be told to go somewhere else. Can I see it? I ask.

She won't show it to me. She looks at me like I might snatch it. I say: haven't I been good? Haven't I allowed you to sit down? Haven't I kept your place? She looks at my face for a long time. She still hesitates. Finally her fingers sort of walk towards her bag, open it up. She does this without moving any other part of her body, as if everyone around us might snatch it. She says to me in a low voice, she sold everything for this ticket. She said she even sold her wedding ring, which was the last precious thing in the world. But, she says, handing me the ticket, her fingers still holding on to it: what is more precious than freedom? And I swear to God I will go mad if I have to stay here. I have to leave this place.

I took my eyes away from the ticket and didn't say anything. It was a ticket to the local museum in P——. I recognised it, because I used to take the children there and look at the porcelain collection. They have, or maybe had, a wonderful collection of small towns in porcelain. Farm animals, milk maids in pannier dresses, powdered wigs. The animals are all glossy, with painted mouths which look like they are smiling. Geese, milk buckets, everything complete down to the last impossibly ideal detail. The old lady had exchanged her wedding ring for a day pass to a museum.

Hills like green velvet, she says. I only have to get it franked, she whispers to me, not even really looking at me, but turning to look about her with suspicious eyes.

I wanted to laugh. I wanted to say to her: wake up! Can't you see what's happening to you? But I looked into her old mad face and I thought she was perhaps better where she was, waiting a few hours till she arrived at that counter and then, perhaps, she would start arguing with that man, and telling him he had it all wrong, and that nothing was more precious than freedom and that she had to get to those hills of green velvet.

It is hard not to laugh. It is hard to laugh. I saw a dog the other day, a skinny mongrel. Nobody feeds dogs any longer, everyone is hungry. It was sick, this dog. It had extruded all its innards. Its entire stomach, its guts, were lying there, raw-looking, in the dirt. The dog was sitting there, panting in the heat. It was looking at its own innards, thinking: I am dying, and I am hungry. Shall I eat my own innards?

I have to stop thinking of that dog. Its expression. Not even a sad expression. Just a kind of curious equation. Shall I? What is happening to me? I will die soon. But I am hungry. Can I not have one last meal? I will die, but I won't at least be hungry. That equation. Not even a sadness.

Nothing is happening up ahead. I look at the man behind the

counter. He is one of those hairy men who go bald quickly. His eyes undress you. He sits behind glass. He is bored. He has already said he cannot hurry things along. He sprawls back in his chair. We stand. We wait. Seventeen minutes pass. Thirty-two minutes. Then he simply gets up, pushes his chair back and, without even glancing at us, puts up a sign. 'Closed'.

The crowd pushes forward. I am losing my place. I push back with my elbows. I say some of those words I never used before. We are fighting now, in the queue as we wait. But the man has gone. The door is closed. Perhaps he will be back after lunch. I notice the clock has not moved. It has stopped.

I close my eyes.

You have to remember, I say to myself.

You have to remember.

Remember what?

The ball of his palm. It isn't much to remember. But you have to remember. You have to remember. You have to.

A Prandial Proposition

It was that time after a meal when the plates had been taken away and everyone sat, some fingering the stems of their wine glass, others rolling crumbs across the tabletop which resembled nothing so much as the landscape of a battlefield in which all were victors, the food alone the vanquished.

Each person at the table surrendered to the strange contentment of being no different from an animal in a field, digesting.

As the metabolism of each silently set to work, breaking down what had been fresh, piquant, picked at its peak, there was a brief lacuna, a small fracture in their content. Suddenly it appeared that every meal like this was almost a final repast when there would not be enough food and the numbers of those hungry would become so oppressive that to eat well might become an act of guilt, demanding contrition as much as pleasure.

So this meal, a triumph in its freshness and the combination of its tastes, was also, in its own subtle way, a defeat. For life is so perverse that no matter how well you have eaten, the meal exits your body and you have to prepare for new food, eternally. In this way the best meal in the world is followed by the dilemma of choosing what to eat next, and where it should be served, and with whom, and at what time, and on what plates . . .

Perhaps it was to blot out this unfortunate vision that one of the diners spoke up. It was Dr Kay, a general practitioner. He said he wished to amuse them by telling a tale as they relaxed over a demitasse of coffee.

The waitress, a thin woman with a hungry look, brought them their coffee, then glancing at her watch with significance, left.

'My story is called,' said Dr Kay, 'you will have to forgive me,' he coughed rather delicately, — "The Revenge of the Arsehole".

The diners glanced at each other briefly, then stared at Dr Kay. Each had their opinion of him, but all found themselves under the spell of lethargy which overtakes any animal immediately after engorging. Truth be told, none of them had the energy to leave. So it was as if each were exiled to that table, to hear the tale through; and it was only at its cessation that any of them could break away, running for mythical appointments or claiming they suddenly did not feel well. That is the meaning of a captive audience.

This is Dr Kay's story.

One day he was called in to the most peculiar case. It concerned the son of an acquaintance, a youth who was uncommonly handsome. He possessed every grace known to the male figure, was modest, charming, respectful to elders, kind to the infirm. His parents, who were averagely ambitious, that is to say, avaricious for success, imagined that their only son — he was their sole child — would ensure that their old age was comfortable, and bathed in that peculiar aura of satisfaction that parents feel when they have produced a reasonable human being.

The only problem was that our graceful young man was not interested, in his turn, in adding to the weight of human population on earth. He preferred men to women, and in fact he preferred being pleasured in that part of his anatomy which has long been an object of supreme ridicule and disdain. For a young man so handsome to be so profligate with his looks aroused great anger in his father who, moreover, saw it as a slight on his own masculinity. He tried every persuasion he could to alter this one unalterable thing.

Matters rose to a crisis when one day the father happened to come across his beautiful son in the middle of being pleasured not even by another handsome young man, but in fact by someone whose looks were decidedly average, whose body seemed to possess no charm. His son, as he saw it, was playing the woman's part. This outraged him to the point of lunacy.

The father decided he would lock the beautiful young man inside his house until he saw reason. He would rather his son were dead, he said, than this insult to existence continue. The

181

son smiled, as if he knew something the father did not; as if, indeed, his eyes had seen to a further plane: he said nothing.

Life continued with the young beauty locked away and watched every moment of the day by his obsessive father. A curious calm had fallen between them, as of a struggle so intense it was as if nothing were actually occurring. The first victim was the boy's mother. One day she did not get out of bed, and within a week she had disappeared. It was as though she did not wish to partake in the murderous course her husband was pursuing. Her farewell to her only son was tender, lingering, yet full of the promise they might yet meet sooner than was expected.

The father and the son's duel continued. The strange thing was that the obsessive father could not bear to be away from his son for one single moment. Yet he began to observe a disturbing thing. The young man's looks, of which he was secretly proud, seeing the son as a younger version of himself, were disappearing: being dismantled in front of him. First of all the son began to put on a loose layering of fat, which gathered in momentum until it fell in cascades about his body. Within a month the young man could barely walk: he could not bend over to pick up anything he dropped. The father found himself converted into a servant who had to wheel his increasingly obese master about his captive cell.

He took to watching the young man, never sleeping, trying to find out how his son had become so suddenly and grotesquely obese. Gradually he came to realise that the young man, who had not spoken to his father directly since they had exchanged their apocalyptic words, was not evacuating any of the food that he so avariciously consumed.

The father could not believe his perversity. He decided to cut the young man's food down completely. But his son at this point fell ill; refused to move, would not open his eyes. He would not look at his father. This drove the father into a deeper frenzy. Why, he said to his son, are you doing this? Can you not see what you are doing? You are poisoning your own body!

The son's eyes by now were two tiny seeds under the folds of his lids. Why? came the strange and sweet voice from his vast bulk. Because you have spoken to me so disparagingly of that

182

orifice which I used for my pleasure. You say its sole purpose is for waste, so I have decided not to use it at all. That is all, the son said. And he smiled

The doctor was called. The doctor took the father aside and said the young man's heart really could not stand the pressure. His kidneys were failing. It was quite critical. Yet nothing the doctor or the father could say would alter the young man's serene purpose. The son sat there and gazed at his father with eyes which were now blood-red and jaundiced. The smell emanating from his flesh was so vile the father could hardly be in the same room without vomiting. Finally it was clear that a form of gangrene was about to break out in the young man's lower extremities — parts of his anatomy the young man had long given up any hope of ever seeing.

You have said, the young man at last wheezed to his father, that I cannot use that orifice, which you find so disgusting, for my own pleasure. This pleasure never hurt you, nor have you ever understood the intensity of the delights which can be found in investigating that much maligned organ. In fact you call people you detest by that very name, as if you were describing the lowest of the low. So now, my dear father, you will have to witness what happens to your son whom you have converted into the lowest of the low. Because that is how you see me.

With a huge cry the father threw himself on his knees. Please forgive me, he said. I knew what you were from the day you looked at me and I knew that you wanted to know a man like myself. This made me afraid, as I have known men to find me attractive!

The rotund young man, now monstrous as a rotting fruit, stinking so badly the windows were no use, simply looked at his father and a slow sad smile settled on his face. A single tear rolled down his cheek. His heart was almost stopping as he gazed at the older man.

Please, the father said then: you may have the freedom to use that debased orifice in whatever way you wish. Simply do not take all the joy of life away from me.

There are connections, said the young man, not all of which happen in the right order. Some things start wrongly and others end at what should have been their beginning. It is like that with you and me, my father. And the old man wept bitter tears. I wanted to see children, he said. I realise this is now vanity. I wanted grandchildren to care for me. Now I shall be alone.

Finally there seemed nothing more to say. The young man and the old man sat together in the room and both, it seemed, were looking in the same direction — not so much towards the future as the past, when the young man was no more than a seed inside the father's prostate, lodged near that site of erotic pleasure, the secret of all homosexual men's desire. It was at that point they had been closest; yet now this is what had driven them so far apart. Neither could find any words to say. The room darkened, and at last there could be heard only a shuddering and then the sound of one person, alone, breathing.

Dawn found a surprising thing: the old man had dropped dead in his sleep. Yet it was as if his dying breath had leapt into the young man's body, invigorating him. You can see, said the doctor, draining the last drop of his demitasse and placing it down with a decisive click, this young man around town. He now looks quite svelte and happy. He has all the vivacity of a survivor.

The diners shook themselves as if awaking, shaking their heads even as their eyes furtively found their way to the face of the glorious and handsome young man who was a guest at their table. He sat there, eyes downcast, furiously blushing.

You have embarrassed this young man, one of the diners said, seeking to protect the patina of his freshness.

Not at all, said the young man, speaking up for the first time. For if we look within the body, what do we see? Inside the chest is the spinal column, with its twelve branching ribs. This is like the Tree of Life in the Garden of Eden. In the lower part of the Garden, below the tree, rest the two serpents. One is the plump white worm of the Colon. Beneath it is the other serpent, the Small Intestine. What are we to do with this knowledge then? These serpents exiled us from Paradise, yet entrance through that aperture can be as close to Paradise as we can find in this miserable world. What are we to make, then, of this cosmic joke? Except perhaps enjoy it.

Alone now in the restaurant, Dr Kay and his companion remained. They glanced towards each other and as if reaching an arrangement they smiled.

'Er . . . waitress,' Dr Kay called out.

The waitress appeared through the swing doors, nonchalantly brushing her hair off her face.

'We thought,' said Dr Kay with a prandial growl in his voice which was positively wolfish. He was gazing at his companion as if he might like, that moment, to eat him, every bit of him — but this would come later.

'We want to look at what post-prandial enticements you have on offer,' he said.

The waitress eyed him testily. She had already missed one bus.

'Come again?'

'Bring us your liqueurs, your port, your brandy, your Benedictine . . . '

And so the inevitable moment was, enjoyably, not so much postponed as stretched, elasticated to its fullest extent.

Hot Ticket

'It happened like this. We met on a ferry. He was standing beside me. Desperate, he was desperate. Unhappy in love.'

'You mean you had been dumped on?' Avon said excitedly, suddenly sitting alert in his chair. He handled his pen more easily now. He tapped the table with it.

'You were being screwed round, right?' He liked the idea.

'He was about to jump. He did jump. I threw a life-saver. He caught it.'

'Reeeeeallly?' Avon took a sharp breath then drew, luxuriously, like silk through a tiny platinum ring, all the vowels out. 'You saved him, right? You became lovers then?'

'I took him home, we undressed. We . . . '

'How long ago is that, please?' said Avon, writing this down. 'I want the listeners to know. It helps them to form a picture.'

When they were going out live, Avon asked the question again, but freshly this time, as if he had just thought of it.

'Oh . . . by the way. Where'd you meet him?'

It happened like this.

'He was standing right beside me. On a ferry. I was eating an ice cream. The top scoop fell off. It fell on his foot. His shoe. His shoes were of a particular kind. English. I apologised. I was always a shoe fetishist anyway.'

Avon looked not so much put out as relieved of any obligations of belief.

He didn't really care anyway.

Besides, as he said when the interview was over, he was meant to be covering a forty-year-old go-go boy.

'With the body of a fabulous twenty-year-old. And I mean faaaaaaaabulous.'

Again he drew out all the vowels.

The forty-year-old go-go boy had not showed.

'No one alive has seen me in these glasses.'

'You want to go somewhere hot?' Avon said later to Nathaniel. They were still in air-conditioning.

The duc, a languid Neapolitan fop, murmured, 'But Mommy is so very tirrrrred.'

Nathaniel noticed everyone here emphasised certain parts of certain words, inhabiting them by extending and underlining, either ironically, or simply for rococo effect. It was perhaps a fag thing.

It was a hot night, mid-winter, in Miami.

Out on the streets all the Toms-of-Finland had their shirts off, so their perfect pecs crested the soft Carribean breeze, nipples not yet hardened to a searchlight.

'My personal reads,' Avon said, as if to get better acquainted, '*Fem top seeks butch bottom*. I don't go in for dish. For all the negativity. I try to report. So be frank. Do you want to go somewhere really *hot*?'

Later, quite quickly, the duc led Nathaniel to a bar stool in Café X.

Café X was already mid-performance, with fashionable extras seated at exquisitely lit tables, waited upon by models in between engagements.

It happened like this. Nathanel had hardly lowered his lips to the frosted edge of his cocktail glass — 'Yes. Straight up. No ice,' he had told the beautiful waiter who had recently occupied a page in *GQ* — Nathaniel had hardly let his lip droop on the edge of the glass, when Able appeared. Able was a photographer. He made people famous. With a flashlight.

'I like your jacket. Looks good,' Able said, shaking his hand.

Nathaniel was wearing a pale yellow silk jacket.

Able and he had met that afternoon, on their way to a corporate lunch. Able had entertained Nathaniel with a tale of a model changing his clothes on the plane, coming down from NY. The model had spent a lot of time with his shirt off. A woman had, coincidentally, fainted. The stewardess had asked: is there a doctor in the house? It was just like television. Said Able.

Able said the model's body wasn't *that* good.

187

Able had taken over the task of educating Nathaniel.

'You're joining us, right?'

'. . . I.'

Nathaniel suddenly appeared indecisive. Before that he had been feeling tired. The evening had appeared a labyrinth with so many paths he was exhausted working out which one not to follow.

'You're ready to go out. To meet people. Right? There are people in this room. You should meet them.'

'That is Cindy Crawford in there.'

The duc was leaning in. Special hush in his voice.

'The woman sitting by Bruce Weber? And that is Aldomovar. Right?'

Beside them, an elegant woman dressed like Morticia threw her head back and expressed what was clearly a trade-mark shriek. It sounded good: the signature of a person used to being a cynosure.

Everyone lacking confidence on that stage glanced at her, smiling in appreciation. One day, I will be like that. They take a mental note. One day I will laugh, the room will grow silent in appreciation. Everyone shall look.

A Cuban waiter, shirt draped over shapely pectorals, slid by, a tray on his shoulder.

Eye contact electricity. Customer control.

'Scuse me, sir,' the waiter ululated in a pleasantly basso voice which echoed down his throat, plunging sonic depths till it reached that final pitch, an organ note. In an empty cathedral. Of his looks.

The two men, Nathaniel and the waiter, smiled at each other, a ziggurat of possibilities. Till the look broke apart, pinging like a streamer held between someone aboard a lit, glittering liner, and someone left on dry land. Nathaniel.

'Please . . . ' said the duc to Nathaniel. The duc was Nathaniel's press agent. 'Mommy feels very tired tonight and she wants her little baby to go out and have a nice time. Besides,' the duc's dark and mossy pupils played upon Nathaniel's face like butterflies, swamp beauties. 'Besides, there are some very important people in there. Ones you ought to know.'

'Right,' said Able. 'Come inside. Meet everyone. I'll introduce you.'

So it happened like this.

'What is your room number?' Nathaniel had overheard Able murmur to the duc, just as the duc was about to go.

Able's head was on one side, as if he were only being considerate.

The duc laughed uneasily, silkily.

'Whadderyer mean?' The duc had a New Jersey accent.

'No. No.' Able had said firmly. 'You only have to tell me. What's your room number?'

It was like a game.

'But I'm a happily married woman,' the duc murmured, suddenly alert for the first time that evening. 'My husband is very jealous. *Very*. (Room 527.) He is Venezuelan, see? Very good in bed. But, sweetheart, his temper!'

The duc had disappeared.

'Mommy is going back to the hotel. You enjoy yourself,' he murmured before he withdrew the opium of his slightly Proustian presence. Pleasantly bruised, le duc.

'You don't like these people?' Nathaniel asked him, catching him by the hand before he left. 'Don't go.'

Fingers inert.

'I did too much of that when I was young. I had too much of everything. Now I'm tired. I'm old. I got to get some sleep.'

The duc was nineteen.

'Good night baby. If you can get mentioned in the columns . . . have your photo taken . . . Mommy will be happy.'

They kissed. Almost tenderly.

So it happened like this.

'Can I read your cards?'

The tarot card reader had big breasts softly sheathed in a scarlet dress. She had a vacant expression as if to better receive the emanations sent through the exquisitely expensive ether.

Able was perched on the very edge of a wrought iron chair, tips of his fingers resting on the woman's upturned pads. Her face was soft with empathy.

Able was talking. Talking.

189

'But you see, I get too involved. See? I always want to give a lot. To make it good for other people. I simply want them to have a good time. I can't relax unless everyone around me is happy.'

'Kind of like Elsa Maxwell?' Nathaniel said to Able as they walked into the main room of the restaurant. 'Except of course, you're a thousand times better looking.'

'I don't have her kind of money,' Able said a little glumly.

'I don't think it was her money,' Nathaniel continued. He and Able appeared to be in the middle of a grave, even a profound conversation. 'I think she simply spent other people's. I don't think she had any of her own.'

They stood still long enough so that everyone could register their presence.

So it happened like this.

'There's nowhere for me to sit,' Nathaniel whispered to Able, who by now was his lover.

'Sit beside Betham,' Able whispered back. 'You know he's a gossip writer. Very influential. So watch your step.'

'He'll tell you terrible things about me,' the duc had whispered, before he went away. 'Just don't believe any of it. And tell me what he said tomorrow morning.'

The duc had laughed thoughtfully, eyeing the beautiful, damaged young man, the companion of the gossip writer.

'As for that little club ditz he's brought down from New York. To fuck all weekend. So typical.'

Oh, but he was charming, was Aaron, the little club ditz.

Aaron had perfected the art of looking like he was half way through being undressed, but then he had been interrupted and had hurriedly pulled on some expensive, if slightly soiled, garment and run out the door, to, well, a simply gorrrrrrrrrgeooooooous party.

Betham, beside him, was no beauty.

Betham was very aware of not being a beauty. He had no conversation. He carried round with him a slightly soiled large envelope from which he took sheets and on which he pencilled notes, in writing so tiny you could never read it, even if you managed to look over his shoulder.

Betham always sat with his back to the wall. He could move

with surprising speed. When the party or the room was no longer fashionable. He only spoke in a monotone, and always as if he didn't have much breath.

'Do you have a lover?'

'How old?'

'How long have you been together?'

'I hated *The Piano*. What did you think of it?'

'Where do you stay in New York?'

Nathaniel knew he was being auditioned, so he was on his toes and he gave back light and malicious comments which he could already see typeset and in print and being read by someone in a place as distant and unknown as where he came from. He had almost learnt never to talk of his country, which was unreadable on all these people's radar. It simply did not evoke any impressions. But it helped him to seem exotic.

'I want to go there,' everyone cried, before switching the conversation with practised efficiency. It had a kind of allure, as of a country you could not actually get to.

'But you hear a lot about it — all good,' said someone sitting momentarily to Nathaniel's right — and one day, Nathaniel knew, there was always the possibility you might have enough time, *down time*, to actually get there. So you made a note, a mental note.

A mental note. His country.

'Actually I'm from Canada myself,' whispered a gentleman who looked like a slightly tired Steve Reeves. Sitting to Nathaniel's left. His voice had a sad inflection.

'So I kind of know . . .'

It happened like this.

Cindy and Bruce and Pedro were sitting together. Nobody in particular was looking at them, but everyone in the room was aware of them. The supermodel sat in the middle of the table, approximately where Christ sat. She was languidly beautiful, perceived like a mirage across a lake. She was smoking, and listening at the same time. She was playing with breadcrumbs on the table top. She was pensive with fame.

'What's this?'

Aaron and Betham leant together for a photo.

Flash!

Nathaniel noticed Betham adopted a definite pose, nose to the extreme left, eyes hooked to the camera, hand a small contrapuntal arrow.

'I can never be photographed enough,' Betham murmured to Nathaniel.

'Never.'

He let out a small sigh, like a slightly disappointed child gazing at an almost empty chocolate box, the contents of which he had already consumed.

'What's this?'

A glamorous stranger. Card in hand.

'It's a ticket for the party.'

'Which party?'

'Which party!?'

'Why. The big party. You know. On South Beach. Tomorrow. Everyone is flying in. From all over. It's big.'

'I like big.'

For the first time that night, Betham seemed happy. His fingers closed round the card and he lifted his bag up high and he buried the card deep, deep within it.

So it happened like this.

'But darling, did you hide the cocaine?'

'She is a sex-change?'

A woman had entered the restaurant with maximum impact, so everyone in the room turned, quickly, to glance at her. There was much air kissing accompanied by the occasional dissonant shriek.

Everyone was everyone's best friend, Nathaniel could see that.

Rustle of paper as Betham withdrew his notes. This was written down.

'She looks like a Roman aristocrat. Who sleeps with slaves.' Nathaniel felt like he was dictating.

'I loooooove champagne.' Aaron pushed Nathaniel's glass forward.

Bottles were being brought and opened, and poured.

'I keep thinking I'm on the set of *Laura*. You know? The film with Gene Tierney?'

It all seemed terribly important.

The woman called Crystal and Nathaniel were really getting to know each other well.

'It's like we're on a stage. A wall could almost slide back and an audience could be sitting out there. Like in . . . that film, that film . . . by Bunuel?'

Crystal nodded. Able was worried.

He kept asking the spiritualist, suddenly, as if he might catch her out — 'I was in ancient Rome, right?'

'Was I ever a Nazi? I feel I've been a Nazi, right?'

'Have I ever been an artist?'

'— Rabelais,' the spiritualist said with confidence. 'You were Rabelais.' Then her eyes strayed round the table.

They were all sitting outside now, in the warm still air.

The spiritualist was standing while they all sat.

'Can I pay you a dollar and you go round the table and maybe do, like, an x-ray on everyone here?'

The spiritualist looked momentarily eager then her enthusiasm waned.

'I guess it's asking quite a lot . . . ' Able said, disappointed.

He kept playing with matches, upending the box, then quickly switching it round.

His eyes glazed past Nathaniel.

They were no longer lovers.

'Rabelais . . . ?' she suddenly sounded a little uncertain. 'He was some kind of French writer, right?'

Nobody bothered to answer.

'Have you seen Nathaniel's film?' said Able to the table. 'It's simply ravishing.'

Able hadn't seen it.

'I keep hearing about it . . . '

' . . . I missed it unfortunately . . . '

'Everyone says it's really fabulous.'

'He's an absolute genius . . . ' Nathaniel heard someone say to someone else nearby.

'I must really get hold of the video . . . '

They had a toast to him.

'Let's not clink glasses,' Crystal said to him quickly. It was her turn to educate him. 'It gets to be so terribly unchic. Besides. So harsh on the ears.'

'I'm dying to see it.'

'When can we see it?'

'I want to have a party. Tomorrow night. We'll get hold of a video.'

'I'll *die* if I don't see it.'

Nobody had seen his film.

As the evening went on, the praise grew. The adjectives became more specific. It was as if, in not seeing it, everyone was viewing it that evening, in his person.

They had another toast to him.

Nathaniel was now being photographed.

'What is your name?'

'How do we spell it?'

Other people now spelt out his name.

'He is from Australia.'

'New Zealand.'

'You look like . . . you look like . . . '

It was a game.

' . . . Peter Sellers in that film. You know. The one before *I'm Alright Jack*. The glasses, I think. The haircut.'

'Twelve inches.'

'No. Seventeen. Deep.'

It was snow in New York. Not the waiter.

So it happened like this.

'You must come with us. Come!'

Crystal and Able and Betham and Aaron were off to Club Y.

The streets were en carnaval. The Toms-of-Finland had replicated, and the hot babes and their boys. Everyone was out on lotus patrol, queuing for nightclubs and clueing for pleasures.

They walked past a frieze of people frozen in a queue, waiting to get in.

'Come with us. Stay close.'

Nathaniel entered the nightclub zone.

The queue stayed behind.

It was like a 'twenties film, one of those scenes when they represent the end of the world. The film speed was set too fast.

Nathaniel and Betham shared the same set of eyes. They were looking at a pulchritudinous black man, in neon blue sweat. He was raised above the crowd. He was dancing as if a genie, a good or bad genie, was possessing his body. He was bewitchingly beautiful, perfect; except his face. He didn't have a face.

Everyone was dancing round him like a scene . . .

'That scene, you know,' Nathaniel said to Betham, 'like round the golden calf. You know. At the bottom of the mountain. It's raining. I can see Charlton Heston . . .'

'Let's dance. Come!'

Aaron had already met a man on the dance floor.

As they abandoned that place, Aaron described the man to Betham.

'From Salt Lake City. On vacation. A hairdresser.'

'Puuuleeeze,' said Betham, as if this news seriously upset his digestion.

They were walking now very fast through the heat.

'I haven't had anyone die yet. I'm lucky,' Aaron murmured to Nathaniel. He was glancing sideways up and down the street, as if he were expecting someone.

'You know,' Betham spoke up. He let out his customary small trill of laughter. He laughed like a geisha, as if the act were involuntary and somehow slightly sexual. 'You know,' he said to Nathaniel, whom he was educating now, 'in Manhattan we have support groups for people who test *negative*.' He did not exactly roll his eyes.

Nathaniel turned round to better see a beauty.

'The trick,' murmured Aaron to Nathaniel, following his eyeline, 'the trick is to *be*. Not to *want*. Once you start waaaaaanting —' and here Aaron's eyes did a quick lassoo round the scenic effects of the street, gathering in, then releasing, all the male beauties, 'it's over. You're finished. There's only dissatisfaction left.'

'New Yorrrrrk speed. Keep moving!'

'I knew it! I knew it!'

They were leaving Club Z. Almost the impossible had happened. They had had to pay to get in. And now the ticket, the hot ticket, was missing.

'I knew it!'

Betham was down on his hands and knees. On the nightclub floor. People were walking past. He was searching for his ticket.

The hot ticket.

Nathaniel thought of Betham on South Beach the day before. They were in muscle city, bubble butt heaven. Betham had remained fully dressed. He had placed a towel over his head. He had daubed white zinc over his face. He exposed no flesh. His tee-shirt read: *I look better naked*. They had walked along the sand together. There was a lot of laughter.

The ticket could not be found.

'He's always like this,' Aaron said *sotto voce* to Nathaniel, as if he were passing on a compliment. 'Let's get out of here. Come!'

Later, much later, they were all sitting in a taxi, silent.

It was an expense, this taxi, but Nathaniel was willing to pay. He had noticed all evening that nobody had paid for anything. And now they were going back to the hotel, to their rooms which none of them paid for.

Nathaniel had now been famous for a whole night. It was almost over.

'I just can't wait to stretch my arrrrrrrrse out,' said Aaron, 'and sleep.'

'Pardon?' said Nathaniel, who had slightly misheard.

Betham was silent, looking out through the window at the last ocean liner which, brilliantly lit up, was leaving Miami by night.

Each weekend liners came into Miami loaded with rich people who spent the weekend chasing happiness. They had two days to find it. Now the last liner was floating out, lit up and sad.

It was a toy cork, burning.

'Perhaps you can get another ticket,' said Nathaniel.

'It cost fifty dollars.' Betham looked at him as if he were mad.

'I wasn't going anyway,' he said with a small smile of triumph of his lips, 'Oh no! *Please!* On the beach? Those big parties?! Crowds! I never do that.'

The taxi drew into the lobby.

'It was worth fifty dollars though,' he said. 'That coat check girl. It was her. She recognised me. I know it. She went through my bag. She stole it.'

He looked happier for having solved the crime.

They got out of their taxi, tipping the black man as small a tip as possible. They separated and went to their rooms. It had all been terribly important. And it was over. And it had happened like this. It had happened like this. It had happened like this.

Confessions of a Provincial Pouf

AN EPILOGUE

When my first collection of short fiction, *Dangerous Desires*, was published in 1991, it was often reviewed purely in terms of a sub-category known as 'gay fiction'. To most reviewers, who often write within an overtly heterosexual frame of reference, this sub-category has no history, no *linkage*. It is seen as an artefact in itself, *brave* or *disgusting* depending on where the reviewer resides in the ideological spectrum.

Context does not exist, because the reading of a work of fiction by a queer writer is, for the reviewer, at most a detour, a tourist trip through unfamiliar country, a variant route, or root. Yet it's this very variant on the voyage, the difference in the view, which is one of fiction's strengths; for the voice of the voyager is of fiction's essence.

This lost linkage occurs possibly because gay fiction is seen as a sport, an off-shoot, most definitely a sub-branch: a sport in the sense, too, of being something inherently trivial, concerned, if not obsessed, with matters unimportant to the great and larger debate, which concerns what was once, with rather entrancing naivety, called 'the family of man'.

Queer writers themselves don't see it in quite the same way. Highly literate writers like Alan Hollinghurst and Neil Bartlett refer back to (or rediscover, reclaim) a tradition which on one hand accepts the arpeggio starkness of pornography, but also wells up around the last great outburst of artful fiction self-consciously created by homosexual men — Marcel Proust, Henry James, Oscar Wilde, Ronald Firbank — a rich tradition in anyone's language.

These earlier writers often expressed their vision through a cast of largely heterosexual characters (Firbank and Proust are the exceptions here). But even these apparently exclusively heterosexual fictional worlds were often concerned with characteristic homosexual dilemmas — the importance of a mask, the clairvoyance of irony: being true to oneself has a special meaning when that self is homosexual.

The major difference, of course, between that fin de siècle and our own is that contemporary writers can be overt in their depiction of homosexual passion. Homosexual writers today can, if they want, write about sex in a very charged yet straightforward way. What is more, this isn't seen as pornography. The effects are incalculable. One has only to compare the erotic frankness of Hollinghurst's *The Swimming Pool Library* with *Teleny*, the pornographic fin de siècle novel of which Wilde is one possible co-author: this spoke in terms of scarlet orbs, and Priapean races. *Teleny* was published in minute editions, of two hundred copies. It was considered less fiction than a kind of sexual aid, hiding behind the spurious title of an *Etude Physiologique*.

More importantly, the emotional issues of (homo)sexuality can now be not only investigated but named. In one sense, English-speaking literature has at long last grown up: what Proust endlessly explored — the Cities of the Plains — can now be the terra cognita to writers in English in the present.

Albert versus Albertine

Proust it was who spoke to Gide about the dichotomy of presenting his erotic hero not as Albert but as Albertine: he spoke of it as the one great regret of his literary life. Today this transposition of homosexual sensibility into heterosexual characters does not exist as quite the same problematic. In fact Patrick White may have been perhaps the last great homosexual novelist of the twentieth century whose major fiction was peopled almost entirely by characters with heterosexual personae. Yet even here the inward history of his most signal characters — notably women — often took on a kind of homosexual ring. Who has read *The Eye of the Storm* and not felt a queer throb in the women's voices?

Today this forced act of literary transvestitism, as one might call it, is no longer necessary. Men can write about their feelings and desires without having to pretend that they are women. Possibly this is why current queer fiction does not possess literary respectability. By its very existence, it is found to be offensive.

Lives of risk and invention

In Michael Cunningham's *A Home at the End of the World*, he writes of a character living in a provincial city musing about people flying off to lives, not of constriction, but of 'risk and invention'. This centrifugal/centripetal, push/pull, small town/ metropolis is a major feature in the contemporary landscape of queer fiction: it parallels, often literally, a kind of coming out.

Small towns, as with small minds, represent a kind of imprisonment. Orthodoxy in small towns can replicate itself, or a remembered image of itself, which nearly always excludes the overtly homosexual. The big city, for so long, has been the zone, not only of sexual freedom, but perhaps as importantly, freedom to assume an identity: to create lives, as Cunningham so perspicaciously says, of risk and invention.

The British historian Jeffrey Weekes asserts that the notion of 'homosexual' as a being rather than descriptive of a sexual act was an essentially nineteenth-century invention, a sprig of Darwinism, if you will. One aspect of contemporary queer fiction is that it tracks, in part, the process of a remarkable twentieth century invention: the gay, or, as he is latterly and assertively known, the queer.

I grew up a provincial pouf, a queer on the furthest perimeter of a Eurocentric map: in fact it was a formative experience of a New Zealander of my generation to arrive in an airline office to make some essential connection, only to find one of those elongated maps of the world in which the islands of New Zealand were signally absent. It gives you a certain grit in the soul, to grow up in a country which has slipped off the edge of the world. And like many a provincial pouf (of which, if the truth be dreadfully told, most of us are, and must be: the great cities of the world are endlessly replenished by new arrivals every bus, every plane) I made my pilgrimage to the homosexual Rome of my day — the sultry and sardonic London depicted in *The Swimming Pool Library*.

My pretext for being there was a study of Edward Carpenter, the writer of a work called *The Intermediate Sex*. This was a late-Victorian polemic which argued, in the careful third person, that homosexual men and women were neither sick nor criminal. Carpenter was called the English Walt Whitman for his rather dreadful poetry: but the fact was that Whitman was a coded word for 'homosexual' among Urnings of his period (the semantic proliferation of names for homosexuals points to an orientation not yet redeemed by official language — not for nothing were homosexual acts called 'the unnameable act' in the earlier nineteenth century). Carpenter's poetry, just as Whitman's Calamus poems, were read by homosexuals for their subtext of male affection.

Today if Carpenter exists at all, it is really as a footnote in literary history: it was at Carpenter's 'commune' that E.M. Forster connected with his homosexuality. Carpenter's charming rough trade lover frottaged the schoolmaster Forster's arse. It is like something, perhaps not coincidentally, out of Forster's fiction. ('Only connect' has a slightly different emphasis when one considers that the word 'connection' was a Victorian euphemism for sexual intercourse. 'For god's sake, fuck!' might be its contemporary resonance.)

As an apprentice literary pouf, I was aware of the great homosexual writers of the past, which I read as part of a general liberal education. Here Proust and James stood alongside their sexually ambiguous contemporaries — Lawrence, Mansfield, Flaubert. However, as a provincial pouf in search of the golden road which might lead me out of myself, the trapped identity in a small town (all of New Zealand is a variant on a small town, regardless how large the city), I began to focus on mainly homosexual writers.

I was committing the perhaps pardonable crime of trying to make sense of my own situation by reading fiction. In one sense I was finding out the history of my kind: yet again and again the very achievements of art sat alongside a demi-tragic foreshortening effect — the effect, one might say, of writers so intimate with their own sexual kind yet speaking of it in the third person, that the experience of reading them is made quite alienating.

This is not to deny that this resort to foreshortening, or metaphor — to put it crudely, Albertine rather than Albert — did not lead to good and strong art. Perhaps the very need to create metaphor is closer to the practice of art, safely delivering the writer from the dangerous threat of bathos, which is the bane of art as autobiography. It was Oscar Wilde who intoned, 'There is no "I" in art.' As with so much else, he illustrated it, perilously, with his own life. His plays live on as gloriously self-sufficient art, even though they can be read, on one level, as a very clear comment on the pleasures and pains of the closet. His immensely painful and personal 'Ballad of Reading Gaol' does not achieve quite the same artistic lift-off, even though he is addressing events and feelings directly and personally. The abandonment of the mask does not always best serve the artist's purpose.

Writers like Tennessee Williams and Truman Capote, to a certain extent, in their lives as well as their fiction, played out a role well known in the gay world as the not entirely unenjoyable high drama, the Maria Callas pitch of the tragic queen, or 'tragedy queen'. The downside of this, of course, is that as the scarlet plush curtain descends, the stage is usually littered with the corpses of suicides, or someone being taken away for 'treatment' in a psychiatric hospital. This was not unlike the lives of some queer men and women of that time. Williams's and Capote's works inspired the writer in me: yet what of the human being who the writer was? Their works schematised tragedy rather than triumph.

Another boy's own story

Edmund White was the first contemporary writer I became aware of who was both out as a gay man and who wrote in what might broadly be called a chaste literary manner; that is, he looked at what was central to gay existence — desire, identity, permanence, illusion — and treated it in language which was subtle, allusive, ironic. His language in *Nocturnes for the King of Naples* is extraordinarily supple yet his major commercial success, apart from *The Joy of Gay Sex* which he co-authored, is, of course, *A Boy's Own Story* — a central coming out event which is referred to again and again as a rite of passage in gay fiction.

This book had the shock of recognition for a generation of gay men: and it is a legitimate tribal function of fiction, not unlike the song or ballad in non-literate societies, to give shape to communal experience. One reads, initially, to see one's own experiences shadowed, given shape, and hence meaning. From here the pleasure of art, or fiction, takes over.

Edmund White was important because his work was part of a period which proclaimed the end of a rigidly determinist universe with the world of the 'homosexual' as a problematic, a man fated to a certain schematic formula not dissimiliar, at its highest points (as in Tennessee Williams's metaphorical plays) to genuine tragedy. Now tragedy was no longer the formula. In part it was a literary expression of what was happening socially: the up adjective *gay* had replaced the perjorative, demi-scientific term *homosexual*.

But more importantly, for the writer and the reader, was the artful expression of Edmund White's work: not merely did it cover a certain area and look at phenomena in what might be seen as a disengaged way, but it did so artfully, with a pleasure in language. This is the singular breakthrough that Edmund White — he of the succinct and cutting phrase and engaging humour — made.

At the same time he created (recreated?) a kind of character type in fiction, one exemplifying what might almost be called a latter-day Jamesian point of view — that is, someone infinitely civilised. That it was simply self-civilisation only made the character type more distinctly new world, and engaging — self-construction carries its own moral premises and excitements. He was a sort of flâneur with roots going back to Baudelaire, as at home in the fuck club as much as at the dinner table, a person who can name, who can construct whatever experiences happen to him, through his verbal dexterity. Drollness was another aspect of this point of view, as well as the very essence perhaps of a certain kind of civilisation — a dry wit.

White himself, in his preface to *The Faber Book of Gay Short*

Fiction, talks of how this literary generation, of which he was such an exemplar, came about. Meeting informally in that greatest of all urban settings of the 1980s — New York — a small group of men each week devoted themselves to literature. Their very title, the Purple Quill Club, is fin de siècle by its colouring, its tone — its facetiousness is perhaps what marks it out as peculiarly modern.

From this small group of men came an unconscionably high proportion of future gay writers: Robert Ferro, Andrew Holleran, Felice Picano. They were in new sociological and psychological waters. Freed from the rigidly determinist universe of the homosexual (although helped in this by the scientific triumph, penicillin — just as the pill underwrote women's independence in the same period) this generation existed in suspension, somewhat like a gilded pre-war condition: freedom was its own reward, if not its own responsibility.

We now know, of course, that it was a generation that would come face to face with the chaotic dark agent of a virus.

White himself calls the roll call for the Purple Quill Club. Yet it is important that although tragedy has once again entered the lives of gay men as a determinant, it is part of the strength of this new psychological (and hence literary) modus operandi that 'tragedy' has been steadfastly rebutted as a characteristic means of expression. Indeed, in the face of very real and daily catastrophes, of threatened diaspora, tragedy has been seen consistently as too self-indulgent: essentially dangerous. When survival is at issue, tragedy becomes superfluous.

The dilemma of queer fiction, in this enduring crisis of AIDS, is to act both as a report on experience and be a self-sufficient literary artefact at the same time. Or as White says, to describe as well as to excite.

In the recent past, I think we have seen two responses which mark as significant a jump forward in the queer lexicon as White's once was. These are both novels: Alan Hollinghurst's *The Swiming Pool Library*, and Neil Bartlett's *Ready to Catch Him Should He Fall*. Yet neither of these novels deals, ostensibly, with the AIDS crisis. A better way of saying this would be to say that AIDS is the unwritten presence, and persuasion, behind every word and thought in these novels. Diaspora leans as a great weight against these works of fiction, and both writers, almost consciously, have set out to explore and record a world under threat.

Adam Mars-Jones, the English writer, speaks about the presence of AIDS being not a subject which he chose to write about: in some senses, it chose him. He notes that the big subject seems particularly suitable for the small form of the short story. But he also noted something else: that it takes a sustained will to write about the subject: it attacks the writer from within, as it were — often almost literally. Beyond steeling one's nerves to deal with what newspapers for too long relished in calling 'the killer disease', there is the fact that with such a vast and changing condition, it is difficult to get the distance from it which art, to a certain extent, needs. At the same time, knowledge of it and experience with it is utterly necessary to give veracity.

Knowledge, experience, yet distance also. Fiction needs the shaping influence of metaphor, to give a wider resonance than the purely autobiographical or diurnal. (Salmon Rushdie has attacked contemporary English fiction, perhaps justifiably, for its refusal to face the big metaphors, the huge questions.) Perhaps then it's no accident that up till now, the queer fiction which does work best as art, operates most effectively as description because AIDS is, paradoxically, absent. (Just as Renais' *The Shooting Party*, set before World War II, is possibly the most prescient film about the coming storm; yet on its surface it is all about aristocrats finding solace in adultery and hunting.)

Yet the subject remains, profound, implacable, demanding the mirror of art at least to make some sense of our lives, our pain and our continued existence through this period. Possibly one answer lies in the statement of the Italian writer, Aldo Busi, that: 'Truly high literature as an end in itself, with all the consequences which flow from it, does not deal with the common sexual desires whether satisfied or denied, but with the unleashing of frustration in the character and how it reverberates in its customs and social surroundings. The great passions in the novel are always a metaphor for political sickness.'

For myself I think one of the current strengths of contemporary queer fiction is the fact that it has to deal with such a basic crisis, as much philosophical as sexual, as much political as it is moral. Its strength is that it is both a report on experience and, in its best work, a transmutation into art: creating, I would argue, one of the contemporary dialogues of late twentieth century fiction. And it is testament to the urgency of this dialogue that the volume of gay fiction, so called, daily grows greater. It will not stop.

The most challenging thing for heterosexual readers is simply to experience a world in which their concerns are placed to the side, viewed from a different angle. The priorities of home, family and children are here viewed by people who have often been there, then taken a different route. This is the most challenging experience, perhaps: to experience marginalisation, a curious parallel to the life-long experience of most homosexual men and women.

And where does the provincial pouf, on the furthest axis of the Eurocentric map, find himself in all of this? The answer is: in the Pacific, an emerging fulcrum of power. In New Zealand, a society which is going through a period of dynamic change.

My own voyage, for someone born mid-century, was not to stay in the great metropolis but to return to the land of my ancestors: I mean, here, ironically, New Zealand, Aotearoa, because this was the only place where the lives of my ancestors made sense. My voyage to Britain was the characteristic rite of passage for the Pakeha. A surface sense of familiarity could not mask more ambiguous feelings: a deep dislike for the ills which perhaps sent my ancestors away in the first place.

My model in returning to New Zealand was, oddly, another homosexual New Zealand writer: Frank Sargeson. He it was who insisted on the possibility of a New Zealand voice, of a place to stand. He, with his rundown cottage and garden full of vegetables, and his persistence in pursuing the art of writing, influenced me more than any other New Zealander. He said: yes, it is possible to exist in the land of your birth, and humbly, with whatever persistence, to make art.

This brings me to a consideration of fiction's role for the reader. Earlier and years ago my wish was to find myself, to find someone who had gone before me who could speak, tell me what had preceded me, and release me from the terrible sense of isolation: am I the only one? Part of fiction's role — possibly particularly for a group whose presence is never taken for granted and is constantly challenged — is an assertive presence: to tell stories which in turn keep our identity visible and alive. As White says, 'not just reporting the past but also shaping the future, forging an identity as much as revealing it.'

There is a remarkable history handed from writer to reader, reader to writer — and that is the lesson of efflorescence, threat and survival. A provincial pouf like myself, on the periphery of a global dialogue, can yet participate. A book travels.

Last year, at a memorial quilt display, I met a young Asian man who was in Auckland to attend the big summer party. Somewhat remarkably, he recognised me from the photograph on the back of my book. He told me how, in his country, a Muslim state, such strict censorship exists that homosexual men, reading a review of a likely book in foreign publications, must immediately send away for copies of it. These are then distributed, by hand, among friends.

In this way, the young man saw a review of my book in an Australian paper. He sent for ten copies of it. So the book slipped into his country before the official censor had heard of it, let alone entered it in a canon of banned texts. I felt immensely pleased — a warmth beyond any good review. This is how ideas and books travel. This is how we, dexterously, manage to stay alive. We invent.

And in this sense the writer is no different from the drag queen, the leather man, the young man and woman getting dressed for Mardi Gras: we simply use words, to describe. And by describing, our world stays alive.